CANDLE
FEATHER
WOODEN SPOON

CANDLE

FEATHER

WOODEN SPOON

New Jewish Stories

RABBI ZOË KLEIN

Foreword by Rabbi Sandy Eisenberg Sasso

CCAR
Press

Reform Judaism Publishing, a division of CCAR Press
CENTRAL CONFERENCE OF AMERICAN RABBIS
5783 NEW YORK 2023

Published by Reform Judaism Publishing, a division of CCAR Press
355 Lexington Avenue, New York, NY 10017
(212) 972-3636 | info@ccarpress.org | www.ccarpress.org

LIBRARY OF CONGRESS CATALOGING-IN-PUBLICATION DATA
Names: Klein, Zoë, author.
Title: Candle, feather, wooden spoon: new Jewish stories / Rabbi Zoë
   Klein; foreword by Rabbi Sandy Eisenberg Sasso.
Description: First edition. | New York: Central Conference of American
   Rabbis (CCAR), 5783 = 2023. | Includes bibliographical references. |
   Summary: "A collection of original stories with settings both
   traditional and contemporary. Each story highlights an essential aspect
   of living a meaningful Jewish life"-- Provided by publisher.
Identifiers: LCCN 2022055112 (print) | LCCN 2022055113 (ebook) | ISBN
   9780881233568 (trade paperback) | ISBN 9780881233575 (ebook)
Classification: LCC PS3611.L453 A6 2023 (print) | LCC PS3611.L453 (ebook)
   | DDC 813/.6--dc23/eng/20221206
LC record available at https://lccn.loc.gov/2022055112
LC ebook record available at https://lccn.loc.gov/2022055113

Cover and interior illustrations by Rabbi Zoë Klein.
Designed and composed by Scott-Martin Kosofsky
at The Philidor Company, Rhinebeck, NY.

Printed in the United States of America
10 9 8 7 6 5 4 3 2 1 0

In gratitude to Rabbi Zoë Klein,
for enriching our congregation
with her stories and poetry,
for teaching us new
metaphors and perspectives,
for hearing and holding our stories,
for encouraging us to shape and tell
our personal and communal narratives,
and for helping us see how our stories
are all connected.

Temple Isaiah of Los Angeles

*Dedicated
to storytellers
everywhere*

Contents

Foreword: The Magic of Story

Rabbi Sandy Eisenberg Sasso

O NE OF MY FAVORITE MIDRASHIM (rabbinic interpretations and stories on biblical texts) reflects on what words were actually spoken at
Mount Sinai. The rabbis disagreed about whether God spoke the entire first
commandment or just its first word. Rabbi Mendel of Rymanov, a Chasidic
teacher, asserted, "What was said on Sinai was only the first letter of the
first word of the first commandment."[1] That Hebrew letter is *alef*, and it is
silent—or, more precisely, it is the very beginning of sound. In other words,
what happened on Sinai was the beginning of a conversation, the beginning
of a story—the story of the Jewish people.

"In the beginning" is our way of saying "Once upon a time." "In the
beginning, God said, 'Let there be light.' And there was light." Speech alone
created light on that first day of Creation. Many a Jewish legend suggest
that the light of the first day has been lost. However, I imagine that the first
light embodied the first divine word, and the first word became more words,
many words became story, and story became more stories. If this is so, then
we can once again find the light of Creation through story. The spiritual
experience itself is inarticulate; the first language of the spiritual life is story.
After all, God is cast as the first storyteller.

We are more a people of storytellers than theologians, coming to know
the holy from the tales and legends of our people. There is no holy day without a story, and no story that does not contain a holy spark. From sacred
narratives in the *Tanach*, over which we recite blessings, to rabbinic midrashim, to Jewish folktales from around the world, we share what we believe,
who we are, and who we aspire to become. In this way, the light that was
spoken into Creation is continually renewed.

In this collection of new stories, Rabbi Zoë Klein speaks new light into
Creation as she weaves her magical tales. You will get lost in her stories
and find something surprising and new about Jewish tradition and yourself. Journey through the pages of *Candle, Feather, Wooden Spoon* and you will

---

1. Rabbi Naftali Zvi Horowitz of Ropshitz, *Zera Kodesh* 2:40.

accompany the angels who collect time, as you think about how to make time count. You will discover fairy footprints in your matzah and ride on the back of a dolphin through the Sea of Reeds to overcome fear. You will laugh with Shmooey from Chelm, then look in the mirror to uncover beauty in a retelling of a tender and true experience. You will find the most important person in the world and the most important words. From the magic of a candle, a feather, and a wooden spoon to the mystical shofar that carries the pain of the world, Rabbi Klein invites us into an enchanted world that entertains and amazes.

We accumulate information, but we appreciate stories. That is why we often forget facts, but we don't forget the stories we have been told. They may lie dormant until something happens in our lives, and one of them finds its way to our consciousness. Stories come to rescue us just when we need them. That is the power of stories: they enlighten us as they occupy a place in our minds and inspire us as they make imprints on our souls.

When we are infants, we fall asleep to the gentle rhythm of story, and no matter how old we become, we never tire of them. Stories have the power to transport us through the years, to go far back in time and forward to a distant future. They can transport us from place to place, around the globe, and into space. They invite us to face monsters and defeat them, to get lost and find our way home.

In story, a simple spoon can become an oar that rows us to safety, a feather can stop a giant, and rocks can fall in love. Stories can hold the keys to our homes in Spain and carry the fragrance of Middle Eastern spices and the taste of honey. They speak Hebrew, Ladino, and Yiddish. They weep and laugh, mourn and celebrate. They travel in the belly of a whale, on cobbled streets, in trains, and on foot through villages and towns. They live in orchards and magical palaces. They stand at Sinai and under the wedding canopy. They light candles at the Sabbath table, meet souls about to be born, and soar with angels to faraway places and land sure-footed on solid ground, back home. We remember them, and they remember us. The philosopher Emmanuel Levinas imagined our sacred texts as stretched on the body of tradition like "the strings of the viola."[2] And so, every time we tell and retell a story, we make music. Rabbi Klein has composed a beautiful symphony.

---

2. Emmanuel Levinas, "The Strings and the Viola," in *Outside the Subject*, trans. Michael B. Smith (Stanford, CA: Stanford University Press, 1994), 174.

RABBI SANDY EISENBERG SASSO, rabbi emerita of Congregation Beth-El Zedeck in Indianapolis, is the first woman to be ordained by the Reconstructionist Rabbinical College (1974). She is the founder of the Religion, Spirituality, and the Arts Initiative at Indiana University–Purdue University Indianapolis (IUPUI) and an award-winning children's author of over twenty-five books. She has also written two books for adults: Midrash: Reading the Bible with Question Marks and Jewish Stories of Love and Marriage (the latter with Peninnah Schram). Her newest book is I Am Not Afraid: Psalm 23 for Bedtime. She has written and lectured about women and spirituality, midrash and creativity, and the religious imagination of children.

Acknowledgments

I WANT TO THANK the entire team at CCAR Press for making this publication possible. I am grateful to Rabbi Hara Person, Rafael Chaiken, Rabbi Jan Katz, Rabbi Sonja Pilz, Deborah Smilow, Chiara Ricisak, Leta Cunningham, and Ariel Tovlev for your incredibly thoughtful editing and ideas. Editing is a difficult art to master. It requires powers of vision, telepathy, finesse, patience, and much more. Your insightfulness shaped and shined this collection. You are its dimensionality and depth. I am especially grateful to the brilliant Rabbi Anne Villarreal-Belford, whose editorial skill borders on alchemy, nimbly quarrying gems out of unhewn writing. I am certain you could turn *tohu* and *vohu* into a beautiful new world, and I would want to live in it. Thank you also to Debra Hirsch Corman, Scott-Martin Kosofsky, Michelle Kwitkin, and Raquel Fairweather-Gallie for all you have done to fine-tune and market this book. To Temple Isaiah, and especially those with whom I study Torah, it is a sublime blessing to learn and grow together, through seasons of sorrow and joy, soul to soul, heart to heart. To my husband Scott Miles—I am so grateful to cowrite new chapters of life and love with you. And to my children, Rachmiel, Kinneret, and Zimra, your journeys—whether to the grocery store or to the moon—are the stories I cherish the most.

Introduction

ON THE NIGHT BEFORE PASSOVER, it is traditional for families to hide pieces of bread in a ritual called *b'dikat chameitz* (searching for leaven). Children search for crumbs with a candle and use a feather to sweep them onto a wooden spoon, all of which are then put in a paper bag. The paper bag with the items inside is burned the following morning, signifying that the home is ready for the holiday to begin.

I have always loved the candle, feather, and wooden spoon. While not on par with the royal flush of seder plate sacred symbols (shank bone, bitter herbs, *charoset*, parsley, and egg), in their own gentle way they indicate that we are ready to begin this story of freedom. For me, they represent the process of storytelling. First comes the light of an idea, then the quill with which to write it down, and at last it is ready to be spooned out and shared.

I also love that all three objects are fairly mundane. Candles are common. You can find feathers amid fallen leaves and weeds. And there is probably a wooden spoon floating around everyone's cookware. Judaism is about elevating the mundane to the sacred, helping us transform mindless action into mindful intention. Stories have the same power of transformation. The famous Jewish story of a person scattering feathers from a pillow and then fruitlessly trying to gather them all back together becomes the simple but effective tool to transmit the important value about speaking kindly and not spreading rumors.

There is a midrash that reads: "Through a parable, a person can fathom words of Torah. Consider the sovereign who has lost a gold coin or a precious pearl in their house. May they not find it by the light of a wick worth no more than an *isar* [a Roman coin]? Likewise, do not let the parable appear of little worth to you. By its light, a person may fathom words of Torah" (*Shir HaShirim Rabbah* 1:1). In this midrash, a parable is likened to a candle, which, despite its low cost, is immensely valuable in its ability to illuminate the greatest treasures. Stories light the path to pearls of wonder and wisdom. They convey message and meaning, preserve memory, and spark curiosity. We develop relationships with the characters and engage personally in the lessons. When we get lost in a story, we are bound to find treasure.

Studying Torah and Jewish texts at Hebrew Union College–Jewish Institute of Religion Rabbinical School, I often imagined rabbit holes, like the one that Alice fell into, concealed between the Hebrew letters. A little pivot and perspective, and I would find myself tumbling into a new wonderland. Curiouser and curiouser. Each story in this collection was drawn out of one of those wonderlands.

This collection's first part, "Candle: Stories That Shine New Light on Tradition," explores Jewish texts and teachings from new vantage points. "Empathy: A Whale Tale" imagines the Jonah story but from the perspective of the whale. "The Flying Insect Café" explores the effect of the verse in which Moses proclaims that all flying insects are forbidden to eat (Deuteronomy 14:19) from the perspective of a family whose livelihood is selling flying insect cuisine. I stumbled upon obscure mentions of an angel of the secrets of the Torah in kabbalistic writings, which led to wondering how such an angel acquired this position, explored in "Yofiel." "Shulamit bat Aminadav" visits the miracle of the Sea of Reeds from the perspective of a girl who loves animals. Rabbi Abraham Joshua Heschel's metaphor that Shabbat is a palace in time becomes literal in "Time Palace," with seconds, minutes, and hours having collectible shape and form. Like so many other Jewish stories, "Fairy Footprints" and "Shades and the Rock on the Grave" grew out of questions. The questions were, respectively, "Why does matzah have holes?" and "Why do we place a rock on a grave when we visit?" Questions are the greatest portals to discovery—every question and discovery their own wonderland. "Shmooey and the Shabbat Encounter" pays homage to the classic stories of Chelm. Both "Shades" and "Shmooey" are set in the romanticized forests and small towns of Eastern Europe, out of which so many classic Chasidic tales are born.

The second part, "Feather: Modern Stories That Take Flight," explores identity and relationship through a modern Jewish lens. The characters in these stories may remind you of people you know or yourself. A marriage chuppah on the top of a mountain in the story "Shalom Bayit" expands from being the symbolic sketch of a home for one loving couple to the symbol of a national protest movement. "JEW" is a fantasy adventure seeking to restore the word "Jew" to its full enchantment and beauty. "The Most Important Person in the World" and "Allison Searches for Her Hebrew Name" are stories of self-realization. "Candle, Feather, Wooden Spoon" is at once a quest to find a magical fruit while outrunning the plague of darkness and also a quest to find understanding between a grandfather and grandson. "The Magic Word" is another quest in which the main character seeks to discover the most powerful magical words. "A Pock-Faced Beauty" explores the wisdom shared between generations and the true meaning of beauty. "Catching the Wind: A Tallit Origin Story" celebrates the bonds of friendship.

The final part, "Wooden Spoon: Stories That Stir Food for Thought," mixes story with philosophy in an attempt to taste the transcendent. "Lace Theory" proposes a unique framework for how we are all interconnected. "Radiant Window: A Zoharic Journey," a search for one's true calling, is studded with verses of *Zohar*, the foundational work of Jewish mysticism. "The Goat Keeper" imagines a lost tribe who broke off from the Israelites after witnessing the Revelation at Mount Sinai. "Two Rocks: A Very Long Legendary Love Story," despite its title, is one of the shortest stories in the collection and explores love in geological time. "Abraham's Return" is a true story from my family. I am grateful to Rabbi Anne Villarreal-Belford for encouraging the inclusion of this story. As the only complete work of nonfiction ("A Pock-Faced Beauty" is a fictional portrayal of a true story), "Abraham's Return" is both about the journey of a particular artwork while also being a commentary on how art lives beyond the printed page in the real world. In the last story, "God Chooses a Genre," the Author of All Life shares their creative process. *(Legend lesson)*

I often think about the authors of the aggadic midrashim, rabbinic legends, that have become our sacred stories, like the story of Abraham smashing the idols, the legends about Miriam's well, or the story of Nachshon entering the Sea of Reeds before anyone else. None of these stories are in the Torah, but we weave them into our Torah stories as if they were. When the authors of these stories wrote them, did they sit and write outlines, think about character arc and development, settings and plot devices? Or did the stories appear to them whole, as in a vision? Story writing is a blend of planning and discovery. In my experience, a story feels right when after all the laborious research, writing, editing, and rewriting, it appears as if the story had just sprung immaculately into the world all on its own. The labor is forgotten, and the birth is just one small point on the story's timeline. The story moves on to have its own life, its own relationships, and its own adventures.

The stories in this collection are intended to be shared, interpreted, and discussed. In the same way that musicians use their artistry and unique style to make a known melody their own, you are encouraged to adopt and adapt these stories, add your voice, and make them yours. Judaism has an extraordinary oral tradition evolving from generation to generation, with each new storyteller adding flavor, color, and texture.

You are a storyteller, with your own voice and experience to add. In retelling "Fairy Footprints: Why Matzah Has Holes" to children, you might soften the scary parts about the evil magicians or embellish the jumping frogs and itchy lice. You might add darker elements to "Shades and the Rock on the Grave" around a campfire with young adults. You might condense stories like "The Most Important Person in the World" or "Allison Searches for a Hebrew Name" to fit in a lesson plan, or rework "Lace Theory" into a sermon. You might retell "Catching the Wind: A Tallit Origin Story" in your own words as a bedtime story, act out "Yofiel" as a play, or add your own magic words to the lists in "The Magic Word." The stories want to dance with you, to share with you their rhythm, and to know yours.

At the end of each story in this collection, there are a number of questions designed to encourage self-reflection, conversation, and engagement. So take a candle (or a reading light!), a feather, and a wooden spoon and search these pages for morsels, parables, and words of Torah. And keep telling your stories.

CANDLE

Stories That Shine New Light on Tradition

Time Palace

THERE ONCE WAS A LEGION OF ANGELS called the Cassielites. Their empire was built on the altostratus altitude range of the sky. Now and then, you still may see fragments of their abandoned kingdom, enormous cloud structures skating ten thousand feet over the earth.

The Cassielites absorbed energy from moonbeams and quenched their thirst on sea mist. As a sunflower's face follows the path of the sun, the Cassielites were aligned with the moon and the tides and felt strongest when the moon was full. They were sparkly as an updraft of fresh powdered snow. When the moon was nothing but the faintest silver sliver, the Cassielites shrunk until they hardly amounted to a wisp of steam off a cup of tea.

More than anything, the Cassielites loved to collect time. Every moment that was wasted on earth drifted upward into their realm, and they would rush to catch it in their crystalline nets. When a Cassielite caught a moment, they rushed it to their sanctum and wrapped it in a swath of feather-soft tropical breeze, bound by star rays. Every week, the Cassielites would unwrap their treasures, polish them to a mirror-shine, and admire them.

Time was so beautiful! Each moment was luminous and multifaceted, reflecting the infinite heavens and the vivid, vibrant earth in one compact kaleidoscopic prism. Yet people seemed to have little idea how precious time was. They spent it meaninglessly. They spent it arguing when they could be caring for each other. They spent it complaining when they could be making positive change. They spent it feeling sorry for themselves instead of appreciating their lot. They spent it counting other people's mistakes instead of counting their own blessings.

The Cassielites reveled in the people's dawdling and delaying. People were so careless, sometimes they even lost time! They lost it idling in stupors. They lost it distracting themselves with loud things and fast things. They lost it hemming and hawing and yawning away nature's beauty by laying around their domiciles doing nothing.

The Jewish people, however, did honor the sanctity of time. They studied and recorded it. They tracked the phases of the moon and had great ceremonies when a new moon appeared in the sky. They counted the days between their spring festival and their harvest festival. They had long debates about when evening ends and when day begins. They marked the rainy season and the season of dew. They marked the blossoming of the almond tree. They woke with a prayer on their lips and went to bed with a prayer on their lips.

Despite the efforts of this one tribe, the Cassielites were ecstatic about how much time they were amassing. Their sanctums were stuffed with time. Seconds were pale little chips. Minutes were petal pink. Hours had silver linings. Days were gold-dusted. Weeks were tinted azure. Months were a whole armful of clear cobalt. An unbroken wasted year was a wonder to behold. A whole decade shimmered like the sea. One Cassielite spent over a hundred years constructing a crystalline net as wide as Madagascar. It filled the sky like a giant spider web. The Cassielite positioned the net at precisely the moment when the moon was full and a human monarch died, and that strong Cassielite managed to catch an entire epoch, an exceptional marvel, spiraling with iridescent rainbows.

Meanwhile, this tribe of Jewish people not only kept time, they also actually *made* time for the things that were truly important. They made time for community gatherings. They made time for family meals. They made time to discover new things and explore big questions. They made time to study great thinkers and dream up new ideas. They made time to listen to others and work for justice and freedom. They made time to witness and appreciate God's goodness.

Still, there was so much wasted time that even with the meaningful moments the Jewish people made, the Cassielites could not keep up with all the squandered hours. Time tumbled out of the Cassielites' sanctums. The Cassielites hardly wrapped one new find in tropical breezes and star rays when another wave of ennui would crest into their kingdom, spilling months and years all over the place. The Cassielites became frenzied in their lust for time, greedily grabbing moments. They didn't realize that the weight of all this time was starting to change their realm. Their empire was sagging.

The people below noticed that the sky was growing heavy and dark. The once-welcomed clouds had become thick and blocked the sun entirely. The people were cold and afraid. The heavens began churning with ominous thunderheads. The people feared their time was over, and they wept.

Despite this terrible impact of catching time, the Cassielites could not stop hoarding each lost moment, until one night, when the moon was faint and the Cassielites were wispy and weak, their cloud kingdom broke apart. All their treasures plunged to the earth and sea. The Cassielites could not withstand the fall, and overnight their wispy forms blew away. The sky was clear, and their legion was no more.

Time began to wash up on the shore. There were tiny instants and rocks (Hannukah) of ages. The people knew they did not deserve this great gift of time they received from the heavens, and they didn't want to squander their chance to now use time more wisely.

They assembled a council to discuss how to protect their time so that it would not run out again. After deliberating for many weeks (they were still learning how to use time correctly, after all), the council decided that there should be a people tasked with keeping time, a trustworthy tribe in tune with the cycle of the moon and the changes of seasons. And that's when they remembered the Jewish people—a people who sanctified time.

So the Jews got to work. They collected the moments that were scattered across the land and lodged into the earth. They took shards of hours and timber of days, and they built a great palace of time. It was a beautiful palace of luminous, multifaceted, kaleidoscopic prisms of time that reflected the infinite heavens and the vivid, vibrant earth. Inside this palace, people discovered that time stood still, and they could freely take the time they needed to reflect on the lessons of the past, the possibilities of the future, and the wonder of the present. The Jewish people created portals to this palace of time that could be opened by anyone from anywhere in the world, to refresh and renew and remember. Then the Jews gave this great palace a name. They called it Shabbat. And the Jewish people, who had been entrusted with keeping time, keep Shabbat to this day, and everyone who enters the palace shares something no Cassielite ever experienced: a glimpse of eternity.

QUESTIONS

1. The Jews in the story were known for noticing and marking time. Why do you think that was—and still is—so important for Jews? How do you mark time in a Jewish way?

2. What does it mean to "waste time," and is "wasting time" ever actually a good thing?

3. The Cassielites hoarded time, but they didn't spend it. If you could take time for yourself, what would you do with it?

4. Rabbi Abraham Joshua Heschel called Shabbat a "palace in time," which stands in contract with the rest of the week, when we are obsessed with the "acquisition of things in space." How can Shabbat affect our relationship with others and the world?

Yofiel

"**W**HAT ARE WE GOING TO DO about Yofiel?" asked Gabrielle, shaking her head.

Uriel pealed the neon-orange Post-it Note with Yofiel's name off the whiteboard. The whiteboard was covered with multicolored Post-its, each bearing another name. The 10^{18} angels in the southeastern host of the Alpha Quadrant of Ursa Minor had all been assigned tasks. All but one.

Uriel stuck the Post-it Note under the section titled PLANTS. "We could assign him to a blade of grass. All he would have to do is command it to grow. How could he possibly mess that up?"

"He could turn the dial too high and we could end up with a single blade of grass the size of Orion's Belt," Raphaela said. They knew she wasn't exaggerating.

Michael removed the Post-it and stuck it under the section titled SHABBAT. Gabrielle couldn't help but guffaw.

"Now wait," Michael said. "Hear me out. The Shabbat angels always travel in pairs, so he would never be alone. All he would have to do is help accompany one worshiper home from synagogue."

"And tell me what happens," Gabrielle said, "when he gets distracted by a dandelion spore, leaving the worshiper unbalanced enough to trip into a river?" "So we assign him to a place where there are no rivers," Michael said.

"Or a road?" Gabrielle added.

"And no roads," Michael sighed resignedly.

The archangels took their job assigning tasks very seriously. They had been assigning tasks to angels since the very beginning, when they instructed two angels to guard the gates to the Garden of Eden. There were big tasks, like intercepting Abraham's knife on Mount Moriah. Telling Sarah that she would have a child. Answering Hagar in the wilderness. Wrestling with

Jacob. Stoking the fire at the Burning Bush. Blocking the path of Balaam's donkey.

Then there were the innumerable smaller tasks. Telling the geese to fly south. Coaxing the cicadas out from their seven years underground. Helping the newborn foal to its feet. They were small tasks, but when they were carried out incorrectly, the consequences were dire. For everything is connected to everything else. There was no room for sloppiness. And oy, Yofiel was sloppy.

"Ah," exclaimed Raphaela. She took the Post-it and stuck it under the section titled LADDER UP.

"Oh, this should be good," Gabrielle said, crossing her arms.

"Yofiel could carry intel from bottom to top," Raphaela explained. "He just has to climb, and we know he likes climbing." Michael nodded. Raphaela continued, "He wouldn't even have to go down, just up. It is much easier to lose your footing on the way down than on the way up."

"But if anyone could lose their footing up or down," Gabrielle said, "it is Yofiel. And then what do we end up with? A fallen angel avalanche. The world could not withstand it."

"What then?" Uriel said, exasperated.

The archangels reviewed Yofiel's thick file, spreading it out over the boardroom table. They weighed and considered every note submitted by his instructors from the Earth Simulation Sphere. *Snagged robe on mountain peak and spilled a generation of wombat spirits into volcanic lake. Slipped on slick of engine grease in Safeway, Inc. parking lot, causing a twenty-shopping-cart pileup, with multiple bruised elbows, plumcots, and persimmons. Instead of telling the robins to chirp cheerily, he told them to burp beerily. Forgot to turn off the geysers. Got a speck of pepper in his nose and sneezed a clearing in the rainforest.*

They also reread the letter of recommendation from his direct supervisor: *To Whom It May Concern: About Yofiel, just don't.*

They also noted, however, that Yofiel had a very happy disposition. He wasn't intentionally causing chaos. His intentions were always good. He got along with the other angels. He was friendly and curious and fun to be around. He was sweet and kind. He was first to volunteer to help whenever it was needed. He had a natural enthusiasm for learning. He just got mixed up and befuddled and clumsy.

"He has straight A's in effort, straight A's in participation," Gabrielle said, "and all F's in mastery, poor thing."

"He really is a good angel," Michael sighed.

"He's just not good at doing angel tasks," Uriel said.

"There *has* to be a task for him," Raphaela said. "We can't just leave him all alone in the Alpha Quadrant."

The archangels sat silently until their coffees turned cold.

Suddenly inspired, Gabrielle whisked the neon-orange Post-it off the table. She went to an empty section of the whiteboard, where she stuck the Post-it. Above Yofiel's name she wrote "KEEPER OF THE SECRETS OF THE TORAH." All the archangels stared at the task. It was a giant task for any young angel, especially one as clumsy as Yofiel. They argued with Gabrielle that it was a ludicrous suggestion, absolutely ludicrous. But Gabrielle countered each argument with logic and patience, and one by one, the archangels came to understand the cleverness of the assignment. So it was done.

Gabrielle brought the news to Yofiel herself. When she arrived, Yofiel, who was covered in asteroid glitter, greeted her with a big smile.

"Gabby!" he exclaimed, his eyes twinkling. He immediately flew to her and gave her a big hug.

"Yofiel," Gabrielle said. "I am here to share your assignment with you."

"Did you know that helium is ticklish to angels?" Yofiel asked.

Yofiel released a spray of helium, and indeed it was ticklish. Gabrielle and Yofiel giggled together until the playful gas wore off. Gabrielle couldn't help but feel happy whenever they were together. This little angel was truly special.

"You are being given a very serious task, Yofiel," Gabrielle said, brushing glitter off her suit jacket. "You are going to be the Keeper of the Secrets of the Torah."

Yofiel suddenly looked very serious. "You can never tell a secret," he said slowly, shaking his head, "or else it wouldn't be a secret."

"That is correct," said Gabrielle, smiling. "And you are going to do great."

She gave Yofiel a kiss, and he clapped his hands, flying off to tell his friends.

Gabrielle, Michael, Raphaela, and Uriel perched where they could watch Yofiel on his first day as Keeper of the Secrets of the Torah. Yofiel landed on the rooftop of an old *beit midrash*, accidentally loosening a clay shingle.

The shingle slipped and shattered on the ground. Uriel gasped and moved to intervene, but Gabrielle said, "Shh, just watch. It's going to be okay."

Yofiel hopped to the ground and slipped under a windowsill into the study room. Pairs of people were seated around the room, leaning over pages of Torah and commentary. Yofiel knew that those pages held lots of beautiful secrets. He knew that there were treasures hiding in the letters and even in the blank spaces between. He also knew that it was his job to keep them safe.

None of the people seemed to be aware of Yofiel's presence. If they felt a shift in temperature or a flutter in the air, they did not show it. Yofiel knew that people could not see angels, but some could sense their soft presence. Yofiel hovered over one pair of learners, who were puzzling over the beginning of the Torah. One asked the other, "Why does the Torah begin with the second letter of the alphabet instead of the first?" Yofiel squeezed his mouth shut, wiggling with excitement. He knew there was an exquisite secret right there in that question, so close to them! Oh, it was a really big, juicy, delicious secret. If they were hungry for wisdom, a bite of this secret would really hit the spot. But no, Yofiel clasped his wings over his mouth. A secret is a secret, and it was his job to protect it. But what a secret it was!

Raphaela smiled. "Here we go," she whispered.

"He looks like he is going to burst," Michael said.

Yofiel saw that the closer the learners came to the secret, the more their eyes twinkled. As they exchanged ideas, they were serious and, at the same time, joyful. Yofiel wanted to feel those feelings too, so he made himself minuscule and dove into the page, frolicking and splashing in the sea of letters. He found the juicy, delicious secret and hugged it to his chest.

"I can't look," Michael winced.

Yofiel hugged the secret a little too tightly, and it slipped out of his arms, bouncing directly into the ear of one of the learners. At first, Yofiel was terrified as he watched the secret dislodge and travel off the page. But then he saw the learner's face light up with wonder and awe, and he knew this "accident" was not an accident at all. It was a beautiful spark of revelation.

Yofiel lay on a raft of letters with his hands behind his head and a פ/pei for a pillow, watching the people in the *beit midrash* sharing the secret with each other. Their faces shined with holy light. Yofiel thought about what a good job he had done. The people clearly understood how special the secret was. He trusted them wholeheartedly. In fact, Yofiel realized, the more people there are who know the secret, the more people there would be to help him keep it safe!

Watching from their perch, the archangels smiled.

"What do you think is going on inside his head?" Raphaela asked.

Uriel shrugged, "That is undecipherable."

"Are you crying?" Gabrielle asked as Michael wiped away a tear.

"He's a good little angel," Michael said, and they all agreed.

The Guardian – Celestial Edition

December 20, 2030 / 24 Kislev, 5791

Yofiel Blunders His Task—Again

Jerusalem, Israel—Fifteen hundred years after shocking the realms with his assignment, Yofiel continues to muddle it all up. Two students, Leon Mandelbaum and Amy Evanston, were studying the weekly Torah portion at the Pardes Institute of Jewish Studies when they stumbled over an inconsistency. They puzzled over it. They delved into Rashi, Radak, Rashbam, Rambam, and Onkelos. They explored Chasidic, Reconstructionist, and Reform commentaries. They applied *g'matria*. They cross-referenced Kabbalah. They examined the trope. Then, at 8:06 p.m., the text flowered right before the study-pair's very eyes.

Sources confirm that for the twenty-sixth thousandth time this week, Yofiel dropped a hint, and yet another Torah secret was revealed. Two more students of Torah are now radiant with revelation.

Reportedly the All Knowing is well informed of the ongoing blunders and is very, very pleased.

QUESTIONS

1. Throughout history, people have believed that great ideas come from outside of them, through muses, inspiration, or divine revelation. Have you ever had an idea that seemed to appear out of nowhere?

2. Why do you think the Torah begins with the second letter of the alphabet instead of the first?

3. At the end of the story we read that God was very pleased with Yofiel and Yofiel's "mistakes." Have you ever made a mistake that turned into something good?

4. The Hebrew word for angels is *malachim*, which is usually translated as "messengers." This opens the possibility that "angels" could be any kind of messengers in our lives and not just the supernatural angel of this story. Who are the messengers in your life, and what messages have they brought?

Shades and the Rock on the Grave

THERE HAVE BEEN MANY NOBLE ATTEMPTS to catalogue life. Thinkers such as Aristotle, Darwin, and Goodall have devoted themselves to the task.

Some have concluded that there are four kingdoms: animal, plant, fungi, and bacteria. Some say there is a fifth kingdom, the protist kingdom. Some have gone so far as to say there are six kingdoms.

With all due respect, there are actually 746 kingdoms in the universe.

For example, there is a kingdom called the shade kingdom, and it has elements of animal, fungi, and bacteria, but it is not entirely any of these things, because it is also shadow. And dark matter. And ash. And nightmare.

Once upon a time there was a solitary woman living on the outskirts of a small town. Lily Redwoods was kind and gentle and kept to herself. She lived in her grandmother's old home, a little cottage covered in ivy, with a wood-burning stove and stone chimney and a pebble path that wound through a lush garden of sunflowers, squash, strawberries, and spinach. She spent much of the day working in her garden, coaxing iridescent vegetation out of tiny seeds with water from her rain barrels and love from her heart. She foraged roots, mushrooms, berries, and bark in the forest. She loved the bright splashes of pink and purple wildflowers that sprung up between mounds of soft green and brown moss, perfuming the air. Baby daffodils were her favorite. She would weave through the giant pillars of trees, looking up at the high branches spread like a chuppah against the sky. She loved the spongy carpet of leaves and soil beneath her bare feet and the vast lacework of leaves above her that sifted the sun into dappled light and the air into diamonds of freshness for her to breathe.

People in the nearby town were afraid of her. They did not understand why she lived alone or walked barefoot through the woods, with her black hair loose and her apron full of herbs. They did not remember that the sages of old would wander too, meditating upon rocks and communing with God through bushes and brooks. Then one misty dusk some children took a dare to spy through her kitchen window and saw her bustling amid jars and steaming pots. They ran back to town and told everyone that Lily was a witch, making potions and casting spells. The townsfolk did not know that what the children had seen was Lily preserving fruits and transforming them into jams and jellies and pickling cucumbers and radishes. They did not know that Lily might live alone but was still a little bit lonely and a lot shy. So whenever she came into town to purchase a little cream or cloth, the townspeople kept their distance.

One day, a sickness crept over towns and cities across the country, and eventually it closed in on the little town. People started coughing and shivering. Their muscles seized and cramped, and then their brains fizzed and popped like lightbulbs bursting from an overload of current. People hunkered down in their beds. Doctors and nurses rushed from home to home with remedies and instructions to rest, hydrate, and keep warm. But the virus was powerful, and many people died.

When the plague finally passed, the people who survived were stricken with a sorrow so deep that they slumped when they stood, dragged their feet when they walked, and sobbed day and night. Their hearts were broken. They wondered why this terrible thing had happened to them. But sometimes the question "why" is itself a whirling wasteland, and when the people could find no answer (because sometimes there is no answer), they started asking "who." Who was to blame for their pain?

So the whispers began: Maybe it was that Lily Redwoods, the woman who lived on the outskirts. Maybe she had cast a spell on the town for shunning her. After all, she was still beautiful and healthy, while their loved ones had grown pale and sickly. Surely that was evidence enough that she was a witch.

It was at this time, in this grief-ridden town, that the Shades were born. Like vultures to carrion, mold to old fruit, lactic acid to sour milk, Shades fester and feed on the shattered pieces of broken hearts. The Shade is invisible to most human eyes. At first, a young Shade, in its larval stage, will fasten itself to a person like a barnacle upon their chest or back, but it cannot simply be scraped away. Then, it will grow into a gloomy bubble around the person's broken heart. As the Shade grows, it will spread across its host's spirit like an ink stain, lapping up lifeblood and draining energy. This is what happened to the people of the little town. The Shades fastened themselves to the people one by one, preventing their broken hearts from mending. The people were eventually so consumed by despair that they could hardly move.

Despite what the people said about her, Lily loved the little town. Lily had moved into the cottage many years ago to take care of her aging grandmother. It was her grandmother who taught her to understand the soil and the seasons. She loved her grandmother, and when her grandmother passed on, Lily made the cottage her home. Even now, Lily could still sense her grandmother's spirit in the changing hues, ancient textures, and buzzing life of the forest.

But after the plague had passed, when Lily returned to the town to purchase a cup of cream and a bolt of cloth, she noticed the heavy sorrow that saturated the residents there. With eyesight made keen from years of foraging, she discerned a shadowy ripple in the air around a weeping old woman. Lily looked closer and saw it: a wobbling phenomenon, existing somewhere between vapor and slime, leeched onto the body of the old woman. She walked through the town and suddenly saw the shadowy ripples everywhere. The townspeople did not seem to be aware they were in the clutches of diaphanous Shades. When Lily saw a Shade on the back of a young boy as he walked solemnly down the street kicking a rotten potato, she became so upset that she picked up a stone and threw it at the Shade to scare it away. The stone went right through the Shade as if it weren't even there, as if it were in a separate dimension. Instead, the stone hit the child squarely on the back. Lily was horrified and hurried toward him, gasping her apology. The boy turned to see who had thrown the stone, and seeing Lily moving toward him, he screamed, "It's the witch! The witch is attacking me!" Fueled by fear, loss, and Shades, the townspeople stormed out of their homes toward Lily, shouting, "Get her!" and "She wants to kill our children!" A mob of angry townsfolk swarmed after Lily.

Lily was faster than them all and ran to the safety of her cottage. Once she was inside, Lily collapsed on the floor and tried to catch her breath. Her heart was racing with the shock of the accusing mob and even more from the terror of the alien parasites that seemed to have taken hold of every person in the town. The people had always been cautious and distant toward her, and she knew about that silly rumor she was a witch. But this was different.

"It must be those things," Lily thought. "Whatever they are, they are taking over the people in the town. It is almost as if they were possessing their hearts."

Lily could not simply watch as the shadowy beings hollowed out her town, so she went where she always did her deepest thinking—the forest—to consider what to do. She walked through the trees, feathery pine needles grazing her shoulders. Would the strange ectoplasm infecting the people also spread to the flowers, trees, and animals she loved so much? Would they choke the life out of her garden? She tried to think clearly. She remembered her grandmother teaching her which plants were invasive and how to pull them up by their roots from the garden. But the blob on that boy wasn't a plant. It had no roots, and a rock went right through it!

When she turned to head home, Lily saw smoke winding through the trees. Her first thought was that it was the strange invasive shadow swallowing up the forest! She gathered up her skirts and started running toward the smoke, without any plan as to what she would do when she arrived. As she came closer, she could see that the smoke was coming from a crackling fire. It wasn't the Shades after all. It was the townspeople. They had set fire to Lily's cottage.

Lily could see a group of them walking away from the fire back toward the town, laughing and cheering. The inside of her cottage was engulfed in flames, and fire burst through the windows, catching the ivy that had taken so many decades to grow. Lily had basins and tubs of rainwater she used to water her gardens, and she hurried to douse the outside of the cottage so that the fire would not spread to the forest. Under showers of sparks she worked furiously, throwing water all around the perimeter, rushing to extinguish sparks that landed on bark and leaves. She knew she could not save the cottage—that was lost—but she could stop the fire from destroying the trees.

As the day turned to night, Lily sat before the burned-out remains of her cottage. Everything had turned into a heap of black ashes. Only the stone chimney remained, charred black. Ash covered the pebble path and the garden. Lily looked to the trees in the light of the setting sun and thought about how they were already hard at work cleaning and freshening the air. She marveled at their beauty and resilience.

Lily rose, not quite sure what to do next. She walked aimlessly away from her burned cottage. It grew chilly, and she drew her shawl closer around her. She felt the tears welling up in her eyes. She was alone in the world. Her heart was starting to crack when she felt something nuzzle against her leg. She looked down and saw a thin dog, its ears flattened against its head and its tail between its legs. She looked closer and could see that there was a Shade around its neck too. The dog whimpered, and Lily scratched its head.

"Something very sad happened to you," Lily said to the dog. "I am guessing you lost your human, and you loved them very much. And now you are lost and alone."

Lily scratched the dog on its neck, noticing how her hand went right through the Shade as if it weren't there. She sat next to the dog, and it rested its head on her lap. Lily tried to clasp her hands around the Shade. She tried to pinch it. She tried to blow it away. But it remained there, a black wreath around the dog's collar.

"Poor little doggie," she said.

The dog licked her cheek and then stood up and loped slowly away. Having nothing better to do and nowhere to go, Lily followed it. The dog drew her toward the outskirts of the little town, then trotted into an abandoned house at the end of a lonely street. Lily followed it inside. There were no people living in the house, but there were half a dozen dogs, a litter of kittens, and a racoon. In the moonlight gleaming through the dusty windows, Lily could see that all the creatures were hosting Shades. The animals all looked matted, uncared for, and bereaved—a bit like her, if she was honest. Deciding she had no other option, Lily settled down among the animals and slept.

In the morning, Lily found old clothing that had been left in the house. She disguised herself so she could walk through the town. The Shades that people carried had grown larger. All the people were bent as if they were carrying boulders. No one else could see the Shades they were carrying, but they could see their effects. People swerved and lost their balance under the great and growing burden of grief. Avoiding them all, Lily rummaged through the town, finding scraps of food for the abandoned animals to eat. Over the course of a week, she befriended each animal, even the raccoon. When she wasn't foraging, she experimented with the animals' Shades. She poured water on them, but that only irritated the animals. She held a match to a Shade, but it was unaffected. She prayed, sang, and danced. She snuggled with the dog that had licked her cheek, thinking love might loosen the Shade; indeed, the Shade seemed to flicker and shrink a bit, but it did not disappear. She went back into the forest for spices and herbs, which she mixed and burned, filling the abandoned house with sweet perfume. She tried to saw through the Shades to separate them from the animals, but it was like sawing through air. She piled bricks upon them, but it was like putting bricks on a shadow. When the animal would move, the Shade went with it. No matter what Lily tried, the Shades remained on all the animals. Meanwhile, the Shades on the townspeople kept growing bigger until each person was fully enclosed inside a mournful dark sphere.

Feeling frustrated by her lack of progress removing the Shades, Lily visited the remains of her grandmother's cottage. She picked through the ashes and found a small rock. It was meaningless, really, but it fit snugly and warmly in her hand. She held onto it as she sat looking up at the chimney and the melted metal of the pots she had used to make soups and stews, the same pots her grandmother had used to cook for her. She started thinking about her grandmother. Not the sad things, not the fact that she was gone, but all the happy times. The sound of her grandmother's singing. The fresh flowers she would put on Lily's nightstand so that she would wake to something pretty. The way her grandmother always made Lily take seconds when she was already full. How much her grandmother liked eating sesame toast with butter and honey. The way her grandmother's hair was filled with leaves after their walks.

Then Lily started thinking about her parents. The way her father was so gentle taking a splinter out of the palm of her hand. The way he put his arm around her mother's shoulders and her mother put her arm around his waist and they leaned into each other as they watched Lily play. The way her mother kissed her.

The rock grew warmer in Lily's hand as she remembered happy times, silly times, meaningful times. Finally, she stood and walked back to the abandoned house on the lonely street, still holding that warm rock. A medium-sized red dog was sleeping fitfully in a patch of sun. On its back was a particularly active Shade, wiggling and wobbling, a leech sucking the spirit of the dog.

She sat next to the sleeping red dog. It was whimpering and twitching, like it was having a bad dream. The Shade was flopping around it, growing bigger. Lily looked at the stone in her hand. Without much thought, she lay the stone upon the Shade. The Shade went berserk. It started squirming and wriggling, jerking and jiggling, like an insect pinned to a board. Lily was shocked. She had tried bricks and fire and blades and boiling water and spices and herbs and prayer and cuddles and incantations, but nothing had worked. Now, the Shade was staked to the ground by a simple stone.

But it wasn't just any stone, Lily realized. It was a stone she had found in the ashes of her grandmother's cottage. A stone that she held in her hand as she meditated on the memories of the ones she had lost.

Lily gently poked the dog, and it woke up. It took a long, delicious stretch in the sunlight and shook its body. It looked quizzically at Lily and then moved away. The Shade did not go with it, but continued to frantically writhe on the ground. The dog looked back, and Lily could see that the dog knew it had been released. The dog's ears suddenly perked up, and its tail lifted and started wagging. It made a happy little bark and ran off to play.

Lily was overjoyed. She knew how to get rid of the Shades! She immediately got to work. She hurried back to the remains of the cottage and sifted through the rubble for stones. She held them one by one and dreamed and remembered. The more space and time she gave herself to dream and remember, the closer she felt to her grandmother and her parents. One by one, Lily trapped the Shades that clung to the animals in the abandoned house. She experimented as she went, and she learned. She learned that once a Shade was trapped, it lost its strength over a day or two, until it finally disappeared. She learned that the stones did not have to come from the burned cottage. She learned that when a Shade was young, when it was born out of a new grief, it was often too strong to anchor with a stone. She had to wait weeks, sometimes months, before the Shade could be anchored with a memory stone.

One day, Lily was walking out of the town toward the forest. Some of the dogs liked to follow her there to chase squirrels and rabbits and to jump and splash in the brook, their tails wagging with delight. The dogs ran ahead of Lily, when she noticed an elderly woman wearing a black dress standing alone in the town cemetery at the edge of town, bent over a tombstone and weeping. Lily could see that the Shade leeched onto her was large, weighty, and mean. Lily was nervous to approach her even though she was still disguising herself. She worried that if she drew closer, the woman would recognize Lily and scream for the townspeople to "get the witch!" Still, Lily mustered her courage, stepped over the low stone wall, and approached the woman.

The woman looked at Lily with eyes red from crying. Lily quietly laid one of her memory stones on the woman's Shade as it wobbled over the grave. It went right through the Shade as if it were air. It didn't work! Lily wondered whether it was different with animals than with humans. She reached her hand out to the grieving woman. The woman looked at her for a moment. Lily was frightened that the women would push her away or scream. But instead, the woman took her hand. Lily quietly said to her, "Would you hold this memory stone for a moment?" The woman took the stone in her other hand and still held onto Lily for support.

The woman looked at Lily through hooded eyes. Then she said, "I told my grandson that you were just different. There is nothing wrong with being different."

Lily startled, momentarily afraid she was in danger. But the woman continued.

"I know that being different is what sets you on a hill and helps you see further than anyone else." The woman squeezed Lily's hand. "I know you are not a witch."

Lily was amazed that this woman was so kind to her, despite the mean Shade that shrouded her. Lily thought for a moment and then smiled. "What is a witch but one who loves nature and is misunderstood," Lily shrugged. "Maybe I am." She paused. "Maybe you are too."

The two stood in silence, and then the woman said, "Maybe that's good."

"Maybe," Lily said.

"I miss him," the woman said, looking down at the grave. Lily looked, too, at the name on the gravestone and the years the person had lived, which were few.

Lily observed the Shade darken and shimmer like an oil slick. "Tell me," she said.

The woman blinked back tears and began to speak. "He was my light," the woman said. "He was my hero."

Lily looked into the woman's glimmering eyes and felt the glow of her heart.

The woman started to share stories. One after the other. Some of the stories made Lily laugh, and some of the stories made her cry. Some of the stories reminded Lily of her own experiences. She listened so long that she forgot about the memory stone in the woman's hand. When the woman let go of Lily's hand to wipe her eye, Lily remembered. She saw the Shade wobbling and swallowing the woman and the tombstone in its whirling murk.

Lily said, "Why don't you lay your memory stone on the tombstone? It will let others know that you visited and that your loved one is remembered."

The woman looked at the stone in her hand. She nodded and carefully laid it down, right on the Shade that she could not see. But Lily saw it. She saw the Shade tremble violently, thrashing against the little stone. When the woman stepped away, the Shade detached, and the woman gasped.

"I feel . . ." the woman said, "different." She smoothed her dress and wiped away another tear.

The two women embraced, the woman thanking Lily over and over. A week later, Lily visited the same grave. She saw that the memory stone was still there and that the Shade was very small and withered now, still struggling against the power of the stone. The Shade, she knew, would soon disappear.

The woman who had hosted this particular Shade returned from the cemetery with light in her eyes and tenderness in her heart. Knowing the townspeople still did not trust Lily, she told her friends about a mysterious woman she met in the cemetery and the power of the memory stone. The woman told her friends about holding the stone and sharing stories about her loved one, and how placing the memory stone on the grave brought great healing to her heart. "I am still sad," she explained to them. "I miss him so very much. The pain is big. It is a part of me, but it is no longer eating me alive."

Her friends were intrigued. One by one, they each found their own stone. Some found colorful pebbles. Some chose rocks from the river, large and smooth. One experimented with a cockle shell from a pink-sand beach many miles away. Another painted a flat stone with patterns and polka dots. Soon, townspeople were filling the streets and squares with stories about their loved ones. They laughed, and cried, and dried their eyes, and brought their memory stones to the places their loved ones had been laid to rest. And one by one, as they laid their stones upon the graves, the grief that had paralyzed their hearts began to give way to a new feeling. A feeling of closeness to one another, gratitude for the love they had shared, and something else. Something tiny and flickering, like a candle in a dark cave or a star whose light is only just reaching us after a hundred thousand years. Hope.

It was only then that the elderly woman revealed that the mysterious woman was really Lily Redwoods. The townspeople remembered what they had done to Lily, and they felt remorseful. They found her living in the abandoned house, caring for animals. Together the townspeople rebuilt her cottage, stone by stone. Children worked alongside Lily, learning to garden. They planted sunflowers and squash, strawberries and spinach, each in its season, and Lily passed the wisdom of the forest that she had learned from her grandmother down to them.

The townspeople were never able to see the Shades. However, they did understand that somehow the stones were weighing down their grief and anchoring their pain. And as time passed, they also learned that the stones could be moved and used for other things, like building towers or skipping across streams. The Shades were gone, and the stones did not become idols to weigh down the townspeople.

Lily lived a long, meaningful life. She died peacefully surrounded by many friends. And the place where she was buried was always covered with memory stones.

QUESTIONS

1. How does sharing stories help alleviate grief? If you were holding a memory stone, what memory would you want to share? How would you like to be remembered?

2. Loss is something that is universal, but our grief is expressed in unique ways. Some people in this story expressed anger, while others expressed sadness. How do you feel when you experience loss? How can you be more compassionate for the strong feelings of others?

3. There are many practices associated with grief and mourning in Judaism, including tearing a ribbon, washing one's hands, covering mirrors, lighting a candle, leaving a stone on the grave, and many more. What ritual or rituals, if any, have brought special meaning to you?

4. Lily Redwoods was different and was treated as an outsider. It took a remarkably kind woman to see through those differences into the heart of who Lily really was. How does our society treat people who are different? What does that say about us?

Empathy

A Whale Tale

I T WAS STORMING in the sky-world. The clouds were heavy and battleship gray. Lightning lit the ocean's surface, followed by rippling, thundering sound waves that Owen felt down to his flukes. The wind whipped white-capped waves into wild turbulence. Rain pierced the water like harpoons. This was more than a storm. It felt like an omen of bad things to come. This was the kind of weather that shredded sails and sunk ships.

Most of the calves in the pod were thrilled by the storm, but not Owen. Owen wanted to swim into the depths where the current was gentle and the water was dark. But all the other calves were playing in the storm. Twyla and Wynn were breaching, seeing who could leap the highest. Wallace torpedoed through a curling wave right before it crashed. Lawanda did a vertical twirl, causing a cyclone of bubbles and foam. Wiley did a beautiful full twist over the water, generating a rogue wave with his great splash. Wilhelmina leapt over Ewing in an incredible sparkling arc. Willard smacked his tail against the water in applause.

Their play lessened Owen's worry, and soon it was his turn to do something. He was planning to breach the surface and blast a fantastic fountain, so he dove down to get a good head start. He turned to head back to the jagged surface, picking up speed. He was encouraged by the resonating song of the calves, their long sonic a's and o's intoning over the ocean roar and echoing throughout his giant body. A school of small fish darted out of his way, flashing their scales silver and purple. Faster and faster, Owen raced cloudward. He was going to soar higher than Wallace! Climb a ladder of rain beyond the firmament, and dive into the cosmic ocean! Soar through the constellations! He was about to break through the water when a terrifying whip of lightning cracked across the sky-world. Owen tried to slow down and turn back, but he was already moving too fast.

Owen closed his eyes as he breached, his mouth opened wide as he gasped in fear. He sloppily flopped onto his side as a wave crashed over him and threw something absolutely vile down his throat and into his belly. It was definitely not a fish—it was not cool, slick, and small. It was big, and Owen swallowed it whole. Its tentacles flailed and kicked inside of him. Owen sunk back into the water, feeling his stomach seizing with this strange, awful-tasting thing wriggling inside of him. He felt his face turn green, and he knew he was going to throw up.

All around him, his friends were laughing. Owen hurtled past the other whales as fast as he could. Behind him he heard Lawanda call out, "Hey Owen! Wait up!" And Ewing said, "He is fast!"

Owen did not slow down until he was sure no one could see him. Even though it took just moments in whale time, it felt like it took three days of swimming for Owen to find privacy. He finally broke the surface near a beach, startling a flotilla of seagulls that had settled on the sea. Astonishingly, the storm had completely subsided. There wasn't a cloud in the sky, and the sun warmed the air. The ocean was eerily calm, but Owen didn't have time to pay attention to this odd phenomenon. Still feeling sick to his stomach, he heaved himself onto the beach and threw up. He immediately felt better. When he turned to swim back, Owen was aghast to see Lawanda was right there behind him. She had seen everything.

"Whoa. Did you see that?" she said, swimming to catch up to him. "That thing you threw up just stood up on its tentacles and walked away!"

Owen was so embarrassed, he swam away faster than ever.

"Are you okay?" Lawanda called, but Owen was too far to hear her. He raced to his family pod and took shelter hiding underneath his mother's giant fin.

"Owen!" his mother said. "What in God's blue ocean is the matter with you?"

"Did you see that?" Owen's father said. "One minute, the sea was savage and stormy, and then, in the snap of a clam, it was perfectly calm!"

"Wayne!" Owen's mother said, "There is something wrong with Owen."

Owen was sobbing so hard that he could hardly speak. His father nuzzled him gently. Owen's cousins and grandparents also came in close. Being surrounded by his family pod made him feel safer.

"I got sick, and everyone was laughing," Owen said.

"What happened?" Owen's grandmother asked.

"I swallowed something big and gross, and when I vomited it out on the beach, it stood up on its tentacles, and it had whiskers all over its face."

Owen's grandfather's eyes got wide. "Owen, you swallowed a human being!" he said.

"I've never heard of such a thing!" Owen's father said.

"Cool!" said one of Owen's cousins.

"Nautical," said another.

Owen cried. "But everyone laughed at me. I'm a joke. I'll always be a joke." He ducked under his mother's fin, away from his family's staring eyes.

"I'm sure they weren't laughing *at* you," his mother said.

"They were probably just laughing *with* you," said his father.

"We all do mortifying things," his mother said. "Sometimes, when you do something embarrassing, the best thing to do is to laugh at yourself."

Owen's grandmother nodded her head. "Getting sick is nothing to be ashamed of."

Owen's parents tucked him into a bed of soft kelp with a bowl of brown algae and mashed krill.

Owen thought about what had happened. He thought about his friends all laughing at him, and it made him groan. But then he remembered the day when they had all laughed with Twyla and Wynn after they both had leapt at the same time and bumped into each other, flopping back into the sea. Even Owen had laughed with them, and come to think of it, Twyla and Wynn had laughed too. "I wasn't laughing *at* them to make them feel bad," Owen realized. "I was laughing *with* them because it was funny."

Then Owen remembered them all laughing when Wallace had a long trail of seaweed stuck on his dorsal fin. And when Wilhelmina belly-flopped. And one time when Ewing got spooked by a manta ray. All those times made everyone laugh.

He also remembered when Willard had sea lice, and that wasn't funny. And when Wynn got injured when he ventured too close to a ship, and they all circled him and sang.

Maybe his friends were laughing because Owen's attempted jump went completely kerflooey. Maybe they didn't know at the time that he had been frightened by the lightning and had swallowed a rancid human.

Lawanda knew he threw up, Owen realized, and she hadn't laughed.

Owen's grandfather peeked in to see how he was doing. "How ya feelin', O?"

Owen said that he was feeling a little better.

His grandfather settled next to him and said, "Do you know what empathy is?"

Owen shook his head no.

His grandfather thought for a moment. "Empathy is when you feel the feelings of another. Like when your friend is excited because they are going on a trip, and you feel excited with them. Or when someone is feeling sad, and you understand their feelings and feel sad with them. When I see you feeling sick to your stomach, I have empathy because I remember times I felt sick to my stomach too. I understand how you feel, and I feel your feelings."

Knowing that his grandfather could feel his feelings made Owen feel stronger. It helped him remember that he wasn't alone.

His grandfather added, "It takes time to learn empathy. But experiences like you had today help you to learn. Now when you see someone who is embarrassed, you will feel their feelings and you will be able to comfort them. A bad experience can be a great gift, because it helps you care more deeply for others."

Later that afternoon, Lawanda came to visit.

"Are you okay?" she asked Owen.

"I am feeling better," Owen said.

"Phew! I was worried," Lawanda said. "Since you're feeling better, do you want to meet the others at the reef?"

Owen nodded and together they rode a warm tide to where the waters were the clearest. Below them they could see towers and bridges of coral, dotted with spiny sea urchins.

"What *was* that thing?" Lawanda asked as they drifted.

"I think it was a human," Owen said.

"No kidding!" Lawanda said. "What was a human doing in the sea during a storm like that?"

"Who knows," Owen shrugged, and then he smiled. "Maybe he fell off a boat."

"You know," Lawanda said, bumping him playfully, "you probably saved that landlubber's life."

When they reached the reef, the other whale calves rushed up to Owen. Ewing exclaimed, "That wave totally rolled you!"

Owen laughed at himself, and they all laughed along.

"Where'd you go?" asked Twyla. "The storm ended, and you were gone."

Owen looked at Lawanda and then at all his friends. "You are *not* going to believe what happened," he said. Owen told them about spitting a human up on the beach, and they listened with amazement. Afterward, they played together with a bob of seals, a bale of sea turtles, and a squadron of pelicans until the sky-world faded from pink and orange to indigo and black. The shimmering stars far above mirrored the bioluminescence far below, and the pod of young whales followed the silver moon path home. Soon the story of Owen swallowing a human, and the storm that suddenly subsided, was woven into the whales' sonorous songs, encircling the world.

QUESTIONS

1. What is the difference between sympathy and empathy?
2. This story looks at the Book of Jonah from the whale's perspective. What other perspectives could you imagine in the Book of Jonah? What might their story be?
3. How does it feel to be laughed at versus laughed with?
4. Judaism places a strong emphasis on doing rather than just feeling. Empathy is usually understood as a feeling, but are there actions you can take to express empathy? Are there ways to increase empathy in the larger world?

The Flying Insect Café

And every flying insect is impure for you; they may not be eaten!
—Deuteronomy 14:19

I REMEMBER THE VERY INSTANT my family almost fell apart.

Moses was going on and on with the rules, and we were listening because we didn't want to get swallowed up by the ground or buried under a mountain. And he said these very words: "And every flying insect is impure for you; they may not be eaten."

My thirteen-year-old cousin Avinoam immediately opened his mouth to shout "Amen" when a gnat flew into his throat, and he gagged.

"I swallowed a bug! I swallowed a flying bug!" he gasped, spitting on the ground, tears streaming down his face. We were terrified, waiting for boils to break out all over our bodies or hailstones to pummel us to death.

People moved away from our family, covering their mouths in case they too accidentally inhaled a flying insect. But nobody looked more stupefied and dismayed than my aunt, uncle, and parents.

The reason that my cousin was so enthusiastic about shouting "Amen" to Moses's proclamation about not eating flying insects was not because he was particularly zealous about the law. Instead, it was because he hated his mother's butterfly broth. It was bitter, to be fair, but it was also believed to have medicinal qualities.

In fact, my family made a decent living operating the Flying Insect Café, which was really a simple kiosk, easy to move with the camp. We would set it up whenever the camp settled in one place, then cook up our goods and sell them. We were always busy, with customers lining up to enjoy the daily specials on the menu. The very day Moses made that pronouncement, the specials were mosquito mush, dragonfly pie, and baked beetle basket. Hearing Moses's new rule, however, made everything uncertain.

That night, my aunt, uncle, and cousin came over to our tent. I hugged Avinoam, happy he wasn't covered in leprosy for transgressing a commandment the very moment it was spoken. I figured God understood that mistakes happen. My aunt and uncle were not feeling nearly as appreciative. They were stomping around, offended that Moses would take such a direct shot at our livelihood.

My father was scrolling through his notes. "Right here!" he said. "This is what he said a few months ago, that there are, *however*, some winged insects you *may* eat: those that have jointed legs for hopping on the ground. You may eat any kind of locust, katydid, cricket, or grasshopper."

"So, we can keep these things on the menu," my mother said.

"Okay," said my aunt, pacing nervously back and forth. "So, the locust lasagna, katydid crunch wrap, Cajun cricket casserole, and grasshopper goulash stay."

"But no more butterfly broth," I whispered behind my hand to Avinoam, and he gave me a secret thumbs-up.

"But *this* time," my uncle said, "Moses *clearly* said *every* flying insect is impure. Every one! We will be washed out!"

"Here, wait!" my mother said, pulling my father's note-scroll from him. "Moses said: Every swarming thing that swarms upon the earth is detestable; it shall not be eaten. Upon the earth! Not flying. Worms, spiders, centipedes."

My aunt threw her hands in the air. She said to me and Avinoam, "Such a shame! Your grandmother's centipede stew was delicious!"

"Yes," my uncle said, agreeing with my mother's point, "but *then* he forbade swarming insects, and today he forbade all FLYING INSECTS!"

"Shraga!" my aunt scolded. "There is no need to shout!"

"Shraga, sit," my father said. "Let's all sit."

We sat in a circle with my father's parchments in the middle.

"What about the fruit fly?" my aunt said.

"It's a FLYING INSECT, Carmella!" my uncle raged, his whole head turning bright red. "Do you want that serpents should bite us?"

"No, but hear me out," she continued. "What if we collected fruit flies that we find *inside* a fruit that is still on the tree. They are not flying, nor are they swarming upon the earth."

"What do you think a tree grows out of, Carmella?" my uncle said. "A cloud!? It grows out of the earth!" He dropped his head into his hands. "We're done! Back to shepherding we go!"

"Stop catastrophizing," my mother said.

"Stop catastrophizing? My sister wants me to simply stop catastrophizing!" my uncle exclaimed. "Oh, okay. I will just erase from my mind what happened to Nadav and Avihu. Or when there was so much quail, two cubits deep we were wading in quail! And we were skipping around like children, yelling 'Yay! Quail! What a gift! Thank You, thank You, God!' and then when the quail meat was still between our teeth, God's anger blazed out against us and we were struck by PLAGUE?!"

"Shraga," my aunt said, handing him a wet cloth for his face. "You're going to make yourself pass out."

"Avinoam's still okay," I pointed out, "and he swallowed a gnat."

"Well," my father said, "that is interesting. But maybe there is a difference between accidentally swallowing a flying insect and intentionally *dining* on insects, yes?"

"If accidentally swallowing a gnat meant you broke God's commandment," my mother mused, "then there would be no more camel racers! I mean, you've seen them galloping around with their mouths hanging open."

"What, are we supposed to wear masks all the time now?" my aunt asked.

"And what happens," Avinoam piped in, "if I am drinking some goat milk, and I look away for a second, and a gnat flies into my milk, and I don't see it, and I drink it? *Plus* I'm the firstborn. Am I dead?"

"Listen," my mother said. "If a drop of cream falls into a pot of meat, it is still kosher as long as the drop of cream is less than a sixtieth of the meat. But you are telling me that a tiny *gnat* in a pot of soup renders the whole soup unkosher?"

"I think to be safe," my father said carefully, "we would have to strain the soup."

"That's ridiculous!" my uncle said.

"What about bugs we can't even see?" I asked.

"I'm afraid to eat *anything* now," Avinoam said.

"Oh great!" my uncle said. "Now everyone is going to be terrified of every speck. How is Omer going to bake his manna birthday cakes? We live in the desert, people! There are specks *everywhere!*"

My aunt suddenly lit up. "What about chopped bugs?" she said. "The law applies to whole bugs, but what if a bug has been chopped up, do the laws still apply?"

"Now you sound like Korach," my father said. "And that didn't end well."

"I'm not challenging Moses," my aunt said. "I'm just trying to understand the particulars."

My uncle stood up. "I need some air," he declared, stomping out of the tent. We could still hear him outside talking to himself: "We didn't have enough time to bake *bread* when we escaped Egypt, so we had to eat *matzah*, but now in the wilderness we *can* eat bread, but we are supposed to *make* time to sift all the *flour* for swarming things and flying things. Somebody please explain to me how *that* makes sense!"

My mother leaned forward, resting her elbows on her knees. "Moses is reasonable. God doesn't expect us to do something impossible. Maybe Carmella's right. Maybe chopped bugs are the way to go."

My parents and my aunt began looking through their recipes, adjusting the ingredients accordingly.

Just then my uncle barged back into the tent waving a loaf of bread. "Partial bugs! Partial bugs!" We all stared at him.

"What are you saying, Shraga?"

"I went to Omer's tent, and he said that he found out that partial bugs *are allowed*. You sift the flour, you strain the soup, but if a bug gets ground up when you're grinding your wheat, what can you do?"

So my family got to work that very night making changes to our business. We made a new sign and changed our name from the Flying Insect Café to Le Insect Café, thinking that removing the word "flying" would be good under these troubling circumstances. We wrote in smaller letters underneath the new name: "100% Partial Bugs." We put an asterisk next to every item on the menu and at the bottom of the menu wrote: "*All of our bugs are ground up and chopped."

We hung a smaller sign in the front of the kiosk that said, "Number of people who have eaten at Le Insect Café who have gotten swallowed up by the earth: 0," and the zero was really big.

The café looked great. The menu looked great. And each day, my family prepared multiple savory and sweet specials, including spaghetti and moth meatballs* and bumblebee biscuits*. But even with our new look and new menu, fewer customers came every day. We tried promotional tactics, like passing out coupons at the Tent of Meeting, but the truth was, people were just not coming.

"That's it!" my uncle said after two weeks. "The café is kaput."

My family was terribly upset. Insect cuisine had been in our family for generations.

"Let's go for a walk," I said to Avinoam. The tension was high in our tent, and I knew it would be best to get out for a while.

We wound through the encampment, running into friends along the way. We reached a pen filled with goats, and we played chase with them for a while. Then we walked further, to a cluster of palm trees.

"Hey!" Avinoam called to me. "Check this out!"

I hustled over to him, and there on the ground was a beehive, cracked in half.

"It must have fallen out of the tree," I said, looking up.

"The bees are gone," Avinoam said.

We knelt to look closer. The hive was broken in two, and each half was filled with dark-gold hexagonal gridding. It was beautiful, like the jeweled breastplate of the High Priest. I touched it with my finger.

"Don't!" Avinoam shouted, knocking my hand away. "Bees are flying insects!"

I looked at the golden drop on my fingertip. "But I'm not eating the insects. Moses didn't say anything about the *product* of flying insects."

"What if there's a leg in there," Avinoam asked, "or a wing?"

I waved my arms around, imitating my uncle, "Partial bugs! Partial bugs are okay!"

Avinoam laughed. Then he stopped as I moved my finger toward my mouth. I could see he was holding his breath. I tasted the golden nectar, and it was delicious.

We both waited to see if the earth was going to swallow me. After a few moments, I said to Avinoam, "You want some?"

He nodded and we both enjoyed the sweet, sticky golden goodness.

We each carried a half of the large hive back to my tent, where our parents were bemoaning their fate.

"This is incredible!" my uncle declared after tasting a drop.

"A miracle!" my mother cheered. "A sign!"

"This is our new direction," my father said. "Honey!" That was the first time Avinoam and I heard what the golden nectar was called.

"And maybe," my aunt pondered, poking at the honeycomb with a spoon, "we just concentrate on one thing and do it really well."

"No more daily specials and long menus," my mother added.

"It's brilliant," my uncle said. He leapt up and started pacing in a circle around us. "But we have to be deliberate. We've already changed our name, menu, and look once, and it didn't work. We need to really plan this transition."

"We need to debut it," my father said, "at a time when people are feeling good."

"Yes," my mother said. "This sweet nectar should be associated with good."

"What about Rosh HaShanah?" I asked.

"Rosh HaShanah," my uncle repeated, still pacing. He rubbed his head. "Rosh HaShanah. I like it, Oreet."

"But are we just selling honey?" my father asked. "Or is there something else, something that makes it unique?"

My aunt tilted a spoonful over the hive, and we all stared as it slowly dripped mesmerizingly down, with its gorgeous amber glow.

Avinoam licked his finger and said, "What goes well with honey?"

"Cucumber, melons," my mother wondered aloud, "leeks, onions, garlic?"

"I don't know," my father said. "I'm not sure that's the right direction for Le Insect Café. Those were things we ate in Egypt. I'm thinking it should be paired with something new."

"Manna is too flaky," my uncle said. "Don't get me wrong, it's delicious." He looked up at the roof of the tent and shouted, "You hear that, Most Praiseworthy God? Manna is delicious! You will never hear me complaining about manna!" Then he put his hand over his mouth and spoke softly to the family, as if to prevent God from hearing him or reading his lips, "But, it is very flaky. We want something new. Something no one else sells. Omer makes the manna cakes and bread. We'll make the honey and . . . and . . ."

"Olives!" my aunt shouted.

Avinoam groaned and held his stomach.

"Okay, okay," my aunt said. "Then how about dates, hmm?"

"Too sweet," my mother said. "Date honey and bee honey, it's too much."

"Figs? Grapes?" my aunt sounded exasperated.

"We need something strong enough to hold the honey," my father said. "It has to be structurally sound. Like a wedge."

"A wedge of what?" my mother asked.

"A wedge of something that complements the sweet but doesn't overwhelm it," my uncle said.

"A wedge of what?" my mother asked again.

We all sat in silence, glancing around for ideas. Day had turned to dusk, and I was getting hungry. My stomach growled.

"At this point I would eat honey on just about anything," I whispered to my cousin. "Even mixed into butterfly broth."

Suddenly, my aunt stood up. She looked like she had been struck by a bolt of Revelation straight from Sinai. We all waited with anticipation for her to present her epiphany. Then, with all the confidence of a High Priest, she pronounced the words: "Fish heads."

"Fish heads, Carmella?" my uncle shouted throwing his hands in the air. "Really?"

"Yes," my aunt exclaimed. "Fish heads. For Rosh HaShanah. Fish and honey. It is perfect. Rosh HaShanah is the *head* of the year, and we will serve *heads* of fish. How can you not see the genius in this?"

"I think it has potential," my father said. "I like fish heads as a symbol. A little sweet honey glaze might give it that zsa zsa zsu."

My uncle shook his head in disbelief. "I think 'zsa zsa zsu' are all out of your minds."

"Listen," my mother said. "We don't have to decide right now. Let's pause, have dinner, and sleep on it."

The next morning, Avinoam and I took a walk, kicking stones.

"Wanna ride donkeys?" he asked.

"Maybe later," I said. "I heard there's a trading caravan in the Zebulunite camp. Wanna check it out?"

"Sure."

We walked into the Zebulunite camp and looked at merchant shops selling crimson yarn tunics and tanned leather sandals. We looked at the pyramids of pottery and reed baskets. We admired the copper incense altars, silver trumpets and hammered gold nose rings. We reached the caravan, with traders from faraway lands, where the air was filled with the scent of cumin, mint, cloves, frankincense, and myrrh. We sampled their oils and vinegars and beheld their dolphin skins, agates, and pearls. And then, at the very end of the caravan, I saw a wagon filled with round colorful fruits.

"What are these?" I asked the merchant. The fruits were red, green, pink, and yellow.

The man didn't answer, but he sliced a red one and handed Avinoam and me each a piece.

"A wedge," Avinoam said, lifting it up.

We each crunched into our wedge at the same time. It was tart and crisp. It was structurally sound. It was crunchy and cool.

"Who grows these things?" I asked. "The Perizzites?"

The merchant shook his head.

"The Hittites? The Canaanites? The Midianites?" I asked, but the merchant continued to shake his head. "The Ishmaelites? The Girgashites? The Moabites? The Amorites? The Jebusites?"

"No," the merchant finally spoke. "They are apples. And they come from a place even farther away."

My cousin puzzled over what could be farther away. "From *space*?" he asked. The merchant laughed.

We bought two apples, one yellow and one red, and ran home.

Like I said, I remember the very instant my family almost fell apart. I also remember the exact moment we persevered: it was when Avinoam and I walked into the tent with those apples.

My mother took the first bite. "It's tart."

My aunt took the second. "It's crisp."

My father took the third. "It's structurally sound."

My uncle took a wedge and said, "But how does it taste if we dip it in honey?" He dunked the wedge into the honeycomb and tasted it. He closed his eyes with delight, and a small tear ran down the side of his face.

"Well?" I asked.

"It tastes like what the new year should be," my uncle said. "Healthy and sweet."

We repainted the sign for Le Insect Café to read "Apples and Honey," and in smaller letters underneath we added, *L'shanah tovah um'tukah*—"A good and sweet year."

And it was good and sweet for our family, for many happy and fruitful years.

QUESTIONS

1. What is a sweet memory you have about Rosh HaShanah?
2. It is said that necessity is the mother of invention. Do you agree? Is there something you've thought of inventing?
3. There is a custom of eating specific foods besides apples and honey on Rosh HaShanah, as a way of asking God to increase our blessings in the new year. Fish heads are one of these foods, as are leeks, beets, pumpkins, and dates. What special food would you pick to start the new year? What would it represent?
4. This story takes one innocuous commandment of Torah (*Every flying insect is impure for you; they may not be eaten!*) and imagines how it might have affected a particular family at that time. Choose another commandment in the Torah, and imagine another family wrestling with its effect on them.

Fairy Footprints
Why Matzah Has Holes

L ONG AGO, in the land of Goshen, east of the river Nile, there lived many children whose parents were slaves to Pharaoh. Their parents were forced to work from early in the morning until late at night. The poor children were left all alone with no one to take care of them, and when their parents were finally allowed to return to their homes, the parents were too sad, tired, and broken to do anything but sleep.

So the children would cry and pray for help. After many tears were shed and many prayers were prayed, something miraculous happened. Out of their salty tears and pure prayers, beautiful little fairies sprung up!

The fairies played with the children every day. They taught the children how to take care of themselves. The children became much happier and healthier, and their homes were filled with singing and giggling. The children would roll out dough to make bread for the return of their hungry parents, and the fairies would dance for them, leaving little footprints in the flour. When the parents would finally return home, the fairies went away, but in the morning, after the parents went to labor, the fairies would always return.

It wasn't long before it was reported to Pharaoh's court that the children in the land of Goshen seemed joyful and well-fed. They were seen singing, playing, and picnicking together, and it didn't make any sense at all. Why were the children of slaves so happy?

Two of Pharaoh's magicians, Jannes and Jambres, became curious and investigated. They spied and took notes and checked their ancient books. They realized that this could only be the work of very rare fairies. They also knew that the fairies' magic could be useful to them, so they set about to build a fairy trap.

This is how they did it: In the middle of the night, under the constellation of the scorpion, the magicians planted a field of hibiscus flowers and watered it with the blood of wild beasts. While the flowers were growing, the magicians sought out an acacia tree that had been struck twice by lightning. They finally found one in the Nubian Desert. When the hibiscus flowers started to bloom, the magicians brought beehives to the field, and the bees took nectar from the flowers and made honey. The magicians smeared the enchanted honey inside a trap made from the wood of the burned tree, and it was ready.

The two magicians took their trap and went to the land of Goshen when all the parents were gone. The bewitching perfume of the red hibiscus honey filled the air, and the fairies all stopped singing. The children watched with fright as the fairies were helplessly lured into the trap, and the evil magicians stole every last one of them away to the palace.

The children were devastated. They knew they had to do something to rescue their tiny magical friends. Day after day they tried to think of a plan, but it all seemed impossible. What could the children of slaves do, especially now that they'd lost their fairies? When they were about to give up hope, one girl, Miriam, said, "We cannot wait any longer. We must sneak into the palace and rescue them." The children were very afraid. But two brave children volunteered to join her.

Early the next morning, just after their parents trudged off, Miriam, Caleb, and Joshua climbed onto one donkey and headed out of the land of Goshen. By the time they reached the palace, it was nearly night. The three children hopped off the donkey and hid behind reeds, watching the gate. The gate was made of giant stones, with thick, heavy doors, iron bolts, and fiery torches, guarded by twenty men.

"We'll never get in!" Caleb cried.

"And even if we did, how will we find the fairies?" Joshua asked.

"I don't know," Miriam whispered. But she could feel in her heart that the fairies were near.

And then, something strange happened. Out of nowhere, a frog leapt onto the steps of the palace, and one of the guards tried to step on it. Then, another frog leapt out of the shadows and landed on a guard's leg. Then another frog leapt out from a date tree and landed on a guard's head! Soon, there was an army of frogs swarming the palace gate, and the guards were jumping from foot to foot trying to shake them off.

Miriam, Caleb, and Joshua didn't have to speak to one another. They knew it was now or never. The three children bolted toward the gate while the guards were pulling frogs off their faces and shaking them out of their clothes. The three children ran through the great corridors of the palace. Everywhere they turned they saw palace royalty running from frogs. The palace echoed with the sound of frogs croaking. Frogs leapt onto the walls, climbed statues, and dropped from the ceiling. But they didn't touch the children.

"I can feel the fairies," Miriam said when they reached the top of a stairwell. "I know they are down here."

The children hurried down the stairs even as Egyptians in fine linens and gold jewelry hurried up the stairs, chased by frogs.

Miriam led Caleb and Joshua through a small door, and inside they saw a horrible sight: walls lined with cages and cages of fairies, their faces filthy and their wings drooping. Under each cage was a bin that collected their powdery glitter. In the center of the room on a stone pedestal was a large glowing crystal. The crystal drained the magic out of the fairies. The children saw the shimmering vapor being pulled out of the fairies' little bodies and how weak and fragile they had become.

Joshua took off his ragged cloak and threw it over the crystal. Immediately the fairies perked up. They cheered as the children struggled to open the locks on their cages.

Suddenly, the evil magicians, covered in frogs, rushed into the room. One of them thrust his hand into a bin, grabbed a handful of fairy glitter, and threw it into the air, saying, "By the power of Ra and the golden throne, turn these frogs into stone!" Instantly, all the frogs turned to stone and fell to the floor.

It was then that the magicians saw the children. The children ran toward the door, but the magicians were fast and strong and grabbed them by their clothes and hair. In their struggle to escape, Joshua's cloak slipped off the crystal, and the crystal began again to drain the fairies' magic. Jannes grabbed Caleb and Joshua, Jambres grabbed Miriam, and they quickly tied the children together with a glowing rope. The fairies began to cry.

Jannes thrust his hand into a bin and grabbed a handful of fairy glitter.

"No!" cried Caleb.

"Please!" shouted Joshua.

The fairies shrieked.

Miriam closed her eyes and prayed.

Jannes threw the handful of glitter into the air and pronounced these words, "By the power of Ra and the golden throne, turn these children . . ."

All at once, Miriam kicked one of the stone frogs at Jannes, and he stumbled. Caleb and Joshua also started kicking the stone frogs they could reach toward the magicians.

Jambres reached for fairy glitter, tossed it over himself, and cried out, "Heat of fire, chill of ice, turn these stones into lice."

All of the frogs that had turned to stone exploded into billions of lice all over the room.

"You nincompoop!" screamed Jannes. "You said the spell wrong!"

Jannes jerked to the side and started scratching his legs and stomach in a frenzy, shouting, "Get them off me! Get them off me!" Jambres frantically started to scratch his hair and screamed, "They're eating me alive!"

Before Jannes could reach for more fairy glitter, the lice swarmed all over the magicians until they were completely blanketed with bugs. However, the lice passed over the children and fairies.

The ropes around the children stopped glowing, and Joshua pulled his hands free. He untied Miriam and Caleb. The three children returned to struggling with the locks on the cages, while trying not to get hit by the magicians, who thrashed miserably about. By this time, the magicians were so covered with lice that the children couldn't tell them apart. Caleb shouted, "I got it!" He showed Miriam and Joshua how to undo the locks, and soon all the cages were opened.

One of the magicians stumbled into the stone pedestal holding the crystal. It tumbled over and shattered. Now the fairies were truly free.

"Follow me!" Miriam yelled, as she ran out the door, up the stairs, and through the corridors of the palace. Behind her were Caleb and Joshua and a twinkling purple and green cloud of fairies, while all around them palace royalty and guards rolled on the floor covered in itchy insects. When they got outside the palace gate, the fairies gathered together, lifted the three children, and flew them all the way back to the land of Goshen.

Finally home, the children wanted to celebrate, but Miriam stopped them. She said, "It won't be long before the magicians are back. We will never be safe here! We must tell our parents that the time to leave is now. And only when we are truly free will we sing and dance."

And that is what happened. It was the children who told the parents that they had to leave Egypt. It took many more trials and miracles before the day finally came, but when it did, the fairies were so excited, they danced. They danced while the children packed up their sacks. They danced while the parents loaded the donkeys. They danced on the donkey's ears, making them twitch. They danced while the parents hurriedly rolled out the dough. They danced on the children's arms, tickling them and making them laugh. They danced on the dough with their tiny pointed slippers, making holes in every matzah.

Eventually, the fairies went to other children who needed them. But every Passover they return to honor Miriam, Joshua, and Caleb, the brave children who set them free, by dancing on the dough, impressing it with their happy steps.

QUESTIONS

1. It was the children in the story who told the parents they had to leave Egypt. In what ways do children teach and inspire adults?

2. Although not named in the Torah, Jannes and Jambres are the names given in later texts to the two magicians who served Pharaoh to deceive the people into thinking God's power wasn't real. In this story, they want to take away the children's fairies to make sure the Israelites remain oppressed. In what ways are trickery and deceit used today to keep people from making positive change?

3. This story imagines Miriam, Joshua, and Caleb's adventure freeing the fairies, and ultimately themselves, and doesn't mention Moses. What freedom movement is happening now, and who are the people making a difference?

4. Matzah is called "bread of freedom" and "bread of affliction." What does matzah represent to you?

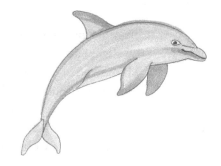

Shulamit bat Aminadav

Shulamit bat Aminadav had a special connection with animals. When the land was covered with frogs, Shulamit caught a big, squirmy, slippery one in her hands and snuck it into her home so she could study it. She kept it in a giant bowl by her bed and fed it locusts. When the cattle in the neighboring homesteads became ill, Shulamit snuck over the wall and experimented using different herbs to heal them. She could identify different baboons and hippos by their markings and personalities. She once found a wild young jackal that had become separated from its pack, and she fed it fish. Soon the jackal followed her wherever she went.

Then came the day when Shulamit's family left their home and marched with the rest of the Israelites out of Egypt. Shulamit's frog came along, snug in a satchel on the side of their camel, and her jackal pranced behind her. The Israelites were told that they were marching toward freedom, except none of the adults really knew what freedom was. They were burdened with worry. The children, however, ran with the goats over the hills, laughing and somersaulting.

Shulamit had never understood that she hadn't been free. She was too busy enthusing over a tiny biome of insects on the leaf of a blue lotus in the wetlands or exhilarating with gazelles running through the forests on the plateau. Because of her relationship with animals, she never felt confined.

Suddenly, everyone on the march stopped. The air was salty. Shulamit lifted her head. She heard a primal sound, one she had never heard before, but somehow felt she had always known. She looked to the east and saw a spectacular silver sea mirroring the sky. Shining waves crested and crashed against the shore. The ebb and flow made the whooshing sound of blood rushing through arteries. It was magnificent. She looked to the west and saw a dusty cloud rising up from the stampede of soldiers on horses sent by Pharaoh to stop them. Her jackal whimpered at her side.

"What are we going to do?" wondered Shulamit. Her older brother, Nachshon, waded into the water. He paused for a moment and then lifted his head high, striding until the water reached his neck. Suddenly, the waters of the sea blasted straight up to touch the clouds. Cool white foam glittered like diamonds as the sea opened a dry path. Her brother was standing on dry ground. He continued walking, and the Israelites slowly followed, marching between the sparkling walls of water. Then they went faster. They were afraid of the water closing in on them and rushed to get to the other side.

But Shulamit was not in a hurry. She was intrigued. This was nothing like water of the Nile delta. She ran her fingers along the wall of water, feeling the vibrating energy. She had heard about the sea, tales about parrotfish, clown fish, and angelfish. She had been curious about stories of bigger creatures, like spotted whale sharks. She had heard tales from travelers who had seen spinner dolphins leaping out of the water and spinning in the air. While everyone looked straight ahead, Shulamit peered into the wall of water like she was looking through a giant window. There she saw fluorescent fish darting among swaying banners of seaweed. She saw translucent jellyfish dancing a graceful ballet. She saw a dark creature with many legs whirl past.

And then, she saw a face looking right back at her. She stopped, and the face stopped too, studying her just as she was studying it. It was the face of a dolphin! A long-beaked spinner dolphin, its length nearly twice her height.

All at once, the dolphin winked at Shulamit and turned to swim away. But Shulamit thrust her hands into the water and took hold of the slick animal's tail. Whoosh! Shulamit was zooming through the water grasping the dolphin, feeling the dust of the desert wash off her. Together they zipped through the water, and Shulamit saw glints of radiant colors she never could have imagined. She and the dolphin shared the same force, as does every living thing, coursing with the same electricity, animated by one spirit. Just when Shulamit remembered she needed to breathe, the dolphin shot up through the water, twirling into the air. Shulamit took the deepest breath she had ever taken, filling her lungs the way the wind fills a giant sail.

The dolphin dove back under the waves with a splash and then leapt again, and as they flew over the water, Shulamit shouted, "Wheeeeeeee!"

She had never felt so good, so happy, so alive! They fell back into the dazzling sea, and again they flew, spinning through the air, and Shulamit shouted, "Whooooooo!"

The Egyptians all stopped and stared. The Israelites stood on their new shore staring. Everyone was stunned by the sight of a girl flying over the shimmering sea on the back of a dolphin, shouting joyfully.

"Now that's freedom!" the Israelites said, and with Shulamit's shouts of joy echoing, the Israelites took up their timbrels and danced. When the dolphin delivered Shulamit to shore, her jackal leapt upon her to lick her face. Then she ran to join the community in dance, grasping hands and spinning in circles, with freedom ringing in each spirit and songs of praise on all their lips.

QUESTIONS

1. This story mentions Shulamit's brother Nachshon, who was the first to take a step toward freedom. The Rabbis wrote midrashim about Nachshon, and this story about Shulamit is a midrash—a commentary in story form—as well. Why do you think so many stories—and stories about stories—are part of the Jewish tradition?

2. At the Sea of Reeds, the Israelites became free from their oppressors. Shulamit demonstrated another level of freedom—freedom from fear. How does one move from physical freedom to freedom from fear?

3. Jewish tradition teaches that everyone, even babies, who crossed through the parted Sea of Reeds saw visions even greater than anything the prophet Ezekiel saw. Why is the crossing of the sea so essential to the Israelites' journey?

4. When people hear the word "miracle," they usually think of something like the splitting of the sea, but Judaism considers everyday events like breathing, getting out of bed, and even going to the bathroom a miracle. What different miracles have you experienced?

Shmooey and the Shabbat Encounter

A Lost Story from Chelm ⟶ town of fools

THIS IS THE STORY of Shmooey of Chelm. He was among the sages and the wise people of Chelm, which was a town known for being . . . well, unconventional. Shmooey was there when the people of Chelm tried to catch the full moon in a barrel of water. In fact, it was Shmooey who later discovered that they had caught only the moon's reflection! He was also there when the synagogue attendant got too old to go house to house knocking on the shutters each day to wake everyone for morning prayers, so the people decided to take all the shutters down from the windows and bring them to the attendant, so he could easily knock on them from his own house. It was Shmooey and his wife, Malkah, who woke up early every morning, had a quick coffee, and went around calling "Morning prayers!" to make sure they always had a minyan. Shmooey was also there when the people of Chelm put the synagogue *tzedakah* box on the top of a pole to protect it from thieves, but then built a staircase so that the poor could still reach it. It was Shmooey who made sure the money got distributed to the right people.

Everyone knows that the people of Chelm were special. They may not have been the most logical or the most intelligent, but they were earnest, kindhearted, and creative. And there were certain things they never forgot: the importance of community, hospitality, and the beauty of Shabbat. In fact, some say that when Albert Einstein said, "I'd rather be an optimist and a fool than a pessimist and right," he was thinking of the people of Chelm.

But what people don't know is that it was really Shmooey who kept things safe and running for these beloved fools. Shmooey loved them dearly, and tending to the needs of the community brought him a sense of great purpose and joy.

However, Shmooey noticed over time that he was beginning to forget things and to mix things up. When the people of Chelm dug the foundation for a new school, they pondered where to put the dirt from the hole they had dug. It was suggested that they dig a second hole to put in the dirt from the first. But then someone asked, "Where would we put the dirt from the second hole?" It was Shmooey who said, "Let's just make the second hole twice as big as the first." But that didn't work out too well. More and more of the things Shmooey tried to do did not work out. He was beginning to forget names, faces, and even the Torah he learned. It was as if everyone in Chelm was genetically predisposed to foolishness, and even Shmooey was not immune.

Then came the terrible day when Shmooey no longer remembered his own address—27 Schildberg Lane—where he lived with his wife Malkah. He was bewildered when he opened a door he thought was his own and saw a woman he did not recognize inside. The woman stared at him in surprise.

Shmooey apologized for the mistake and walked away. When he reached a fork in the road, he paused. A sign pointed one way to Prague, and another to Lvov. Shmooey asked himself, "Do I live in Prague or in Lvov?" He had not just forgotten where his home was; he had forgotten all about Chelm. He forgot his parents, who had named him Shmuel, the voice of the *chazan*, the taste of matzah ball soup, his wife's smile, and the sound of the shofar. He even forgot about Shabbat. The only thing he remembered was how to walk, so that is what he did.

Shmooey did not leave Chelm with much, and what he did have wore out quickly. He had a tattered shirt with two missing buttons. He had a jacket that did very little to keep out the cold, though it did have two good pockets for the coins and morsels people would sometimes give him. He had a pair of pants with hems that were frayed and knees that were almost worn away. He had a pair of woolen knickers, a pair of woolen socks, and shoes as thin as newspaper. Shmooey also had a floppy hat, which he crumpled up as a pillow. That was all he had as he walked from town to town.

But Shmooey also had a dream that someday he would find home.

Shmooey knew he had a home somewhere, a home where he was known and loved, a home in which someone he loved, loved him very much, a home where he was comfortable and happy. He always felt like it was nearby, just around the corner, just past the field, or in the next town over. Until that dream came true, Shmooey spent his days wandering, asking the good people he met for a spare coin or a slice of bread.

One day, Shmooey happened upon a little town in which all the people were bustling about. Shmooey did not know it at the time, but it was Friday afternoon, and they were running around trying to prepare for the arrival of Shabbat.

Shmooey stopped a woman who was hurrying home with a cart filled with a great assortment of sumptuous groceries: chicken, fish, meatballs, cabbage, carrots, onions, flour, eggs, noodles, and apple cake.

"Excuse me, ma'am," said Shmooey. "Might you spare a morsel for me to eat?"

The woman hurriedly gave Shmooey a delicious meatball and a slice of apple cake wrapped in paper. She said, "Here, enjoy! I must run! Shabbat is coming, and I need to prepare a feast!"

Then Shmooey stopped a man who was hurrying home with a bouquet of flowers and two loaves of braided bread.

"Excuse me, sir, might you spare a coin?" asked Shmooey.

The man fished into his pocket and gave Shmooey a coin. "I am sorry, stranger," the man said, "but I must rush. Shabbat is coming! And I must put on my best clothes!"

"Hmmmm," thought Shmooey. "This Shabbat must be a very important person! Everyone is rushing about to prepare feasts for Shabbat! I wonder who Shabbat is? Perhaps Shabbat is a noble or a wealthy merchant. If I could just meet this Shabbat person whom everyone knows, perhaps Shabbat can point me in the direction of home!"

All day, whenever Shmooey asked someone to spare a little of this or a little of that, they would spare what they could and then rush off to prepare for Shabbat. Finally, Shmooey asked a boy for a coin or a morsel to eat.

The boy said, "I don't have any coins or morsels to give you. But come with me. I will take you to my family's home, and you can sit at our table, eat a festive meal with us, and celebrate the arrival of Shabbat."

"Perfect," thought Shmooey. "Just the opportunity I was hoping for!

When Shabbat comes over, I'll go sit right up close. I will say, 'Excuse me, Shabbat. Everyone seems to know you in this town, which means you must know everyone in this town, and I am also in this town. Perhaps you can tell me who I am and where I belong.'"

As they were walking to the little boy's house, the boy said, "I can't wait for Shabbat to come."

"Me neither!" said Shmooey, with a sparkle in his eye.

The boy led Shmooey to a modest little house. Inside, there was a beautiful table covered with a tablecloth that glistened like snow. The table was set with sparkling china, crystal, and silver.

The boy's family welcomed Shmooey kindly. The mother said, "Shabbat won't be here for about an hour. Here are some newly scrubbed clothes, and there is a washbasin in the back room filled with hot, soapy water. You can get nice and clean to welcome Shabbat. And if you want to take a nap before Shabbat comes, there is a little bed and some blankets in that room over there."

"Perfect!" thought Shmooey, as he thanked the family. "Now I will be able to charm Shabbat into helping me, with these nice clothes and a fresh face."

Shmooey washed up. The hot, soapy water felt wonderful as he squeezed it over his face and hair.

Shmooey slipped on the clean clothes, and they fit just right. "Now don't I look like a real somebody," Shmooey said to himself, as he smoothed out his pant legs.

Shmooey stretched out on the little bed. He could hear the mother setting an extra place for him at the table. "I hope it is next to Shabbat," he thought. He stared up at the ceiling and wondered about what Shabbat would look like and how Shabbat would act. Would Shabbat be friendly? Or mean? But how could Shabbat possibly be mean if so many people were celebrating the arrival of Shabbat!

With these thoughts in his mind, Shmooey drifted off to sleep. And then he had the most remarkable dream.

In his dream, Shmooey was lying on his back on a green, emerald slope. The sky had the gleam of twilight. Stars began to peek out of the darkening blue, one by one. Finally, the whole night sky was filled with twinkling stars, like bushels of diamonds tossed into the sea. Shmooey stared up at the Milky Way, and he felt very peaceful.

All of a sudden, Shmooey saw the Milky Way move! How can that be? Shmooey bolted upright, rubbed his eyes, and looked again. There it is! The Milky Way was moving!

In fact, it was moving toward him!

The Milky Way seemed to ripple in the sky as if it were a long sheath of deep blue silk covered in diamonds. It was like a beautiful gown. In fact, Shmooey realized, it *was* a gown!

Soon it was approaching the very hill upon which Shmooey stood. A moment later, it was walking in the very same meadow, and Shmooey could see that wearing the gown was a woman.

She was a bride, and she wore a shimmering veil of starlight.

Shmooey's eyes were wide with wonder. He gasped, "Who are you?"

The bride leaned toward him. "I am Shabbat," she said, and her voice soothed away all the aches and pains in Shmooey's body from years of wandering and years of loneliness.

"I know," Shabbat said, "that you want to ask me something . . ."

Of course, Shmooey had planned to ask Shabbat to point him in the direction of home. But at the moment, all he could say was, "I just want you to stay with me forever."

"I will stay with you," said Shabbat, "until tomorrow night, and then I must return to the heavens. But I will leave a spark for you to have with you always. And I shall come to you every week at this time, if you open your heart to me."

Shabbat then held out her hands and there, cupped in her palms, was a twinkling little spark, a speck of sparkling star. She placed it into Shmooey's open hands, and he watched it dissolve into his skin. He could feel a new vitality zing through his spirit, setting his face aglow. Suddenly a faraway memory flickered in Shmooey, like a candle flame in a gusty room. There was a moon and a barrel and a reflection, and Shmooey was surrounded by all the people he knew and loved. But before it became clear, the memory disappeared, the way a reflection of the moon in a barrel disappears when the water is disturbed.

"That spark is your *n'shamah y'teirah*," Shabbat said, "your extra soul."

"Thank you," Shmooey said, his eyes welling with tears. He held his hands to his heart and thought, "Reflections are illusions, but this, this *n'shamah y'teirah*, is real."

Shabbat withdrew and moved across the landscape, draping it in night and glints of light. Tears of joy ran down Shmooey's face, and his eyes were filled with her beauty.

Just then, there was a loud knock, and Shmooey awoke from his magical dream. It was the little boy.

"It is time to join us at the table," he said. "Shabbat is coming." The smell of challah woke memories that had been dormant inside of him since he was small. Looking past the boy, Shmooey could see candles glistening on the table. Shabbat candles, yes. He remembered.

Shmooey smiled to the boy and said, "Shabbat is already here." He could feel Shabbat's presence warming his heart and stirring his memories. He remembered the friendly face of Mayor Mottel and the time the mayor was on his hands and knees searching all over the floor. What was he searching for? Shmooey wondered. Ah, yes, he remembered. The people had lost heart, and Mayor Mottel was trying to find it. "I have lost myself," Shmooey thought. "But Shabbat found me."

At the table, the family began singing *Shalom Aleichem*, and Shmooey found that he knew all the words. There were still things in his mind that were fuzzy around the edges. He was still piecing together who he was and where exactly he was from, but he knew with certainty where he belonged. He belonged in Shabbat, and Shabbat was always going to be there, right around the corner. That aching desire for "home" Shmooey felt for so long drifted away like a star fading in the sunrise.

"*Bar'chuni l'shalom, malachei hashalom, malachei elyon*," Shmooey sang. "Bless me with peace, messengers of peace, messengers of the Most High." When the prayer was complete, Shmooey said to the boy and his family, "Thank you. Thank you all. You have fulfilled a great mitzvah. A blessing on your home. A blessing on your lives. As a great teacher once taught me, more than Israel has kept Shabbat, Shabbat has kept Israel. May Shabbat keep watch over you, over me, and over all who have lost their way."

To which the family responded, "Amen."

The next morning, Shmooey woke up before anyone else in the family. He washed up and put on his old, tattered clothes. He folded the sheets, blankets, and clothing they had given him. He kissed the mezuzah as he stepped out of the house into the morning light. He walked to the end of the walkway and leaned against the mailbox, closing his eyes to feel the warmth against his eyelids. When he opened his eyes, he noticed the words on the mailbox: 26 Schildberg Lane.

"Hmm," Shmooey said, scratching his chin. He contemplated the words, which were strangely familiar. Soft, downy memories drifted past him like feathers from a torn pillow. They tickled his mind. And then he heard a woman's voice from the house at 27 Schildberg Lane.

"Shmooey?" the woman said. Shmooey turned toward her. She was wearing a faded checkered nightdress, a matching flannel sleeping cap with a pompom at the end, and fluffy old slippers, and she was holding a steaming mug of coffee. She was as beautiful to Shmooey as the Sabbath Bride herself. She stared at Shmooey for a moment longer and then screamed with joy, "Shmooey!!!" The woman threw the mug onto the grass and ran toward Shmooey, with her arms open wide, laughing, weeping and praising God. Shmooey opened his arms and ran toward her. In their zeal, they ran a little too fast and knocked each other over onto the ground. But they quickly scrambled back up, and as they clung to each other, Shmooey whispered into her ear, "Malkah, my love, I am home."

QUESTIONS

1. What is the difference between wisdom, knowledge, and intelligence?
2. In the story it is written, "It was as if everyone in Chelm was genetically predisposed to foolishness, and even Shmooey was not immune." How does thinking of the people of Chelm as suffering not from foolishness, but from something like dementia change how you see them?
3. This story references a famous quote by the Jewish Zionist philosopher Ahad HaAm, who said, "More than Israel has kept Shabbat, Shabbat has kept Israel." What do you think this means?
4. Have you had a dream that changed your life?

FEATHER

Modern Stories That Take Flight

Shalom Bayit

Mateo Cardozo closed his laptop and took off his glasses. He rubbed his eyes. He remembered what his mentor had taught him, that the job of a school counselor was to see the unshed tear and hear the unasked question. And today a student, Shiloh, had come to his office, and Mateo watched as they struggled to hold back tears. Shiloh had asked, "How many days can I miss and still graduate?" but Mateo knew from the way the student balanced themselves gingerly on the edge of the chair, as if they didn't belong, as if they were accustomed to making themselves smaller, that the unasked question was closer to "Would anyone care if I disappeared?"

There had been a marked increase in students in need of help. Young people were suffering an unprecedented mental health crisis. All the systems that Mateo hardly thought about when he was young now seemed unstable and untrustworthy: education, business, media, health care, government, police, world powers, the environment, you name it. Even technology, which once was this magical portal to knowledge and connection, now was a window that allowed misinformation, predators, bullies, and trolls to crawl right into their brains and bedrooms. Mateo remembered how he had believed his parents when they would tell him, "Everything will be okay." But that wouldn't comfort kids today. They were too smart. Too informed. They knew it was a promise adults couldn't necessarily keep.

But when students stepped into his office, whether they were courageous to do so on their own or they were sent by a teacher or parent, Mateo tried to create a respite. He put a lot of effort into the design of the space. Art that covered the drab cinderblock. A rug to warm the century-old linoleum. Big leafy plants. Colorful acrylic cubes that students could stack or peer through when they were fidgety. Over time, however, he learned that what mattered more than all that was presence. Even after a sewage pipe burst and the school moved him temporarily to an office that was no better than an interrogation room, with folding metal chairs and glaring fluorescent overhead lights that flickered every fifteen minutes, it didn't matter. It wasn't about the location or decoration. It was about the listening. His students knew that when they spoke with Mateo, Mateo would hear them without the distraction of phones pinging or alarms ringing. They knew he would hear them, respect their experience, follow through, and follow up. Mateo felt that when he was counseling a student, they created a sacred space. Sometimes he felt like a rabbi officiating a ceremony under a movable chuppah, except rather than a wedding between two people, his task was to help just one remember that they were worthy of love.

Mateo took the bus home, thinking about brokenness and fragile family systems. When he arrived at the door to his apartment, he kissed his two fingers and touched the mezuzah, saying, "*Shalom bayit.*" Peace in the home. It was in part a prayer for his students and in part a commitment to himself to try to leave the troubles of the week outside. After a week of caring for others, once he stepped over the threshold into his home, he needed to focus on his own spirit. Good food, music, rest. Tonight was Shabbat, and after a particularly draining week, he thought he would hike a new mountain trail tomorrow. Get some fresh air, exercise, and perspective.

Isaac Blau was only half listening to his friends at the restaurant. Harris had just finished a long saga involving a neighbor who seemed hell-bent on getting him evicted for having a dog, even though the HOA allowed pets.

"The poor dog is twelve years old!" Harris exclaimed. "If she ever barks it sounds like, I don't know, stepping on a dry leaf. I mean, we live under a flight path, and the neighbor is okay with the roar of jets but not *Sadie*?"

Rob was laughing.

"Why can't people just let people be happy?" Harris shook his head.

"Speaking of happy," Rob commented as the waiter delivered large bowls of ramen to the table.

The half of Isaac that wasn't listening to his friends was meditating on the ice in his tea. The cubes balanced one on top of the other in the tall glass. The center of each ice cube was a little cloudy and held a cluster of tiny bubbles, which meant that the restaurant made their ice with ice trays instead of an ice machine, and the minerals in the water had been pushed to the center as the cubes froze, leaving the center porous. He stirred the iced tea with his straw and took a sip. He looked at the bowl of ramen, which was its own kind of ecosystem, a delicate balance of flavors and salinity joined to create the tasty brine. He thought about the mathematics of the soft-boiled egg, the measurement of heat needed to coagulate the yolk, that circle of protein inside an ellipsoid.

"Uh, hello, Professor Blau," Rob said, bringing Isaac's mind back to the table.

"Yes, right," Isaac said. "I'm sorry."

"You haven't changed since college," Harris teased.

"Except then he was just little Yitz," Rob said, "and now he is professor of mathematics and structural engineering."

"Chemistry, actually," Isaac said. "Structural chemistry, not engineering."

Isaac reflected on his friends as he drove home. It had been good to see them. However, he realized, lately he always felt a little lonely, even in good company. When people learned he was a mathematician, usually the first thing they said was "I hate math." It made him sad, because the thing he loved the most, the internal structure of literally everything, was so misunderstood. More than misunderstood—maligned.

Isaac's research was in carbon capture, the theory that carbon dioxide could be taken out of the atmosphere and insulated for millennia in natural petroleum reservoirs. Isaac's work was about cleaning the troposphere, that improbable region of breathable sky enwreathing the planet, and repairing the stratospheric ozone, which hung over that sky like a chuppah. His work hoped to bring the concentration of carbon dioxide in the atmosphere back under 350 parts per million. Achieving this required partial differential equations, nonlinear equations, statistics, and computer modeling. It required factoring in the uncertainty of carbon and methane release from melting arctic permafrost. It required studying heat, momentum, time, fluid inclusions, and the geometry and parameters of porous mediums. In other words, it required *math*, which everyone says they hate.

Isaac unlocked his front door and paused to touch the mezuzah, bringing his fingers to his lips. A blessing in the doorway, a liminal space. Isaac loved these liminal, in-between spaces. The things that lived in the in-between were a barometer of the health of the larger biome, like amphibians, living between water and land, or polar ice, living between sea and sky. These things were so vulnerable. Data concerning these fragile lifeforms and places told the story of the past and predicted the future. Thinking of liminal spaces and the power of math, Isaac felt like a rabbi, pouring over a cryptic scripture of *alefs*, x-variables, golden ratios, and infinities, deciphering revelations and trying to preserve *shalom bayit*, peace and harmony in our only home, earth. But tomorrow, he thought to himself, he would pull himself away from the numbers and theories and get outside for some fresh air.

Mateo began his hike from the east in a flowering field. Wild poppies opened their orange faces to the morning sun, and bees filled the meadow with movement and sound. It felt good to stretch his legs as he traversed the flatland and began the trail that led up the mountainside. It was a clear day, and he knew the view at the top would be wonderful. He thought about his last student, Shiloh, and how much they would benefit from stepping away from the high school habitat and being in nature. Great branches of sycamore and oak stretched over the path as he climbed, and while beautiful, Mateo was more enamored by the unseen network of roots beneath the ground, the great sharing of nutrients, signals, and sweetness that was happening under the ground where he passed. "We could learn a lot from you," he said to a stately oak as he went by.

Isaac began his hike from the west in a parking lot. He passed through a wooden horse gate that looked like it was a hundred years old, which led to an olive tree grove that looked even older. It felt good to push himself as he began the switchbacks that led up the steep mountainside. Halfway up, he paused to drink water under a eucalyptus tree and take in the view. A fluttering made him look up. There, just a meter or so above him, was a roost of monarch butterflies. Isaac stood watching how the roost seemed to breathe as if it were a single organism, with its topography of gently fanning wings. "A butterfly flaps its wings in California and causes a hurricane in the Caribbean," he said, thinking about his studies in chaos theory and how sensitive the atmosphere is to little changes. Everything affects everything else in one way or another.

Mateo drank from his canteen and poured a little water over his head. He ate a power bar while he pushed himself the last mile to the summit. The day was getting hot.

When the switchbacks emerged above the tree line, Isaac could see the summit. He drank from his canteen and dampened the bandana he wore around his neck as the sun crossed the meridian.

Finally, Mateo reached the top, a wide flat clearing with little vegetation. He stood, reveling in simple accomplishment, looking over the valley while his heart and breath recovered from the exertion.

Finally, Isaac reached the top. He looked back over the trail he had taken to get here. It had been a lot longer than he originally estimated, and he felt the satisfaction of having set out a task and completing it. He felt his pulse rate decrease as he looked out, his eye resting on a cloud of smog that settled over the southern valley.

"I remember when clouds were white," Mateo said.

Isaac noticed the other hiker for the first time. He smiled.

"Maybe gray," Mateo said, shaking his head, "but definitely not yellow."

Isaac nodded. He put down his backpack and took out an orange. He unpeeled it in one long spiral, tucking the peel in his pocket to throw out later. He held out half of the fruit to Mateo.

"I'm Isaac," he said.

"It's good to meet you, Isaac," Mateo said, taking the fruit. "I'm Mateo."

They both stood listening to birds and insects, looking at the valley with its tiny houses and layer of smog below.

Mateo held up a slice of orange and said, "Did you hear there was a study where they connected plants to lie detector tests and found that the signals fluctuated just like humans and that the signals responded to the feelings of the people in the room! *And* that when you eat a salad near a plant, the plant gets totally stressed out? But, if you feel gratitude while eating the salad, the plant calms down?"

Isaac looked at Mateo for a moment. He was surprised that he had happened to bring up a study that Isaac was very familiar with.

"Yes," Isaac said. "Cleve Backster was the scientist. In the 1960s." In fact, Isaac mused, at that moment he could relate to the plant attached to the polygraph. This stranger seemed to be picking up signals deep within him, signals that hadn't yet formulated into full thoughts—the desire to connect.

"Well, I don't want to stress out everything living on this mountain," Mateo continued. "So thank you for the orange, and thank you to the tree that produced it."

"The difference between the lifeblood of plants and that of people is only one atom," Isaac offered.

"Really?" Mateo asked, with genuine interest.

"Yes. Chlorophyll is made up of 136 atoms of hydrogen, carbon, oxygen, and nitrogen, all arranged in a ring around a single atom of magnesium. And hemoglobin is made up of 136 atoms of hydrogen, carbon, oxygen, and nitrogen, all arranged in a ring around a single atom of iron."

"That's incredible. It just shows how little things, a single atom, can make such a difference."

"Yes, that's exactly what it shows."

"Well, time to go down," Mateo said, extending his hand. "It was nice to meet you."

Isaac took his hand and shook it. "Yes, it was."

Mateo turned to head back down the trail. The sunlight seemed to caress everything it touched. His spirit felt light. He thought about the miraculous feeling of closeness you can have with someone you just met. His heart felt warm with a feeling of *shalom bayit.*

Isaac also headed back down the trail, moving in the opposite direction. He saw spirals in the whorls of knotty trees and patterns in the leaves. His stride was confident and long. He thought about the mystery of chemistry between two people, the nucleus of *shalom bayit.*

It took Mateo a few days to find Isaac. He had guessed that he was probably a professor. A few internet searches based on their short interaction—Professor, Isaac, Southern California, Biology, Botany, Chemistry—eventually yielded fruit: an email address on his professional page. Mateo took another day to think about what to write. Finally, he just decided to keep it simple: "Hey. I'm the guy from the mountaintop. We shared an orange. Coffee?"

Isaac's response came only two minutes later: "Mateo, who remembers when clouds were white. Thursday morning?"

When Isaac stepped under the chuppah, the wedding canopy, he had a palpable sense that the air in that sacred space was different. Even though the chuppah was open on all sides, even though it was simply a canopy made from his and Mateo's tallitot strung across four poles, something changed when he stepped inside. The air felt measurably charged . . . with something immeasurable. He looked at Mateo and knew. This atmosphere they shared was saturated, a million parts per million, with love.

They had decided to marry in the place they had met, on the mountaintop. A small wedding, surrounded by a dozen of their closest friends and family. A couple of stray overnight hikers, who had seen the procession marching up the trail with chuppah poles and schnapps, also joined. Four friends held the poles of the chuppah. One, Isaac's college friend Harris, had his dog Sadie, a rheumy-eyed chihuahua whose tongue was perpetually out, in a carrier on his back like an infant. It had been two years, nearly to the day, since Isaac had that dinner with Harris and Rob, the day before meeting Mateo.

As Mateo stepped under the chuppah, he reflected on the families he had interacted with over the course of his career and how each family had its individual struggle. It was like Tolstoy said, "Happy families are all alike; every unhappy family is unhappy in its own way." Looking at Isaac, he was comforted in the realization that he actually looked forward to traversing the hardships with him. Those would be the times when they would really understand and learn from their strengths and vulnerabilities, and they would do it together.

The rabbi served the Hillel at the university where Isaac worked, and the two were friends. She went paddleboarding or kayaking three times a week in the sunrise hour and jumped at the idea of a mountaintop wedding.

"The roof of the chuppah is a sail; it is a magic carpet. Your two tallitot are the wings of a dove," she said as the wedding began. "This chuppah is the sketch of your home, Isaac and Mateo, open, inviting, beautiful, and filled with love. The poles of the chuppah are easily lifted and carried, teaching that the home you create together is in your palm, your pocket. Anywhere you are together, it is home. Wherever the trail may take you, this chuppah will remain the essence of your home. And as you grow together as life partners, a part of you will always be here, filled with amazement and thankfulness, wonderstruck by the depth of your love for one another. In honor of all the journeys that have brought us to this blessed time, we recite the *Shehecheyanu* blessing."

Mateo listened to the rabbi's chanting and to the birdsong accompanying her. Isaac wondered at the way the early afternoon light filtered through the fabric of the tallitot across Mateo's face. The rabbi was talking about their journey together the last two years, their shared commitment to *tikkun olam*, and the courage that is love. She reported that their friends told her that the two of them were so aligned, they were practically telepathic in an almost spooky way. Their friends laughed. And then she said, "In the words of American poet Archibald Macleish, 'To see the earth as it truly is, small and blue and beautiful in that eternal silence where it floats, is to see ourselves as riders on the earth together, brothers on that bright loveliness in the eternal cold—brothers who know now they are truly brothers.'"

As the ceremony drew to a close, Isaac started feeling anxious. There was a yellowish brown cloud at the periphery of his vision, pollution from the port. He wondered how that was connected to this moment. At the same time, Mateo began to have a feeling of foreboding, and he tried to identify the source. A shadow had moved over them.

There were two glasses wrapped in handkerchiefs at their feet, and the rabbi was talking about the meaning of breaking a glass at a wedding. She talked about how at the height of our joy we still remember the destruction of the Temple in Jerusalem, how we still remember the suffering in the world. She said it also represents the breaking open of a cocoon and the birthing of a new heaven and a new earth through their union. Isaac and Mateo simultaneously reached and took each other's hand, and each stepped on a glass together. Loud bursts of *mazal tov* surrounded them, and in the din of cheer and shouts, Isaac and Mateo spoke to each other at the same time.

"Let's make a stand," Isaac said.

"Let's not leave," Mateo said.

And in that spooky telepathic way they had, they perfectly understood one another. There was so much brokenness out there, as they were both all too aware. So they held fast to each other's hands and decided to stay under their chuppah. This would be their protest. This is how they would start their marriage—in solidarity with all who suffered. They each felt that while they were committing to one another, they were also committing to a covenant they had individually made with the world. They thought of Julia Butterfly Hill, who lived in a California redwood for 738 days to prevent loggers from sawing it down. And they pictured Greta Thunberg, whose solitary protests in front of the Swedish Parliament grew into a worldwide movement.

Leaning toward one another with their foreheads touching, Mateo whispered, "This is our home—open, inviting, beautiful, and filled with love."

"This is a microcosm of what should be," Isaac whispered back. He thought of the countless complicated computer models he had created compared to the simplicity of the chuppah, the wholeness of this moment.

"For the sake of *shalom bayit*," Mateo said, and they both knew that he wasn't just referring to peace in their own home, but also to peace upon the earth, small and blue and beautiful in that eternal silence where it floats.

They turned and raised a toast to their guests, thanking them for being in their lives.

And then Mateo explained, "We are not leaving our chuppah. Everyone deserves a safe place to call home. Everyone deserves clean air and a roof over their heads."

"We want to send a message," Isaac added, "and so we are having a sit-in, here in our chuppah."

Harris, one of the chuppah pole holders asked, "Does that mean the four of us have to stay too? Because I may get tired of standing, and Sadie is afraid of the dark."

"No," Isaac said, "of course not. The soil is loose enough here, so we can dig holes for the poles, and secure them with rocks."

The friends and family argued with them. "Don't you want to spend your first night after the wedding in comfort?"

"We've had plenty of comfort in our lives," Mateo said.

"What about your honeymoon?"

"We will spend it between the earth and the stars," said Isaac.

"What about work?"

"My students will know I am standing up for them," Mateo answered.

"How will you charge your phones?"

Isaac shrugged.

"What will you eat?"

Mateo shrugged.

"This is silly."

"Absolutely," laughed Isaac.

"What will it matter to anyone?"

"It matters to them," said their rabbi, who knelt to take a tin cup out of her backpack and started digging next to a chuppah pole.

Mateo, Isaac, and others soon joined her. The stray overnight hikers joined with their spades, and other guests used sticks, rocks, knives, and even a bottle opener to dig holes for the chuppah poles. Friends and family took pictures of the scene and posted them on their social media pages, each interpreting the protest in their own way.

Mateo's cousin posted: *My cuz and his hubs refuse to leave their chuppah in protest of corruption.*

Isaac's friend posted: *My good friend Professor Isaac Blau just married Mateo Cardozo, then announced that they will remain under their chuppah until the carbon parts per million in the atmosphere goes below 350.*

A friend of Mateo's posted: *My buddy Mateo Cardozo and his new groom Isaac Blau shocked us at their wedding by declaring they will not leave their chuppah until all the homeless are housed.*

A colleague of Isaac's who taught comparative religion posted: *I am at a Jewish wedding but am reminded of the Hindu Khareshwari—who vow never to sit or lie down, abandoning their own comfort—and the Christian stylite—who lived on the top of a pillar exposed to the elements. The grooms Professor Isaac Blau and Mr. Mateo Cardozo are showing their own version of modern asceticism . . .*

The responses came in quickly:

—Srsly?

—First rain, and they outta there.

—Where are they?

—What is a chuppah?

—Cool

—Following

Once the chuppah was secure, Mateo and Isaac sat down underneath, and their friends and family sat with them. While they were drinking, sharing snacks, singing, and laughing, the social media posts were gaining momentum and being shared from one person to another to another, and soon the word "chuppah" rose to the top of the Google search engine. The overnight campers who had joined the wedding party pitched their tents on the mountaintop, a short distance from the chuppah, and sent out messages to their camping community. In a couple of hours, others came hiking to the mountaintop, from the east and the west, with supplies. Two sleeping bags and sleeping mats, jugs of water, clothing and raingear, sunscreen, protein bars, and dehydrated food. One by one their family and friends stepped into the chuppah and hugged and kissed them, then made their way down the mountain. The campers, Josie and Sakura, became fast friends with the newly married couple, and they shared their supplies and left them a lantern as they returned to their tent. Mateo and Isaac rezipped the two sleeping bags into one and shared their wedding night warm and content as could be.

They woke before dawn and huddled together to watch the sunrise. The night's dew evaporated off their tallitot. Josie and Sakura made hot coffee for them all and joined them under the chuppah. They took pictures and then packed up their tents. As they left to continue their own journey, Sakura turned back to Isaac and Mateo and said, "Great wedding!"

Throughout that day, people came to visit Isaac and Mateo. Some were friends, and some were strangers. Mateo and Isaac didn't ask anyone for anything, but people observed what the couple needed and posted about it. Soon there was a network of people working together to provide toothbrushes and biodegradable toothpaste, towels, and clean socks. When one person saw that their water was running low, they messaged someone else to bring water. And so it went, hour after hour, day after day.

In the beginning, the visitors sat with Isaac and Mateo, congratulating them on their marriage and talking with them about their ideals. But soon, the visitors came to talk with each other. Groups of activists sat in circles around the chuppah, sharing stories and plans, hardly talking to the couple.

Mateo rested his head on Isaac's shoulder as they watched the different groups of people sitting together, passionately and respectfully debating and discussing a variety of ideas, and Mateo said, "They've forgotten all about us."

"That's very good," Isaac said, and Mateo agreed, because they both knew their chuppah protest was now bigger than they were.

Five hikers set up tents around their chuppah to spend the night on the mountaintop, and on the evening of that second day, one activist stood on a rock, with the setting sun behind him and a group of people before him recording on their phones. He quoted the Reverend Dr. Martin Luther King Jr.'s words: "We've got some difficult days ahead. But it really doesn't matter with me now, because I've been to the mountaintop. . . . I've looked over and I've seen the Promised Land. I may not get there with you. But I want you to know tonight, that we as a people will get to the Promised Land!" And then he added, "We stand with Mateo and Isaac under their marriage chuppah, and when the world asks you, 'Do you care enough to make a stand?' what are you going to answer?" The people responded in unison, "I do!" and broke into cheers.

On the third day, along with the visitors came reporters, interviewing the couple.

"Professor Blau," asked one reporter, "what are you hoping to achieve with your protest? Are you really expecting world peace?"

Isaac thought for a moment. "Perhaps we could just start with that cloud of pollution over there," he said, pointing to the cloud of smog low on the horizon.

"Mr. Cardozo," asked another reporter, "are you aware that the forecast is for rain this weekend? What will you do?"

"I suppose we'll get wet!"

"Professor Blau, the thing people are asking most of all is, do you leave the chuppah to go to the bathroom?"

"Isn't it interesting how desperately we want to separate ourselves from animals?" Isaac said, while gazing toward a lizard. Then he looked at the reporter and said, "We have a dedicated place just below the mountaintop, and it is the only time one of us leaves the chuppah, but the other remains here, so the chuppah is never empty."

That night there were ten tents set up around the chuppah and on the trails.

On the fourth day, a little entourage of people summited with four poles and a lace canopy. They set up their chuppah next to Mateo and Isaac's, and a minister officiated their wedding. Their guests had brought drums and tambourines. Mateo took a hand drum and Isaac a tambourine, and they all filled the growing campsite with energetic rhythm and dancing for the better part of the day. After the wedding party left, by evening, some of the overnight campers took out guitars and ukuleles. It was a day of music and love.

On the fifth day, the history teacher at the high school where Mateo worked came to sit with them under the chuppah and brought a folder filled with articles from the past few days. The first article had a large photo of protesters in front of City Hall standing under chuppahs. The chuppah canopies were white cloth painted with the words "Sanctuary for All" and "Sanctuario Para Todos." There was another article that talked about protesters raising chuppahs on the US border with Mexico, holding signs proclaiming "Families Belong Together" and "We Are All Migrants." The article talked about the portability of the chuppah as a perfect symbol of families in search of a safe home. There was also an article by one of the climatologists with whom Isaac worked, quoting Isaac comparing the fragile chuppah to our stratosphere, sheltering the planet we love.

The sixth day was Friday, and the rabbi who had officiated their wedding gave a sermon at the Hillel about the history of protests in Judaism. She talked about the Talmudic idea of protesting for the sake of heaven and said that the Exodus from Egypt was a grand-scale protest against oppression. She talked about Abraham smashing the idols in his father's shop and later challenging God, saying, "Shall not the Judge of all the earth do justly?" She talked about the Triangle Shirtwaist protest, the movements to rescue Jews from the Soviet Union, Jewish involvement in civil rights activism. She talked about the chuppah movement and ended with the prayer "Spread over us a shelter of Your peace."

Shabbat morning, it rained. Mateo and Isaac and the community of campers on the mountaintop were prepared. They spread a large tarp over the chuppah and tallitot, and Mateo and Isaac huddled within. The rain was loud against the tarp, and it was cold. The other campers were all inside their own tents, waiting out the storm. Suddenly, the tarp lifted on one side, and a person crawled in with them, wearing raingear that covered their head and face.

The person sat down and pulled off their hood and face shield. They were a young person, looking exuberant and happy. They said, "Hi, Mr. Cardozo!"

Mateo's eyes got wide. "Shiloh!" he exclaimed, and then he said to Isaac, "Isaac, please meet Shiloh. They were one of my students. A wonderful person." He looked at Shiloh for a moment, seeing their bright eyes and glowing cheeks. "I can't believe you climbed up here in a rainstorm! Are you okay?"

"Yes," they said. "I am more than okay. This is amazing. All of this. The courage. The freedom. The community. I've been following the chuppah movement, and it's helped me find my voice. My friends and I, we had a ceremony. We made a chuppah, and we each took turns standing under it. And we each made a private commitment to have a deep, loving relationship with our self. I wanted you to know—I needed you to know—that I am going to take care of me. I am whole. No more self-harm. No more unreasonable self-criticism. I am now a partnership of body and soul. Well, at least I am working on it."

Mateo said, "I am so proud of you, Shiloh. I am so proud of you, and so inspired by you."

"What an honor to meet you," said Isaac.

Shiloh stayed until the rain lightened in the afternoon, and then they headed back down.

The rain didn't stop completely until Sunday afternoon. Isaac pulled the tarp off of the chuppah. Mateo was reading. Isaac looked out over the landscape. The cloud of smog was gone, but he knew it wasn't gone forever; the rain had just washed it away for a bit. It would be back. He thought of the Jewish saying "It is not up to you to finish the task, but you are not free to avoid it."

He looked at Mateo, who sensed his gaze and looked up from reading his book to read Isaac's face. "Is it time?" Mateo asked.

Isaac nodded.

"Have we done enough?" Mateo asked.

"Never," Isaac said, and Mateo nodded.

"But we've done something," Mateo said, thinking about all the chuppahs around the country, thinking about Shiloh.

"Yes," Isaac said. "We introduced an algorithm that can be replicated and followed."

"I suppose we did," Mateo said. He stood up and took Isaac's two hands in his. He said, "What happens when two become one and then that one gets multiplied by other ones?"

"It is all One," Isaac answered. He put his arm around Mateo, and Mateo put his arm around Isaac's waist, and together they stepped out of their chuppah for the first time since they wed.

They looked out over the hills at the beautiful clear air, all the way to the blue ocean, which dipped under the horizon. They could feel the curve of the one earth and its spinning around its one warm star.

"Peace in the home," Isaac said softly.

Mateo said, "*Shalom bayit.*" And they walked down the mountain together.

QUESTIONS

1. Breaking the glass at a wedding recalls the destruction of the Temple in Jerusalem, so that even at the height of our joy, we remember there is pain and brokenness in the world. In other words, it is a form of protest. This story imagines the chuppah as a symbol of protest. What other Jewish symbols could be used in protesting brokenness and injustice?
2. What protest movement inspires you?
3. Shiloh and their friends used the chuppah to each make a private commitment to have a deep, loving relationship with their self. What other ways could the chuppah be used?
4. In this story we see Mateo and Isaac express their love for each other, their love for their work, their love for community, and their love for pursuing justice. What are the ways that you express love toward others, work, community, and the world?

JEW

T HERE ARE ONLY A HANDFUL OF PEOPLE at Elijah's funeral. Not many people really knew him. Maybe they will notice that he is no longer sitting cross-legged on a flattened cardboard box leaning against the wall of the Los Angeles Kosher Market. Or maybe they won't.

I didn't truly know him until one wild day many years before. I had seen him around when my mother took me shopping. She would always hand him a dollar, and sometimes she'd give him a container of cold cuts and a baguette. He always said, "Thank you," and "God bless." Still, he frightened me. His beard was big, straggly, and the color of storm clouds, while the hair on top of his head was greasy and flat. His eyes were gray and murky. His skin was sunbaked and leathery. His sleeves and pants were too short, the hems unraveling. I always looked away from him. Standing at his funeral, it makes me sad to think that there may be people who are relieved he is gone.

The rabbi is speaking words, but I'm not listening. I am looking at Broderick, who is standing on the other side of the grave. The years have changed him. He is no longer that skinny, blond-haired, green-eyed sixth grader who wore jeans and oversized sweatshirts. He is a man now, and his hair has thinned. He wears wire glasses. He has creases around his eyes and laugh lines around his mouth. He wears a long, light trench coat, and he has shiny shoes. His hands are in his pockets. His wife is standing next to him, with her arm looped around his. Her head rests on his shoulder. She has dark, rich skin and wide-set eyes, and her hair and neck are wrapped in a thin camel-colored shawl. Their child stands between them, shifting from foot to foot and clutching a stuffed manga unicorn.

Broderick is looking at me too. I wonder if he still sees the girl I was then. Quiet and introverted, I always sat in the front row in class, wearing my favorite aviator cap with the earflaps and goggles. I liked being close to the board and the teacher. Also, from there I didn't have to look at the other kids. I kept to myself, preferring the virtual world over the real one. I was a gamer. My avatar was a flying mermaid, and online I could wield a sword, dodge a flamethrower, even lead an army—nothing like the anxious kid I was in real life. Broderick, on the other hand, always sat in the back of the class, collecting bad grades as if they were gold tokens. I don't think we said one word to each other in all of elementary school, until that day.

He smiles sadly at me as the rabbi leads the recitation of *Kaddish*. I feel my eyes water. Broderick puts his arm around his wife and pulls her closer. I wish my family was with me, but my partner was not able to take off from work and my father is watching the baby at home. He lives with us now. I feel a tear drop down my cheek. I dab my eyes with my sleeve.

V'imru, amen.

"Amen," I say, and Broderick follows just a beat after me.

Broderick, his wife, and I shovel earth into the grave. There are two other mourners here as well, a homeless couple with their dog. Broderick's wife hugs me and then walks with their child toward their car. The rabbi and the funeral director leave, and then the homeless couple and their dog walk away. Broderick and I remain and stand together, looking down. Three men in blue work shirts are preparing to fill in the grave. Olive trees interrupt the flat landscape, displaying the silvery green undersides of their leaves. In the distance, palm trees stand like fireworks frozen in time.

Broderick takes my hand, and we stand for what seems like a long while in silence.

"Meirav," he says, squeezing my hand, "he changed my life."

"Mine too," I say.

"Yes," Broderick says. "But he *saved* mine."

I squeeze his hand back. "I know."

Instead of driving home, I drive to the shop my parents had once owned, near the corner of Pico and Doheny. It is no longer filled with broken computers. Now it is a kosher sushi restaurant. The painted brick storefront is covered in ivy.

I put my hand up to the wall and draw aside the clinging vines. I smile when I see there are still flecks of red spray paint there, hidden under the leaves. I touch it lightly and then kiss my fingers, as if touching a mezuzah. I can remember every detail of the day I first saw that red paint, as if it had just happened. *As if it were happening now.*

My parents owned a computer and cell phone repair shop. Behind the counter were bins of wires and parts. I loved watching my parents perform surgery on the machines people brought in. I would spend much of my Sundays building little steampunk robots out of old parts, the rustier the better, or sinking into the deep old armchair in the back of the shop, playing Fortnite, Call of Duty, and Sims. One Sunday, my father pulled me up from the armchair and said, "You spend too much time playing games. You should know how to build the machines that make them possible." From that moment on I became my parents' apprentice, and they taught me the mechanics of computers. By fourth grade I had moved from just being able to replace the shattered face of an iPhone to building a hard drive from scratch all by myself. There wasn't a smartphone that was too smart for me to fix! The summer before sixth grade I went to coding camp so I could learn the codes behind the technology and build my own apps and games. My parents called me a "digital native" because I was so comfortable navigating a printed circuit board and reading lines of code.

That particular Sunday morning, when we came to open the shop, my father froze in his tracks. My mother gasped and tried to shield my eyes. But it was too late. I had already seen. The word "JEW" was spray-painted in large red letters on the white brick of my parents' shop.

The word looked angry. It was written like a curse or a swear word. The paint was the color of blood. I wondered at the time how a little word could seem so violent and menacing. The *J* looked like a hook. The *E* looked like three claw marks. The points of the *W* were sharp like fangs. It scared me. I pulled my goggles, with their gear-shaped frames, down from my cap to hide my eyes in case I cried.

My parents called the police, and they arrived fifteen minutes later. Two officers in blue. They looked at the graffiti and took notes. They, too, looked sad.

That's when I saw Elijah. I realized I had never seen him standing up, but I recognized him right away, with his storm-cloud beard and greasy gray hair. He walked briskly up the block toward us. I noticed him before I noticed that he was gripping a boy by his arm. Broderick. The kid who sat in the back of the class and never spoke to anyone. And even though Broderick was young and strong and Elijah looked weathered and weak, Elijah seemed to have a powerful grip on my classmate. I hid behind my father.

Elijah marched right up to my parents and the police and said, "I saw him do it."

"Is that true?" one of the officers asked, looking at Broderick.

Broderick kept his eyes on the sidewalk. But he muttered, "Yes, sir."

I was stunned. Why would Broderick do that to me? What had I done to him? He didn't even know me! At that moment, I was not thinking about my parents or the Jewish people. This was personal. This was about why he hated me.

"First things first," the other officer said. "You are going to clean this off, young man."

My mother went into the store and returned with a bucket of soapy water, a towel, and a large sponge. My parents stepped aside to talk with the police, and I stood watching Broderick as he dipped the sponge into the bucket and started scrubbing at the sharp fangs of the W. I stared at his back, trying to understand. I wanted to say something to him or yell at him, but I didn't know what to say.

Elijah watched him too. After a moment, he took a rag out of his pants pocket and stepped next to Broderick. Elijah dipped the rag into the bucket and started scrubbing the wall as well. He started in the center of the E, moving his hand in a small circle. None of us spoke.

I watched Elijah's hand, and I became mesmerized. Broderick stopped scrubbing and took a step back. He watched the homeless man move his rag in a circle. The circle grew larger, touching the J and the W. The red spray paint trickled along the grooves between the white bricks. I couldn't look away. It was as if I was watching a screen, being drawn into a virtual world I was so used to, except the controls were not in my hand. I lifted my goggles to see more clearly. Still, the edges of my consciousness fuzzed. My parents, the police—in fact the entire street—faded from my awareness. It was just Elijah, Broderick, and me and the spinning red and white circle. Before my eyes, the colors swallowed up the word, and then the spinning wheel became dimensional. It spun inward into a deep vortex, entering the wall.

Elijah was singing softly. *"LaY'hudim hay'tah orah, hay'tah orah . . ."* I knew the song he was singing; in English it meant "For the Jews, there was light." We sang it on Purim and at *Havdalah*. Elijah's singing became louder. I felt the spinning vortex drawing me in. My feet were planted in place, and yet I was getting closer, as if on a conveyer belt.

Elijah's head turned toward me slowly, like an owl. He put out his hand.

My heart raced. I couldn't move. Broderick was frozen as well.

I felt Elijah's hand close around my arm as the vortex spun faster, the red and white blurring into pink. Elijah was holding Broderick with his other hand, and Broderick was bug-eyed and pale as a ghost. I felt terror creeping over me, my body going cold. My heart raced in panic. I knew I couldn't escape. Instead, I told myself it wasn't real. How could it be?

"No, I must be in front of a screen," I told myself, "in a virtual game. I am a flying mermaid," although the grip of Elijah's fingers on my arm said otherwise. As we crossed the threshold of the portal in the wall, I mouthed the words, "Press play."

Broderick broke out of his trance, wresting his arm out of Elijah's grasp. He whipped around and flung himself toward the tunnel through which we had just come, but as he reached the whirling threshold, the vortex collapsed to the size of a PC case fan before sparking and disappearing. Broderick flew face first into a brick wall. He spun back around, wobbled, and tried to steady himself with his hands on his knees. He straightened up and rubbed his forehead.

"Where the freak are we?" he shouted at Elijah.

I wondered the same thing as I looked around. We were not inside Pico Computer Repair. That was for certain. I sensed we were outside, but it was too dark to be sure. I squinted into the darkness and could distinguish large shapes in the distance. My eyes adjusted, and I could see there were large rectangles; no, they were more trapezoidal. And they were moving. Yes, they were vehicles, and they moved like front loaders, with their continuous track wheels. But these were not front loaders or backhoes or excavators.

"Those are tanks," I said, pointing.

Elijah handed a giant bowl to Broderick and another to me. They were solid and the size of our family's breakfast tabletop, but they were light as foam. "You are going to need these," he said.

"What for?" Broderick asked frantically.

The bowls were silvery white and glowed with a faint light. Pearlescent. I ran my hand over the bowl. It was satiny smooth, outside and in. Running my hand along the inside, I felt a handle at the bottom, in the center. I looked at the tanks in the distance. I could make them out more clearly now. I wondered who was driving them. The turret of one of the tanks began to turn its cannon toward us.

I looked to where Elijah had been standing. He was gone. I looked at Broderick. He was standing there bewildered, with a large bruise on his forehead.

"They're shields," I said to him. When I realized he wasn't registering anything, I shouted, "Broderick, they're shields!"

He snapped into the present just as we heard a shattering explosion. Broderick held his shield up in front of his body. I dropped to the ground and pulled my shield over me like a turtle shell. I felt a barrage of pellets rain on my shield. I also heard Broderick.

"My leg!" he screamed.

I came out from under the shield. By the light of the shields, I could see that the jeans on his left leg were torn, and he was bleeding.

I grabbed his hand and said, "Come on!"

"Where?"

"I don't know, but we can't stay here."

The air quaked with another explosion, and we both dropped and hid under our shields. Then we leapt up and ran. My mind was racing faster than my feet. "We can't outrun tanks," I thought. "There has to be another way."

"Meirav," Broderick called. He was a little behind me. I kept running. "Meirav!" he called louder. I turned. He was trying to keep up, but he was limping. His shield wasn't smooth anymore. It was dented and pocked. He pointed up.

I looked up. A fleet of slow-moving spacecrafts hummed across the sky. Massive triangular ships glided like sharks moving through a black sea. Rows of green lights on the bottom of each spacecraft formed giant Xs. I stared at them, unable to look away. A deer in headlights. Then, the four tips of each X began to rapidly blink. All at once, the lights at the tips switched, each line angling at the center to the right, and then every twisted X turned red. Swastikas.

"Why do they want to hurt us?" Broderick cried out.

We each ducked under our shields as red beams of lights shot out of the sky. I could feel the lasers tearing open the ground around me. I could feel their heat through my shield, but it held strong. I worried about Broderick, and then I felt angry. "Why should I worry about him? He doesn't care about me. Why did Elijah drag me here with him? This is his punishment, not mine."

I heard a small whimper. A child. I peeked out from under my shield. There was a young boy standing with his hands up over his head. He was wearing knickers that reached just below his knees and a clean white shirt, and he had a book bag over his shoulder. He looked like he was on his way home from school. I glanced up. The red swastikas were green Xs again. I looked toward where the boy was staring, and I saw a tank with its cannon pointing directly at him. My heart was in my throat, and my body quivered. "I am not Meirav Selah Edelman," I told myself. "I am the Magical Mermaid Menace of Anarchy Acres and I am undefeated!" Well, almost undefeated.

I bolted toward the boy, zigzagging around the pits and craters in the ground. I tackled him and pulled him under my shield. The air exploded with cannon fire. I felt ammo pound against the shield. The boy was curled up next to me. I could see him in the shield's glow. I was disoriented, and then I realized that the shield had become larger to shelter us both. The boy looked at me with large eyes.

"My sister," he pleaded.

I lifted the shield. The landscape was glowing green.

I saw Broderick struggling with his shield. His shield was smaller, and some of the dents and pocks had become holes. I scanned around until I saw a girl even younger than the boy, with two long braids and a doll in her right hand, staring up at the sky. She had to be the boy's sister! The tips of the Xs started blinking. Then the landscape turned red. I looked up at the spacecraft, with their crooked red Xs.

"Stay under the shield," I said to the boy, and I catapulted toward the girl. Incinerating beams of red light dropped from the sky. I felt my hair and flannel shirt singe. I grabbed the girl and pulled her into a smoking trench, holding her tightly while the lasers raked the land. Then everything turned green.

"What's going on! What's going on!" Broderick was yelling.

The girl and I climbed out of the trench. I took her hand, and we sprinted back toward where her brother knelt. The shield was behind him, surrounding him in a halo of soft light. I looked over at Broderick. He was walking in circles, and his hair was standing up like he had been electrocuted. His clothes were torn, and his shield was like Swiss cheese.

"I shouldn't care," I thought. But I did. A lot. He wasn't any different to me than the brother and sister. We were all children. We were all vulnerable. We were all lost.

"Follow me," I called to him. He turned to me with wild eyes and sprang into action. The landscape turned red again. I pulled Broderick, along with the brother and sister, under my shield. The shield grew into a shelter big enough for us all.

Inside the shield, Broderick clasped his knees and wept. I examined his shield. Not only was it filled with holes, but it had gotten smaller. A large chunk was missing from one side. It looked like a waning moon.

The boy opened his book bag. He reached in and pulled out a small gold disc. He handed it to me. It looked like an elevator button, with the number 18 engraved on it. I gave it back to him, and he placed the button on the ground between us.

"What is that?" Broderick exclaimed. "What is going on?"

I smiled at the boy, and he smiled back and nodded. I pressed the button, and a blue ring lit up around it. Outside the shield, a cannon exploded. I whispered to myself, "Level two."

The button opened the ground beneath the shield, and the four of us slid down a steep chute. We landed on soft grass, our shields tumbling down with us. I looked up and saw an overcast gray sky. The spacecraft and tanks were gone. I looked around and realized we were in a graveyard. The tombstones looked old, and some were crumbling. All the stones around us were carved with Hebrew letters. All except one—a newer grave not far from where we had landed.

"Where are we?" Broderick asked, wiping his nose with his tattered sleeve. He struggled to his feet.

"I don't know," I said as I stood as well. I turned to the brother and sister, but they were far away, holding hands and skipping through the graves. I listened to them giggling until they disappeared. I turned back to Broderick. "Why did you do that to my parents' shop?" I snapped at him. He looked pathetic. I felt sorry for him. But I was still mad.

He struggled to find words.

Just then he noticed the newer grave and stepped over to it. Written on the grave were three lines with the words "Carl Roberts, 1935–2022, A Generous Man." As we stared at the grave, the letters on the top line started to morph. Instead of "Carl Roberts," it read "Forgive."

Broderick looked like a ghost.

"Forgive who?" I said out loud. Then I pointed to Broderick. "Him?" Was I trapped inside a storyline where the protagonist can only save herself by discovering her own power to forgive? "No go, Elijah," I thought. Absolutely not.

Then, the letters on the third line morphed as well. Instead of "A Generous Man," it read "Brody."

"Forgive Brody?" I asked the empty graveyard, my thumb pointing at Broderick. "Ha! He hasn't even said sorry."

"No one calls me Brody," Broderick said, "except my grandfather."

I looked at him quizzically. He added, "My grandfather was Carl Roberts."

I looked at the freshly turned earth in front of the tombstone.

"He raised me," Broderick said softly.

"Well, Broderick's grandfather," I announced loudly, "you raised a total jerk."

Broderick held his busted shield close to his chest protectively. "My grandfather died last summer," he said.

Then, the numbers on the middle line morphed into a single word: "Me."

I studied Broderick for a moment. I could see the grief in his eyes. I remembered him back in first and second grade. He had seemed like a happier kid back then. I had a vague memory of Broderick's father. Then, starting in third grade, I remember he was picked up from school by his grandparents. This year, no one picked him up. I would see him walk out of school alone to the bus stop.

Behind us, we heard a soft bleating: "Baah." We turned to see a baby goat nibbling on a tuft of grass. Broderick walked up to the kid and petted it between the ears. His body was turned away from me. I could see Broderick's back trembling. He was weeping.

"My grandfather had chickens and goats," Broderick said. "I helped him feed and take care of them."

"I help in my parents' shop," I said.

I saw Broderick lower his head. "I know," he said.

We both swung around to the sound of a man shouting. Running through the graves was a giant man, at least eight feet tall, wearing a white apron smeared with blood. He was wearing a white triangular paper hat and carrying a gleaming butcher knife. "Get back here, you stupid goat!" he shouted. "Get back here!" In the distance, on the hazy horizon, I saw a factory. Its tall smokestacks puffed clouds into the sky.

"Slaughterhouse," I thought.

Broderick dropped his shield and grabbed the kid into his arms. The butcher ran toward us, his long legs hurdling tombstones. Broderick started running. I grabbed Broderick's shield and ducked down under mine. I heard the butcher stop. I could sense he was standing over me.

"Are you in there, little goat?" I heard him say. Then the butcher knife came down on the shield with the force of a hatchet. I saw my shield dent with the blow. It hadn't dented when struck by the tank fire or the lasers. I braced myself for the knife to come down again.

"I have the kid!" I heard Broderick shout. The butcher stepped away to chase Broderick, shouting, "Get back here, stupid goat!"

I remained crouched under my shield, contemplating the dent. Broderick's shield was in my hands. I looked at it, and I saw one of its holes close. "He could have kept running," I realized. "He could have hidden from the butcher, but he saw I was in trouble and he saved me."

I looked again at the dent in my shield before emerging. Broderick was running with the kid goat in his arms, and the butcher was chasing him. The butcher was not hurdling tombstones now. He was stepping directly on them with his giant black boots. The crumbling stones exploded into dust. Then a song burst into my mind, chilling the blood in my veins:

Once there was a wicked, wicked man
And Haman was his name, sir.
He would have murdered all the Jews
Though they were not to blame, sir.

I shook the song from my brain. The butcher was closing in on Broderick. I couldn't move. There was no way I could reach Broderick and shield him in time. Though at home I was the Mermaid Menace, lightning fast and an ace with a crossbow in the virtual world, here I was uncharacteristically anchored in place, and I had no weapon. The longer I stood, the smaller my shield became, waning like the moon until it was merely a crescent. Something was cementing me down. Meanwhile, Broderick's shield was growing, its surface smoothing.

I remembered one time when I was playing Fortnite in the Battle Royale map, I acquired a boomerang at Junk Junction, just north of the Haunted Hills. I saw that the crescent shield in my hand was roughly the same shape as that boomerang. I took aim at the running butcher and drew my arm back. "Throw," I said, as if voice-activating my own arm, and I threw what was left of my shield. The shield spun like helicopter blades across the cemetery and struck the butcher square in the head. The giant man tumbled, and the shield opened into a half moon and dropped. Broderick grabbed it as it continued to wax larger, and with the kid under his other arm, he ran back to me.

Out of breath, Broderick managed to ask me if I was all right.

I nodded. Broderick put the kid down. He scratched it again between the ears. The baby goat nibbled a buttercup and, with a grateful "baah," leapt away.

"It's so sad," he said.

"What is?" I asked.

He looked at the desecrated cemetery. "All the destruction," he said.

I blinked at him and all the ruined tombstones. And then I had a realization. I looked back toward his grandfather's grave, but it too had been destroyed. I thought of its message, "Forgive me, Brody." It wasn't a message for me. It was a message for Broderick.

"Your grandfather wants *you*," I said slowly, "to forgive *him*."

Broderick wiped his eyes.

"For dying," I said.

Broderick lowered his head.

"You don't hate me," I realized out loud. I looked over at the baby goat leaping toward pasture. The clouds were clearing, and the sky was blue. "You needed a scapegoat," I said.

Broderick was sobbing. "I'm sorry," he gasped and crumpled to the ground. "I am so sorry." I sat beside him. Our two shields lay on the ground upside down, open to the sunshine. I scanned the horizon and noticed that the factory was gone. The butcher was gone. The tombstones were restored, and they were shiny and smooth. Buttercups and bluebells dotted the land.

I wondered what we were supposed to do now. I sat beside Broderick on the grass.

"I am really sorry," Broderick said, and he looked it. "I don't know why I did that. I don't know why I thought 'Jew' was something bad. I don't even really know what 'Jew' means."

"It means 'thankful,'" I said, remembering what I had learned in religious school. "It is from Genesis. When Leah has her fourth son, she is thankful, and so she names him Y'hudah, Judah, which means 'thankful.'"

"Oh," Broderick said sadly. We had sat for what felt like a long while when he looked up at me and said, "It is a beautiful word."

I leaned back on the grass and looked at the clear sky. I felt peaceful. I remembered the song that Elijah had been singing when he was scrubbing the wall, opening the portal. I started singing it: "*LaY'hudim hay'tah orah, hay'tah orah, v'simchah, v'sason, vikar. Kein, tih'yeh lanu*"—"For the Jews, there was light and joy, happiness and honor, and so may it be for us." I sang it again and again, the melody transporting me to happy times. I thought of singing it on Purim, dancing in the sanctuary, wearing an Esther crown. I thought about singing it around the dancing light of the braided *Havdalah* candle, with its multiple wicks, and the sweet smell of cinnamon and cloves in the spice box.

Broderick lay back beside me. He reached over and held my hand, our fingers braiding together, and it felt perfectly natural. He started to sing with me. He struggled with the Hebrew but sang "*hay'tah orah, hay'tah orah*" with confidence. It made me laugh. Soon, we were both laughing. We watched as our two shields rose above us, as if that, too, was perfectly natural. We watched as they came together to form a sphere and then rise as if filled with helium. We watched as the sky turned purple and orange and the sun dipped low. We watched as the sphere became the full moon.

I closed my eyes. I was happy. And sleepy. And light. When I opened my eyes, I was no longer holding Broderick's hand. I was holding Elijah's hand, and Broderick was holding his other hand. We were standing in front of Pico Computer Repair, in front of the white brick wall. "JEW" was still written there, but the word did not seem angry or like a curse. The *J* was a ladle filled with warmth and goodness. The *E* was a ladder reaching for higher ideals. The *W* was the hands of the High Priest blessing the people.

Elijah let go of us without a word and moved down the sidewalk. Broderick stared at the soapy sponge in his hand as if trying to decipher a puzzle.

"It wasn't a dream," he said quietly to himself. He turned to me. He had no bruise on his forehead. His clothes weren't torn. His leg wasn't bloodied. I reached up and could feel that my hair sticking out from under my cap was not singed, nor was my flannel shirt. Still, I agreed with Broderick. It had happened. "No," I said. "It wasn't a dream."

He stared at me wonderingly. He opened his mouth and then closed it again, reconsidering.

"What?" I asked.

He took a deep breath. "I was just thinking," he said, "how thankful I am." He looked at the word "JEW" and then back at me. "For you. For what happened to us."

"I am thankful too," I said.

Broderick touched the sponge to wall. He paused for a moment before scrubbing and whispered, "I'm sorry."

I touched the paint lightly, like I was touching a mezuzah. I contemplated the red on my fingertip. "I know," I said. "I believe you."

Walking into my home, I feel as if I have been away a long time, although it has just been a few hours since I left Elijah's funeral and the site of my parents' computer repair shop. The apartment smells wonderful. Jordannah is standing over a large pot of vegetable soup, ladling it into three bowls. She is wearing her navy suit and the gray silk scarf with silver threads I had bought her in New York. A fresh loaf of crusty rosemary and parmigiana bread is on the cutting board. I laugh to myself. When our friends gave us a bread machine for our wedding, we were sure we would never use it. We had joked about how long we would have to keep it before giving it away, so as not to insult them. But here it is years later, that big machine dominating our small kitchen counter, and we use it all the time. It turned out to be our favorite gift.

My father is at the table with a magnifying glass, dissecting a wireless gaming wand, and the baby is in her high chair, mushing carrots and peas with her fingers.

"Abba," I say, "at the dinner table?" I kiss Nili on the top of her head, and she touches carrots to my cheek.

"Traffic?" Jordannah asks, carrying two bowls to the table.

I fetch the third bowl. It feels warm in my hands. "No," I say from the kitchen. "Memories."

QUESTIONS

1. What does the word "Jew" mean to you?
2. This story touches on different historical periods when Jews have faced antisemitism: the time in antiquity when Haman tried to kill the Jews, the Nazi attempt to eradicate European Jewry in modern times, and a more contemporary example of antisemitic graffiti. Have you experienced antisemitism? Why do you think antisemitism continues?
3. Can you think of any examples when hate was transformed into understanding and community building?
4. Meirav is a gamer, her family works in computer repair, and her experience with Broderick feels like an advanced virtual reality program. How can technology be used to combat antisemitism? How might technology make antisemitism worse?

The Most Important Person in the World

THE STUDENTS WERE RESTLESS. They could feel summer in the air. Peaches and nectarines were appearing in their lunch bags. Sunscreen lotion was on display by the grocery checkout counter. The weather was getting hotter, and the days were getting longer.

Sasha was especially excited. Three weeks left of school! This was going to be her first summer at sleepaway camp. She was going for twelve days to Havayah Arts, a Jewish arts camp. Sasha loved to draw. The desk in her room had cups filled with pencils and markers; she had already filled nine sketchbooks and was starting her tenth. Her grandfather was an artist, and she loved spending hours in his studio, helping him bring large works of art to life. Her grandfather taught her to be free with the paper and to be unafraid of filling up space. He taught her about lines that breathe and how perfection is sometimes the enemy of creativity. Sasha also spent a lot of time watching drawing tutorials on YouTube. That's how she learned about shadow and dimension. But she had developed her own style too, and all her friends wanted her to draw them. Her portraits were playful and dynamic. The art teacher at school told Sasha that she had "great perspective." That meant she saw things from a unique point of view. Sasha was excited to go to camp to learn new techniques and meet new friends who also loved art.

Sasha's friends were extra fidgety in religious school, especially right before *t'filah*. Leah was sitting on one side of her, and she was chatting about what she wanted for her birthday, which was funny because Leah's birthday had been last week. Leah started thinking about her next birthday the minute her last one ended! Even when the teacher put her finger to her lips to let Leah know to quiet down, she kept on chatting. Sam sat on the other side of Sasha, and he was tapping out a rhythm on his legs. He was getting so into his own rhythm that he kicked the pew in front of him, and Nick turned around and pretend-scowled.

Part of being an artist was observing things closely, and Sasha loved to observe people. She paid attention to little details. She noticed that Leah had dimples when she smiled and a face shaped like a heart. She noticed that Sam had an egg-shaped face and always wore band T-shirts. She noticed that Nick had eyebrows that came together and looked like a seagull's silhouette against the sun.

Songleader Ari strummed the first electric chords of a rock 'n' roll version of *Mi Chamochah*, and all the children in the sanctuary leapt up and started dancing. When it came to the chorus, Sasha and her friends spilled out of the pews into the aisles, waving their hands in the air and singing, "Freedom! Free-ee-dom! Freedom's on our way!" Sasha liked how Ari's blond curly hair looked like fusilli pasta bouncing on his head.

The students settled squirmily back into their rows. Leah was still singing the chorus, but she replaced "freedom" with "summer." Sam bounced on the cushion.

Sasha thought about what Shabbat would be like at camp. She would be there for two Shabbats. She wondered who she would be sitting next to during camp *t'filah* and if they sang different melodies for the prayers. In one of her sketchbooks, she had a drawing of her family around two Shabbat candles. Her religious school teacher had taught her that we light two candles because one candle represents the command to "observe the Sabbath" and the other candle represents the command to "remember the Sabbath." Observe and remember—two things that are essential to being an artist. Perhaps being Jewish was all about being an artist and looking at the world from a unique perspective.

Rabbi Rebecca Zissen had spiky white hair, half-moon eyes, and rosy cheeks, and she wore a silk tallit painted with Hebrew letters. She started telling a story about someone named Zusia from a long time ago.

Zusia was a funny name. Sasha wondered how she would draw this person named Zusia. Maybe with a big beard? Perhaps with a hat? Would she draw him large or skinny, standing or sitting? Maybe wearing a helmet in a rocket-powered wheelchair with a turtle in his lap? Anything was possible with art.

Rabbi Zissen was saying, "Instead of trying to be like someone else, Zusia tried to be the best version of Zusia he could be, because there was no one else like Zusia."

Maybe he wore roller skates and a tablecloth as a cape, Sasha thought. That would be fun to draw.

"Just like there is no one like each one of you," Rabbi Zissen continued. "Each one of you has a job, and that is to strive to be the best version of you. Not to be Moses or Miriam, or to look like that pop singer or that TV star. Zusia was Zusia, and you are you!"

Sasha knew that she was unique. She used to have long brown hair, but in fourth grade she decided she wanted to cut her hair super short and dye it bright red. She liked being different. Differences are what made people works of art.

Rabbi Zissen said to the students, "Let me ask you, my friends: Who is the most important person in the world?"

All of the students started calling out answers.

"Abraham Lincoln!"

"Gandhi!"

"Mother Teresa!"

"Martin Luther King Jr.!"

"These are all excellent suggestions," Rabbi Zissen said. "I want you to think about who the most important person in the world is, and we will hear your ideas next week."

Sasha thought about the question when she went to the carpool line to get picked up. She asked Luke, who was standing next to her, about his answer to the question the rabbi had asked. Luke flattened his lips together like a duckbill when he was thinking, and he was always thinking. He said, "Definitely Johannes Gutenberg. He invented the printing press. Without him, we wouldn't have any books."

That definitely was important. Maddie was standing on the other side of Sasha, with her long black hair parted in a white line in the middle. She said, "I am the most important person. That's what the rabbi wants us to say. That the most important person in the world is me because no one else is like me."

That made sense, Sasha thought. Zusia is Zusia, Maddie is Maddie, Johannes Gutenberg is Johannes Gutenberg, and I am me. It also sounded like the kind of thing the rabbi would say.

But still, something about that answer bothered Sasha. Wasn't it a little arrogant to think that we are each the most important person? Didn't they also learn in religious school that Hillel said, "If I am not for myself, who will be for me? But if I am only for myself, who am I?" Maybe Hillel was the most important person.

That night at dinner, Sasha brought up the question to her family. Her older brother, Benji, said, "Definitely Moses. The Torah is called the Five Books of Moses, so there you have it." Benji had long hair in the front that fell over one eye.

"But Torah says that Moses is the most humble person in the world," Sasha's father said, scratching his smooth head. Sasha noticed he had a smudge on his glasses. "Can you be the most humble *and* the most important?"

Sasha's little brother, Micky, asked, "What is humble?"

"Humble is when you are aware of how small you are," answered Sasha's father.

"Then I am the most humble in the family!" Micky exclaimed, and they all laughed because he really was the smallest. He looked like a miniature Benji.

"Maybe being humble is what makes you important," Sasha's grandfather suggested.

"I think the most important person in the world is a newborn baby," Sasha's mother said. "A baby is full of potential and hope."

Sasha thought that was a good idea. But did that mean that once you grew up, you weren't important anymore? She looked at her grandfather, who was sitting beside her, with his paint-splattered pants and the spray of creases at the corners of his eyes. She looked at his strong hands, with the scars on his fingers from so many years carving wood. He was so important to her.

"I think the most important person is the stranger," Sasha's father said. "After all, our Torah is all about how we treat the stranger, because we were once strangers in Egypt."

Sasha thought that was a good idea too. But what happened when the stranger became your friend? Were they less important then? That didn't make sense. Sasha wondered what she would do if there were two hungry people and she had only enough to feed one of them. What if one of the hungry people was a stranger and the other was her mother; would she choose the stranger? Maybe her mother was the most important person in the world. Sasha looked at her mother, her apple cheeks and high forehead, and hair that poofed out like cotton candy. But what about Maddie's mother? Or Luke's mother? Or songleader Ari's mother? Or Rabbi Zissen's mother?

After dinner, Sasha opened her tenth sketchbook and wrote in bubble letters at the top of the first page, "The Most Important Person in the World." Then she started doing quick pencil sketches. She sketched Leah sleeping on a bed that was really a birthday cake, dreaming about cupcakes. She sketched Abraham Lincoln and Mahatma Gandhi riding a two-seated bicycle. She sketched Martin Luther King Jr. and Mother Teresa in a hot-air balloon. She sketched Rabbi Zissen skydiving. She sketched her brother Benji as a cyclops and her little brother as a frog sitting on a mushroom. They all looked funny together on one page!

On the next page she sketched what she imagined Johannes Gutenberg might have looked like, wearing a striped top hat and giant buttons, printing pictures of a teacher with her finger to her mouth, whispering "shh." She sketched a rock 'n' roll band, with songleader Ari on guitar standing in a bowl of pasta, Sam on drums wearing a Metallica T-shirt, Moses playing the washboard, a newborn baby playing trombone, and Maddie on the microphone surrounded by music notes. She sketched Nick and made his eyebrows into the wings of a bird. She sketched Luke floating on a raft in a pond filled with lilies and Hebrew letters. She sketched her parents roller-skating with a bear in a cape. She sketched her grandfather holding out a bouquet of pencils, markers, and paintbrushes.

All week Sasha thought about who the most important person in the world was and added to her sketchbook. She drew a pilot, a garbage collector, a camp counselor, a nurse, a soldier, and a farmer. How could one be more important than another? She drew a firefighter, a mountain climber, a plumber, a baker, a mayor, and a housecleaner. The Torah taught that everyone is made in God's image, so weren't they all equally important? Except that when you are on a bus, the driver is the most important. And if you are at the beach, the lifeguard is the most important. Maybe the answer to the question depends on where you are.

Sasha closed her sketchbook and wondered if an artist could ever be the most important person in the world. "Am I helping anyone by observing and remembering?" she asked herself. She thought about all the people she had drawn, and a wave of insecurity came over her. Had art ever saved a life? Sasha went to bed feeling very small.

The next day at religious school, the students gathered in the sanctuary for *t'filah*. Sasha was sitting between Nicola and Toby. Nicola was missing a tooth. Toby had black nail polish and a birthmark on their cheek. Sasha looked to see where Leah and Sam were. Leah was sitting between Zach and Harris. Sam was sitting between Carrie and Gus. The sanctuary was buzzing with talking and laughter until songleader Ari brought everyone together singing, "You created me, You shaped me, You breathed me into life."

Then Rabbi Zissen asked, "So, my friends. Did you think about who the most important person in the world is?"

Hands went up. Sasha thought all the hands looked like strange flowers, with the arms as stems. The sanctuary was a garden of ideas.

"Adam, the first man," said one student. "If it wasn't for him, none of us would be here."

"Eve, the first woman," said another. "If it wasn't for her, none of us would be here."

"Noah," said another. "If it wasn't for him, we would all be lost in the Flood, and there would be no animals."

"My grandma Stella," said a student. "If it wasn't for her surviving the war, my family wouldn't be here."

"Jonas Salk," called another. "He discovered the cure for polio!"

"Dr. Dorothy Ho," said a student, "because she saved my life when I was a baby and needed oxygen."

"LeBron James!"

"No, Michael Jordan!"

"No, Shaquille O'Neal!"

"No, Kareem Abdul-Jabbar!"

"The prophet Elijah!"

"Albert Einstein!"

"Esther!"

"Jimi Hendrix," suggested songleader Ari, playing a loud resonating chord.

"These are all great answers," Rabbi Zissen said. "Anyone else?"

As students called out names, Sasha imagined what it would be like if all of these important people were sitting in the sanctuary with them. She imagined Albert Einstein, LeBron James, and Grandma Stella sitting there amid her friends. She imagined Jimi Hendrix and Eve and Jonas Salk. Then she imagined all the people in her sketchbook coming to life and joining them as well—nurses, farmers, plumbers, bakers. She imagined the sanctuary teeming with all different kinds of people, squishing together into the pews. Suddenly, she knew why art was important! It was about paying close attention and seeing things in a unique way.

"We have time for one more answer," Rabbi Zissen said.

Sasha raised her hand. Rabbi Zissen pointed to her and said, "Yes, Sasha? Who is the most important person in the world?"

"I think the most important person is the person sitting next to you."

The sanctuary was silent for a moment. Sasha's answer was a new seed in this garden of ideas, and it needed a moment to germinate. And then, Sasha saw her friends all looking on their right and their left, with eyes bright as if observing something new about the people around them. And then the sanctuary erupted in chatter.

"You are really important!" Sasha heard Maddie exclaim to Luke. And he responded, "You are pretty important too, I guess."

Toby pointed two fingers first at their own eyes and then at Sasha and said, "I see you."

Sasha smiled and said, "I see you too!"

Nikola shouted, "I must be important because I am seated next to the most important people!"

"No," Sam blurted out, "this guy's the most important!" He had his arm around Gus's neck, playfully grinding his knuckles against his head. Gus managed to extract himself and tickle Sam while shouting, "No, he's the most important of all!"

Sasha heard Leah exclaim, "Does anyone have the same birthday as me? May 2?"

"I do, actually!" Rabbi Zissen laughed.

"You're important!" Leah shouted.

"You, too!" exclaimed the rabbi, and then she settled the noise with a loud, "*Echad, sh'tayim, shalosh*, hands on your *rosh*!"

Once the students settled down, the rabbi spoke. "Sasha has shared some great wisdom with us. And I want to add this for everyone to think about. If the most important person is the person next to you, that means that you have a responsibility toward that person: to make sure they feel safe and supported." She paused and then said sternly, "Gus, let go of Sam!"

"He started it," Gus quipped.

"Is that how you treat the most important person in the world?" Rabbi Zissen asked.

"You mean me?" Sam asked.

"Or me?" asked Gus.

"Exactly," Rabbi Zissen said. "We have a responsibility to each other because the person sitting next to you, whoever they are, is unique. There is no one like them in the world. They are special and precious, and we must protect that about each other, right?"

The students all looked at the people sitting next to them. Sasha imagined that all her friends had become artists, observing new details about the people around them, details they would remember. For a moment, everyone saw, and everyone was seen.

"God designed each of us for a purpose," Rabbi Zissen said, and Sasha imagined God opening the Book of Life, except it wasn't a book filled with names. It was a sketchbook, and the pages were filled with drawings of people in all different colors and shapes, with lines that were hard and soft, curved and zigzaggy. And then, Sasha envisioned God breathing into the drawings, animating them all into life.

Just then songleader Ari strummed the first notes of a new prayer, and Rabbi Zissen clapped along. Sasha and her friends all stood up, as if the music was God's breath animating them off the page, and they all started dancing.

QUESTIONS

1. Who makes you feel important? What can you do to make other people feel important?

2. Who are the marginalized people in your community, and how could you help support them?

3. Sasha's conclusion—that the most important person in the world is the person sitting next to you—comes from a place of humility. One has to see past one's own ego to recognize the importance of others. Alan Morinis writes in his book *Everyday Holiness*, "Being humble doesn't mean being a nobody, it just means being no more of a somebody than you ought to be." He suggests the following practice: "Next time you sit on a bench, watch how much of it you occupy. There is no need to cringe on the edge because you're entitled to it. Yet there is also no justification for sprawling into a space that ought to accommodate someone else." When is it important to take up more space, and when is it important to make room for others?

4. In the story we read, "Perhaps being Jewish was all about being an artist and looking at the world from a unique perspective." What unique perspective does Judaism offer?

Allison Searches for Her Hebrew Name

ON THE FIRST DAY OF HEBREW SCHOOL, teacher Brett handed out white sticker labels and markers. He asked the students to make themselves name tags using their Hebrew names. Jackson's Hebrew name was Yehoshua. Sam's Hebrew name was Shmuel. Sherrie's Hebrew name was Brachah.

The problem was, Allison didn't have a Hebrew name. She stared at the blank sticker, not knowing what to do.

Brandon wrote "Zev" on his sticker, peeled off the backing, and stuck it proudly on his shirt. "I'm named after my great-grandfather," he said. "It means 'wolf.'" Brandon growled and made his fingers like claws.

Jesse wrote "Yishai." Madison wrote "Miriam." Tina wrote "Tikvah." Ralph wrote "Raphael."

Sarah's name was the same in Hebrew and in English. The same was true for Oreet. But Oreet was from Israel, and Sarah was from Hazelton, Pennsylvania.

Oreet said, "In Israel we don't have two different names. We just have one Hebrew name."

Parker squeezed "Esther-Malka" onto her sticker. "I was born on Purim."

Soon A.J. was wearing the name "Avraham," Becky was wearing "Rivke," Matthew was wearing "Mattityahu," and Kelly was wearing "Kahatya."

Teacher Brett looked at Kelly's sticker and said, "I don't know that Hebrew name."

Kelly said, "It is an acronym. K, H, T, Y. It stands for *Kol han'shamah t'ha-leil Yah*, which means 'Every soul will praise God.'"

"How beautiful!" teacher Brett exclaimed.

There was another girl in Allison's class named Alyson. Their names sounded the same, but they were spelled differently. The other Alyson wrote on her sticker "Aviva."

David was taking his time writing and decorating his Hebrew name, "Dov-Ber." Allison would have thought he would have David as a Hebrew name, but she supposed it didn't always work that way.

"Interesting," said teacher Brett. "Your name is both Hebrew and Yiddish. Dov is Hebrew for 'bear,' and Ber is Yiddish for 'bear.'"

Allison wrote a big purple question mark on her sticker and stuck it over her heart.

"Don't worry, Allison," teacher Brett said, "lots of people don't have Hebrew names. The good news is you can still get one! A lot of Hebrew names start with the same letter as the English name. You and your parents can talk with the clergy about choosing one. It is fun to choose a Hebrew name when you are a little older, because you get to think about what is meaningful to you and what you like."

The other Alyson said, "Why don't you choose Aviva, like me?"

"Aviva is a very lyrical name," teacher Brett said, "and it means 'spring.'"

"It's a pretty name," Allison said. "But I don't really feel like an Aviva."

"How can you not feel like an Aviva?" the other Alyson asked. "You feel like an Alyson, don't you?"

Allison knew their English names sounded the same. But she also knew that they were very different, she and the other Alyson. The other Alyson had wavy blond hair, green eyes, and no freckles, and she always wore dresses and barrettes. Allison had curly brown hair, dark brown eyes, and lots of freckles, and she liked to wear shorts, colorful knee-high socks, and white converse sneakers. Plus, the other Alyson was born in April, which was the spring, while she was born in September.

Allison excused herself to go to the bathroom. When she stood in front of the mirror and saw the question mark over her heart, it made her sad. She took off the sticker and threw it in the trash.

That night Allison asked her parents why she didn't have a Hebrew name. Her parents said that they hadn't really thought about it at the time, but if she wanted a Hebrew name, they could pick one together.

"How about Latke?" suggested her father. "Those are yummy."

"How about Mazal Tov?" suggested her mother. "Or L'chayim?"

"Those are not names," Allison said.

"Why not?" they asked.

Allison opened the browser on her phone and looked up Hebrew names starting with the letter *A*.

Adi: Jewel
Adina: Gentle
Ahuva: Beloved
Aliza: Happy
Amit: Friendly
Ariella: Lioness of God
Ashira: Rich
Atara: Crown
Ayelet: Deer

As she read each name, she imagined trying it on like a beautiful silk robe. She imagined how the name would feel against her skin and in her heart. Each name was beautiful, but none of them felt right. They felt foreign to her, like she was trying on robes that belonged to someone else. None of them fit.

After school the next day, Allison went shopping with her mother. While her mother was in the freezer aisle, Allison wandered to look at the yogurts. There, picking out parmesan and ricotta, was Cantor Tovah from the temple.

"Hi, Allison," Cantor Tovah said.

"Hi, Cantor," Allison responded. "Can I ask you a question?"

"Certainly!" Cantor Tovah put the parmesan and ricotta in her shopping cart next to two shiny eggplants, a jar of tomato sauce, and a carton of eggs.

"How do you choose a Hebrew name?" Allison asked.

"There are lots of ways," Cantor Tovah said. "Some people choose a Hebrew name based on the name of a relative who died. For example, if someone had a great-uncle whose Hebrew name was Yitzchak, they might name their baby Yitzchak to honor him."

"What if their baby is a girl?"

"Well, they could choose a Hebrew name starting with *Y*, like Yael, or Yaffah, or Yardenah. I am named after my grandfather Tuvia." The cantor rested her arms on her cart and leaned forward, studying Allison for a moment. "Are you shopping for a Hebrew name for yourself?" she asked.

Allison nodded.

"Exciting!" Cantor Tovah exclaimed, straightening up. "You could choose a name based on a holiday near your birthday; for example, if you were born near Tu BiSh'vat, you could be named Ilanah, which means 'tree.' Or it could be based on a personality trait. If you are joyous, you could be named Gilah; if you are pleasant, you could be named Naamah; if you are compassionate, you could be named Ruchamah. I know for a fact that you are all three of those things."

Allison smiled.

The cantor continued, "You could also base your Hebrew name on something you really like. For example, if you like the sea, you could be named Galyah, which means 'wave,' or Peninah, which means 'pearl.' If you like music there is Shirah, which means 'song.' Lots of cantors name their daughters Shirah."

"I don't know," Allison said, putting her hands in the pockets of her denim shorts. "I've looked at a lot of names, and none of them really feel right."

"Hmm," Cantor Tovah thought out loud. "You could also choose a name based on a person in the Torah, like Sarah, Rivkah, Rachel, or Leah. Or choose a name after a place in Israel like Moriah, Natanyah, or Carmel. Or you could do what some people do in Israel and get really creative and choose names that don't appear in Torah, like Orah, Vered, Lilach, and Dalyah."

"Allison!" Allison's mother called to her. She came around the corner and smiled at Cantor Tovah. "Is she talking to you about Hebrew names?"

"Yes," smiled the cantor. "I think this is something that deserves more than a passing conversation in the dairy aisle. Let's explore together at the temple. Okay, Allison?"

Allison nodded.

In the car, Allison told her mother some of the ways people choose Hebrew names.

"How about Glidah?" Allison's mother said. "Doesn't that mean 'ice cream'? You love ice cream!"

"Mom," Allison groaned, rolling her eyes.

"You were born close to Rosh HaShanah. How about Shofarah? Is that a name?"

"No, I am pretty sure that is not a name."

"But you said they get creative with Hebrew names in Israel."
Shofarah definitely did not feel right to Allison.

Now, what Allison could not possibly know is that while she was searching for her Hebrew name, there was a Hebrew name searching for her—it had been searching for her for 240 years. In 1770, on the outskirts of the city of Plovdiv in Bulgaria, a poor couple welcomed their only child into the world. She was born on the fourth night of Chanukah, when it was bitter cold and there was hardly a moon in the sky. She was healthy and strong, and her parents named her Yehudit, after the Jewish heroine in the Chanukah story who single-handedly conquered the Assyrian general Holofernes and inspired her people to rise up and fight for their freedom. She was the light of her parents' lives and filled their hearts with joy. Yehudit was Allison's great-great-great-great-great-great-grandmother. That's six greats—eight generations ago.

Yehudit's mother was a seamstress, and her father worked in a tannery. Yehudit was a voracious reader and made a living as a bookbinder. Every year the family attended an annual fair to sell garments and books. It was at one of these fairs that Yehudit fell in love with the man she would marry, a Jewish merchant from Turkey. They married and had two children, a daughter who died young of yellow fever and a son who lived a long life. Yehudit's son had three sons of his own, and his sons had sons. Yehudit lived to be a 102. After she died, her name began searching for a place to land, carrying within it some of the precious light of Yehudit's spirit.

The name darted in and out of history, ducking into shadows to protect itself. It hid when the Ottoman Empire fell and the Jewish community suffered riots and expulsions. It found safety in a coat pocket and migrated back to Hungary. It retreated into the tall trees of the forest when there was danger and rode fallen leaves down the Danube river. It curled up behind the yellow Star of David and stowed away in the bundles that refugees carried on their backs. Most of Yehudit's descendants disappeared in one of history's darkest hours, buried in unmarked graves. Her name slipped into a transit visa and crossed the sea to Palestine. There it sought its lost family, traversing fields and town squares, climbing mountains, fluttering around campfires. It wandered through orange groves, over aqueducts and stone ruins. Eventually it surrendered itself to a drifting cloud and sailed out to sea, where it clung to the mast of a ship. The name reached New York harbor and resumed the long, nearly hopeless search, alighting from mezuzah to mezuzah until it finally decided to stop searching. It looked for a resting place in a small synagogue in a small town, in the folds of an ancient Torah scroll inside a humble wooden ark.

Like the name, the Torah scroll had also traveled across the sea, having survived fires and looting. There was another, newer Torah beside this one, with polished handles and ink bright as patent leather, but the name felt more comfortable amid the fading letters. The name's light was dim now, barely a flicker, and there, inside the stained parchment with crumbling edges, it lay itself down.

Allison sat with Rabbi Reyna in her office on a comfortable couch. On the coffee table was a stack of books and a bowl of Sunkist fruit gems. Rabbi Reyna was the same height as Allison, with a kind face and intelligent eyes. "What is so important about a Hebrew name anyway?" Allison asked her. Rabbi Reyna said, "A great sage, the Chatam Sofer, taught that one of the main reasons we were rescued out of Egypt was because we kept our names. Our names connect us to our history, to our future, and to God. A Hebrew name is like a passport that we keep hidden away in our back pocket, tucked away and ready to be taken out at any time so that we may enter magical worlds. Names have powerful associations in Jewish tradition. God is even called *HaShem*, which means 'The Name,' expressing a belief that God's true name is unknowable and unpronounceable, because a name contains the essence, power, and unity that is God. When Moses asked God what God's true name was, do you know what God said?"

Allison shook her head no.

"God says mysteriously, 'I am that I am. I was that I was. I will be that I will be.' The founder of the Chasidic movement was called the Baal Shem Tov, 'Master of a Good Name,' because he possessed great wisdom of the power of God's name. In the Talmud it is written, 'The crown of a good name excels all other crowns, including the crown of learning, of priesthood, and even of royalty.'"

"I want a Hebrew name, and I have been looking and looking, but I don't know which one to choose. And my mom wants to name me Glidah."

Rabbi Reyna laughed. "Come with me," she said. As they left the office, Rabbi Reyna invited Cantor Tovah to join them, and together they went into the sanctuary. There was no one else besides the three of them there, and it felt big and echoey. "Let's all stand in front of the ark."

Allison felt special being in front of the ark with the cantor and the rabbi. Rabbi Reyna said, "In the midrash, it is written that there are three names by which a person is called. One by which her father and mother call her. One by which other people call her, and one that she earns for herself. The best one is the one you earn for yourself. I have no doubt, Allison, that you and your Hebrew name will find each other."

Cantor Tova started singing, "*L'chi lach*, and I shall make your name great. *Lech l'cha*, and all shall praise your name." Rabbi Reyna sang along with her.

Allison closed her eyes and felt the words and the melody surround her like waves of silk. What Allison, the rabbi, and the cantor did not know is that their words and Allison's search for her Hebrew name had stirred awake the name that had laid itself down inside one of the temple's Torah scrolls. The name felt a rush of joy invigorate its spirit.

It slipped out of the old scroll and alighted onto a curl of Allison's hair.

"You will find your name," Rabbi Reyna said. "And whatever it is, it will be a blessing."

That night, Allison lay in her bed and realized she felt better. She hadn't yet found her Hebrew name, but she was okay with that for now. She didn't want to just slap a label on herself and call it a day. Her soul knew her name, even if her brain hadn't received it yet. She whispered *Sh'ma Yisrael* and turned over, nestling into her pillow. As Allison drifted to sleep, the name that had alighted on her head slipped down to her cheek like the gentlest kiss, and light as a snowflake, it melted into the warmth of her skin.

Allison dreamed she was in a room surrounded by books and candlelight. In her hand was a needle, and she was stitching a soft leather binding of a book. She opened the cover of the book in her lap and tried to read the faded name that had been stamped there. *Ye...* She could not make out the rest.

The next day, in religious school, teacher Brett was talking about how much he liked chopped liver.

"Gross," said Parker.

"Blech," said Matt.

And the other Alyson said, "Yeah, who'd eat that?"

"What did you say?" asked Allison.

The other Alyson said, "I said, 'Yeah, who'd eat that?'"

"Yeah, who'd eat that." The words felt strange but also familiar in Allison's mind. She contemplated the syllables slowly. Yeah-who'd-eat-that. Yeah-who'd-eat. Ye-hoo-deet . . . and then she laughed out loud. "Yehudit," she said in a whisper to herself. And then louder, "Yehudit! That is my Hebrew name!"

Allison stepped onto the bimah during Shabbat services. The congregation rose, and the rabbi opened the ark.

"May the one who blessed our ancestors bless you with life, health, goodness, and peace," said Cantor Tovah.

"Your Hebrew name is Yehudit. May this name be respected and honored for wisdom and good deeds, and may it be a beacon of light in our world," said the Rabbi, and the community said, "*Amen.*"

Allison felt complete. What had begun as a purple question mark on a sticker on her shirt had become a name inscribed in her heart. She would treasure her name always, and her name would treasure her.

QUESTIONS

1. What is the story behind your name?
2. In Judaism, names have power. That is why we do not know how to say God's true name—it would give us power over God! What power do you think names have? Why are names so important?
3. There is a Rabbinic teaching that one of the reasons the Israelites were freed from Egypt was that they didn't change their names (*Vayikra Rabbah* 32). What is the importance of a Hebrew name?
4. It is written, "Every person has three names: One their parents give them, one others call them, and one they acquire for themself" (*Kohelet Rabbah* 7:1:3) What are your three names?

Candle, Feather, Wooden Spoon

Part 1: Grandpa and The Professor

"BITTER, BITTER, BITTER," Grandpa muttered while he stood over the stove, dropping batter into a sizzling pan. "Potato pancakes vere sveeter in the Old Country."

It was the first night of Chanukah, and once again Grandpa was tasked with making latkes for Chase. If Chase's parents were here, they would make the best potato pancakes. But they were working an event. They were always working an event. They were caterers and often were out late making other people's birthdays, *b'nei mitzvah*, weddings, and reunions amazing. So, someone else was having a grand Chanukah feast, while it was just Chase, Grandpa, and The Professor alone in the house. It made Chase mad—and a little bitter himself.

That night, Chase watched his grandfather light the first Chanukah candle. His grandfather never let Chase light it himself, because he was afraid Chase was going to drop the match and set the house on fire. If Chase could build the best snow fort in the neighborhood, he could certainly hold a match! Grandpa was afraid of everything. Meanwhile, it was Grandpa's hand that was trembling so much that he could barely light the candle without knocking the whole *chanukiyah* over. Chase would have liked to help him, but Grandpa didn't like being helped.

Chase opened his gift and found his grandfather's faded blue pillowcase folded up inside. He unfolded it and saw it had messy Hebrew letters written shakily on it with thick black marker. He tried to make sense of the letters and once again wished his parents were there. They would make this less awkward.

"It's Yiddish," his grandfather said. "Vat? They don't teach you Yiddish in fifth grade?"

"They don't teach Yiddish in any grade," Chase thought to himself. The Professor was sleeping on the couch, missing everything.

"What does it say?" asked Chase.

"It says, 'The Fortress of Maccabia.' Like the Maccabees. For that snow fort you've been building outside." His grandfather looked at Chase as if he was searching Chase's eyes for something he had lost long ago. Then he threw his hands up and said, "Feh," as if he was giving up on finding whatever was missing. Grandpa slowly lifted himself out of the chair and returned toward the kitchen muttering, "The first flag of Israel vas made with some fabric and a marker." Chase sat alone, watching the candles reflect against the dark window.

Chase knew that back in the Old Country, his grandfather had experienced long winters of war. Chase had even heard that his grandfather had lost a toe because of frostbite in the Old Country. But Grandpa never wanted to talk about that. And he didn't want to talk about Grandma, who had died when Chase was a baby. In fact, Chase's grandfather didn't talk much at all, except to mutter and complain about how bitter everything is.

"Bitter, bitter, bitter," Chase could hear his grandfather muttering again from the kitchen. Maybe it was these sounds that finally woke The Professor up, or maybe it was the smell of the frying oil. The Professor stretched, hopped off the couch, and stood in front of Chase, with that same beseeching gaze his grandpa had.

The Professor had been part of Chase's family since long before Chase was born. Chase's father met The Professor in college one brisk September, when Chase's father saw him wandering around campus as if he was lost. The Professor was trembling and scared. He had patches of bald skin, there was caked mud in his long beard, and he was covered in fleas. Chase's father shared his corned beef sandwich with The Professor, and after that, he would wait for Chase's father outside of every class. Soon, Chase's father decided to adopt him. He took The Professor to the vet, got him all cleaned up and healthy, and gave him a bed right next to his. Chase's father named him "The Professor" because he said he learned more about life from that dog than he learned from any teacher he'd ever had.

But The Professor was a big problem for Chase. First of all, he was nearly as big as a pony. Second of all, he was unaware of his large size, and so he tended to knock things over. The Professor had destroyed many things in the house, including the catapult Chase had built for the science fair, the three-tiered cake Chase's parents had made for a wedding, and the painted ceramic tea kettle that Chase's grandfather had brought from the Old Country (and apparently had made only the sweetest tea, unlike the replacement kettle, which made everything bitter). Last but not least, The Professor had a habit of sneaking into Chase's room and messing with his stuff. Like last Chanukah, when Grandpa had given Chase a collection of bottle caps, which he'd said could be used for all sorts of games. But Grandpa never told Chase what kind of games used bottle caps, so Chase said, "Grandpa, I have video games to play with." That night, Chase found The Professor chewing on his video game controller! Then there was the time Grandpa cut an empty plastic milk carton in half and gave it to Chase, saying it was a planter. Chase sneakily threw it into the trash, but that night The Professor came into his room with the cut-up milk carton in his mouth, and he placed it right on Chase's bed. Or when Grandpa gave him the small piece of driftwood because it was shaped vaguely like a dreidel. That time, Chase actually threw the driftwood for The Professor to catch, but instead The Professor just sat and looked at him before walking away. Now, Chase kept the bottle caps, milk carton, and driftwood on a shelf in his room, and it looked like a collection of garbage. It made Chase embarrassed.

That Chanukah was the beginning of a long winter, and Grandpa was complaining more than ever. Chase had heard that Grandpa had an iron rod in his arm from when it had once been broken and that it hurt when it was cold. But Grandpa didn't talk about that.

"Bitter, bitter, bitter," Grandpa muttered while he warmed broth in a pot. "Chicken soup vas sveeter in the Old Country."

When Chase spent too much time in his snow fort, Grandpa limped around saying, "Vy build so many valls ven you can make snow angels instead?"

"Angels are boring," Chase said.

"Valls are boring," Grandpa replied, and then he added, "Feh," and walked away.

On Purim there was a new gift for Chase from Grandpa. Inside was another pillowcase. The frayed edges and tiny hole in the corner made Chase feel sorry for his grandfather.

"What does it say?" asked Chase.

"A boy your age can't read?" Grandpa snapped.

"I can read," Chase said. "I just can't read Yiddish."

"It says 'The Palace of Ahasuerus and Esther,'" Grandpa said. Then he held out a plate of extra hamantaschen Chase's parents had made for a synagogue party. The dough was light and buttery, and the apricot filling was deliciously sweet.

"Ven I vas your age I could read upside down!" Grandpa said angrily. When Grandpa bit into one of the cookies, crumbs got stuck in his beard and dusted the front of his shirt. Chase looked away from him. Grandpa tried to brush them off and muttered, "Bitter, bitter, bitter. Cookies vere sveeter in the Old Country."

Suddenly Chase became frustrated and shouted, "If everything was so much better in the Old Country, why don't you just go back there!"

Chase's grandfather sighed and sank lower into his chair. He said softly, "Because it isn't there anymore." Then he lifted himself out of his chair and limped off to his room, with The Professor following him, leaving Chase alone again.

Despite his grandfather, falling tree limbs, and snowball fights with his friends, Chase's amazing snow fort and its snowman guards managed to survive until the first week of March, all except for that one poor snowman upon which The Professor kept peeing, so that it was perpetually half-melted in the most humiliating way.

All in all, it had been a successful winter, and Chase was not disappointed when the spring sun started to thaw his icicle gate and melt away his bricks and towers. Soon daffodils would poke through the puddling remains of his snowmen, and their family would start the slow process of cleaning for Passover. The parsley seeds Grandpa planted in the half milk carton had grown into dark, frilly greens.

One spring afternoon, Chase came home from school to find his grandfather emptying the refrigerator and spritzing the shelves with Windex. "Bitter, bitter, bitter," Grandpa muttered. "Matzah vas sveeter in the Old Country."

Chase reached his breaking point. "Matzah?" Chase said, throwing down his backpack. "Really? Matzah doesn't even have any flavor!"

His grandfather turned to him. He said, "You know the sandvich ve make at the seder, ven ve put the sveet *charoset* and the bitter horseradish betveen the matzahs?"

"The Hillel sandwich," Chase said.

"In life, there has to be just enough bitter to make you appreciate the sveet. And there has to be enough sveet to make you think that the bitter vas vorthvile. Vell, in my life, there hasn't been a balance. And now, it's all horseradish."

"Even me?" Chase asked, feeling suddenly hurt. "Am I horseradish?"

Chase's grandfather looked sad too. He shuffled over to Chase and put his heavy hands lightly on Chase's shoulders. "You may be the sveetest boy in the vorld," Grandpa said, with his eyes swimming in tears. "But I knew a lot of boys like you in the Old Country. And they are all gone now."

Chase ran to his room and dove into his bed. The Professor came dashing after him and laid his big head close to Chase's tear-streaked face.

"How could things be better in a place where the dreidels had splinters and didn't even spin?" Chase asked the dog. "Where bottle caps were used for games? Where plants grew in sawed-off milk cartons?" The Professor licked Chase's face, and for the first time, Chase was glad to have the big sloppy dog around. Soon Chase fell asleep.

When Chase woke, the dog was still there looking at him. Chase stared into The Professor's kind, brown eyes. The moon was almost full, and it cast a silvery light into his room. He stroked The Professor's beard, thinking how funny it was that both his dog and his grandpa had long gray beards.

"Who cares about Hillel's stupid sandwich," Chase said to The Professor. He patted the dog's head and closed his eyes, feeling the dog's hot breath on his face. For the first time, he didn't mind The Professor's musky smell. It was nice to have company.

And then Chase heard, "You know, a sandwich once saved my life."

Chase opened his eyes. There was no one else in his room except for him and The Professor.

"What?" Chase asked.

"I said, a sandwich once saved my life," the dog said. "It was a corned beef sandwich."

"Excuse me?" Chase said, sitting up. He stared at the dog. The dog's eyes were emerald green.

"I was a few hours away from starving to death. It was the most delicious thing I have ever tasted."

"You are talking," Chase said to the dog, incredulously. Then he looked toward the moon, remembering learning that the vocabulary word "lunatic" means someone who is made crazy by the moon.

"You're not a lunatic," said The Professor. "And you're also not horseradish," he added with a wink.

"I don't understand," Chase said. "You've never spoken before."

"*Kol han'shamah t'haleil Yah*," the dog said.

"I don't speak Yiddish," Chase said.

"That wasn't Yiddish. That was Hebrew," explained The Professor, scratching himself behind his ear with his back paw. "It means, 'Every breath shall praise God.' It is from Psalm 150."

"Oh," said Chase, not knowing what to say.

"Every living thing that breathes can also speak. And praise. We just don't understand each other. Ever since the big meshugaas with the Tower of Babel, we don't understand very many languages. You don't speak squirrel, or spider crab, or woodpecker, do you?"

"But how come I understand you now?"

"Because I have a message for you," the dog said, as if this was just a matter of fact.

Chase hugged his comforter around his shoulders. "From whom?" he asked.

"Ah," said the dog. "Some mysteries simply cannot be named."

"Listen to me carefully," The Professor suddenly said in an urgent whisper. "There is a fruit that grows in only one garden and on only one tree. It is sweet, and full of memory and the nectar of peace. If you find this fruit for your grandfather, he will be cured of his bitterness."

"But how?" asked Chase.

"It is a perilous journey. You will have to gather three things and carry them in a magic satchel. And you must beware the Plague of Darkness. It brings a darkness so thick that one person can no longer see the other person standing in front of them. And when you can't see the person standing in front of you, and you know they can't see you, your heart hardens and you do terrible things. The Plague of Darkness will swallow your goodness like a snake swallows a rodent."

Chase shivered and pulled his blankets up over his mouth and nose so that only his eyes peeked out. "But, what do I have to do?"

"Ah," The Professor said. "Wait here." The dog trotted out of the room. A moment later, the dog returned with a faintly glowing satchel in his mouth. The dog laid it in front of Chase.

Chase picked it up. It was soft as velvet, and it glistened like a starlit puddle.

The Professor looked toward the window. The moonlight glowed around his face like a silver lining around a storm cloud.

The Professor said in a faraway voice:

"Candle, feather, wooden spoon,
Passover will be coming soon.
Candle, feather, wooden spoon,
Follow the light of the silvery moon."

Chase didn't know what that meant, and he opened his mouth to ask The Professor, but something had changed in the room, and Chase became afraid. The dog pushed his nose against the window and nudged it open. Then he stuck his head out and howled long and loud. Chase became even more frightened and shrunk back, clutching the glowing satchel to his chest. When the dog looked back at Chase, Chase could see that his eyes were no longer emerald green. They were kind and brown. The Professor put his front paws on the bed, licked Chase's face, and then ran out of the room, wagging his tail.

Part 2: You Have to Gather Three Things

CANDLE. Chase sat in his bed in a nest of blankets and looked around his room. He wondered if he had just woken from a dream. Then he felt the fabric of the shimmering satchel in his hand and the warm night air through the open window, and he knew he was awake.

He thought about what The Professor had said. He had talked about the Plague of Darkness. He had also talked about gathering three things and putting them in a magic satchel.

"I have the satchel," Chase said to himself, holding it up. "What makes it magic? And what three things am I supposed to put into it?" Then he remembered the poem. Candle, feather, wooden spoon. Should he get a Shabbat candle from the cabinet perhaps? A feather from inside his pillow? A wooden spoon from the kitchen? What would happen then?

"Candle, feather, wooden spoon," Chase whispered. "Follow the light of the silvery moon."

Just then, a silver ray of moonlight spiked through the open window like a laser beam. It hovered there in the middle of the room while Chase mustered the courage to step out of his bed. Chase reached out his hand to touch the moonbeam. He expected his hand to go right through it, but instead it felt taut, like a violin string or the wire of a zipline. Hanging off the end of the moonbeam was a silver triangle with a bar on the bottom.

"It *is* a zipline," Chase said. What would happen if he took hold of it? He remembered The Professor's words about the Plague of Darkness, and he shivered. But then he heard his grandfather mutter from the kitchen, "Bitter, bitter, bitter. Life vas sveeter in the Old Country," and he realized how very much he loved his grandfather, how sad he was that Grandpa was always bitter, and that he would take a perilous journey if only to find him the sweet fruit full of memory and peace that grew on only one tree.

Chase swung the satchel over his shoulder and took a deep breath. With the rallying cry, "For Grandpa!" Chase took hold of the bar at the bottom of the triangle, and without a sound Chase was suddenly rocketing through the window. There was a faint whiff of wet grass as he soared over his backyard, and then the air was clear and beautiful as sapphire. Below him, moonlight lay on the rooftops, treetops, and meadows like frosting on a cake. Chase held the moonbeam tightly, but somehow, he also felt as if the moonbeam was holding him with invisible hands that supported his body. He was not afraid of falling.

Chase looked up and realized the sky was filled with stars. He saw constellations he'd never seen before. And they kept changing. He saw a lamb surrounded by bursts of flowers. He saw six constellations circling one another and realized they were symbols of the seder plate. He saw the stars gather into the cup of Elijah. Then the stars twirled out all at once until every star had six points like the Star of David. They surrounded him on all sides, above and below, behind him and in front of him, until it felt as though he were soaring through a meteor shower, shooting stars whirring past him like a hailstorm.

Chase closed his eyes and only opened them when the moonbeam slowed down. Looking down, Chase saw that he was low to the ground now, gliding over a narrow cobblestone street. It reminded him of a photograph Grandpa kept on his bedside table. In the photograph was a woman, but Grandpa never spoke about who she was. Chase's mother said she thought it might have been Grandpa's sister. "Is this the Old Country?" Chase wondered as he felt the invisible hands of the moonbeam release him, and he also let go and landed before an open window.

Inside the window, Chase saw someone who looked like the woman in Grandpa's photograph. She was standing at a wooden table. She lit a match, just like Grandpa did on Friday nights to light the two Shabbat candles. However, this woman was using a very long match, and the candles were stuck into black bottles. Chase could see only the little flicker as she lit them, and then the lights were hidden.

Chase heard a rumbling. It sounded like a train roaring over a track or thunder rolling over the sky. The woman heard it too. She threw on a jacket and rushed through the door out into the little street, bumping into Chase. Their eyes met for a moment before the woman turned and started running down the street. The moonlight started to dim as the rumbling grew louder and louder. "The Plague of Darkness," Chase remembered The Professor telling him. Chase could see shadows turn the corner into the narrow street, as the rumbling became a roar. In the midst of the noise, Chase heard the Plague speak:

"Run, run, through the night.
We'll blow out your little light."

Chase started running, and the Plague of Darkness followed him. He could feel its coldness brush against his ankles. He could no longer see the woman. Chase pushed himself to run faster, turning one corner, then another corner. The streets were a tight little maze. The darkness was closing in. The moon was nearly snuffed out when suddenly Chase turned another corner and the Plague turned a different way. The sound of a woman's scream made Chase stop in his tracks. He turned around and yelled at the top of his lungs:

"Go away and let her be!
Instead of her, chase me!"

The Plague turned back and thundered toward him like a stampede of wild beasts. Chase ran, his heart beating through his chest and up into his throat. He turned another corner and found himself running toward the same window where the woman had been lighting candles in black bottles. He remembered the words of The Professor. Candle. Feather. Wooden spoon. The door to the woman's home was swung open from when she had run out. Chase ran through the door and picked up one of the bottles. He put the bottle with its precious light into the magic satchel.

A long ribbon of moonlight tumbled down through the doorway like a trapeze. Chase grabbed on, and the light of the silvery moon whooshed him up, swinging into the sapphire sky.

FEATHER. Chase was lulled by the kaleidoscope of stars all around him. Soon, he was swinging gently over a peaceful garden, beautiful in the moonlight. When the swing was close enough to the ground, Chase hopped off at the garden gate. Just inside the gate was a woman kneeling. She was planting something. Chase could hear her singing to herself:

> "Sweet berries, bitter roots.
> Pretty flowers, sour fruits."

Chase walked toward the gate, but before he reached it, an angel leapt out and screeched:

> "Turn back, turn back! Do not walk forward!
> Or I will use my fiery sword!"

The angel had a human body that was smooth like marble, and in the angel's hands was a sword of whirling lava. Surprisingly, the woman didn't seem to hear the screeching angel. She just continued planting and singing.

Chase had stood up to the Plague of Darkness, and he felt braver than when he started this journey. He stood up tall and spoke clearly to the angel:

> "Move aside, I beg your pardon.
> I need some fruit from this garden."

The angel spread out its large gold wings. Suddenly, in the distance, Chase heard rumbling. The Plague of Darkness had followed him here, hurtling through the air like a swarm of locusts. Through the noise, the Plague said:

"Run, run, through the dark.
We'll blow out your little spark."

Chase and the angel were suddenly surrounded. The angel's sword flared brighter. Behind the angel, Chase saw the woman in the garden still peacefully planting. What would happen to her if the Plague broke through the gate? Chase and the angel exchanged a glance. Suddenly Chase understood how important the guardian angel was in protecting the garden.

Chase stood up tall and yelled at the shadows:

"Go away and let her be!
Instead of her, chase me!"

Chase swiftly jumped onto the angel, and the angel shot up into the sky. The Plague raced after them, away from the garden. Chase could feel its coldness brush against his neck. Chase felt dizzy. He tried to hold onto the angel, but the angel's body was so smooth that Chase started to slip. He remembered The Professor saying that the Plague would swallow him like a serpent swallows a mouse. He tried with all his might to grip the angel when he remembered something else The Professor had said. Candle, *feather*, wooden spoon . . . maybe the feather could come from the angel! Just then the darkness swelled over the angel and Chase like a wave about to crash down. They would be drowned by the Plague of Darkness. The darkness brushed the tip of the angel's wing, and it screeched as feathers froze and fell away. The angel suddenly flipped upside down and scooped Chase toward its chest, folding its wings around him. With Chase cocooned inside, the angel somersaulted through the shrinking opening just before the Plague of Darkness crashed down. As the angel reopened its wings, Chase snatched one of the frozen golden feathers that was fluttering in the air. It instantly warmed in his hand. He tumbled out of the angel's grasp and landed on a moonbeam that held him like a saddle, and he rode the silver light straight into the ever-deepening night.

WOODEN SPOON. Chase put the feather in his magic satchel and checked on the black bottle. He lifted it out and saw that the candle was still flickering inside. "You really are a magic satchel!" Chase said. He made himself comfortable in the moonbeam saddle as silver Stars of David spun around him in sparkling pinwheels. He wondered if Grandpa ever looked at the stars in the Old Country. Thinking about his grandfather made him hungry. His grandfather often made him something hearty and warm to eat. Chase missed him.

Soon the moonbeam slowed. Chase dismounted and found he was standing in a dark wood. The canopy of leaves above him was thick and let in very little moonlight. Chase was nervous to be so alone, but then he smelled something cooking. It was an unpleasant smell, like moldy cheese frying in vinegar with moldy vegetables. "Bitter, bitter, bitter," Chase said to himself and then laughed at how he sounded like Grandpa. Chase knew the smell meant that someone—or something—must be nearby. Chase followed the smell, stepping over rocks and roots until he found himself standing outside a house with a giant door. The door was three times the size of a normal door. And it was open, as if to invite Chase inside. When Chase peeked through, he saw a giant as tall as a telephone pole, with his back to the door. He was standing in front of an open oven, stirring a giant cauldron with a spoon the size of an oar. As he stirred, he chanted:

> "I stir my stew with a spoon of wood
> Stolen from one who was poor and good.
> I stir in crickets and chunks of bone.
> This spoon was all she ever owned."

Chase was frozen in fear. A gust of wind came in from the open door and blew out the fire in the giant's oven. Slowly, the giant turned around. The giant's eyes were dark as lunar eclipses. Chase started trembling from head to toe. His knees vibrated like gongs. In a voice that chilled Chase's heart, the giant said, "Give me your fire."

"I . . . I . . . I don't have any fire," Chase managed to say.

"Give me your fire, boy!" roared the giant. "The fire in the bottle in the bag on your back!"

The giant thrust his long arm out the door and grabbed Chase by his sleeve. The giant dragged Chase into the kitchen. Chase tugged away so hard that his sleeve ripped; then he wiggled out of the giant's grip, crawled under the kitchen table, and scrambled to the other side. Chase felt like a fly compared to the giant. The giant threw the table against the wall and reached across the room for Chase. Chase felt the giant's long nails brush against his chest before he again ducked and tried to run toward the door.

"Oh no you don't," the giant snapped, blocking the door with his giant foot. "That fire belongs to me."

Chase could see there was no other way out of the kitchen. The Professor's words once again echoed in his memory. Candle, feather, wooden spoon . . . wooden spoon! He had an idea.

He stood up tall and said to the giant, "You'll have to cook me first!"

The giant laughed. His laugh made Chase's bones go cold. He pinched Chase by the back of his neck and held him over the cauldron. Below Chase the stew bubbled and belched. Crickets were leaping around the rim. The giant was laughing. Chase stretched out his hands to try to grasp the handle of the wooden spoon, but he couldn't reach it. He started to swing himself to get closer as he dangled from the giant's fingers like a worm on a hook.

This made the giant laugh harder. "Where do you think you are going, boy?"

With all his strength, Chase lunged toward the wooden spoon and grabbed it with both hands. The giant was still laughing when a moonbeam whipped through the door and wrapped around Chase's waist like a lasso. The giant shrieked as the silver ray whisked Chase out of the giant's home. Chase could see the giant rush after him, howling and stretching toward Chase. His legs, torso, and arms all seemed to grow longer and longer as the giant strode over trees pawing at him. Chase thought he would be caught, but the moonbeam picked up speed, hurling him out of the dark woods and into the diamond-studded air.

Part 3: Bitter, Bitter, Bitter

Chase opened his magic satchel and checked on everything inside. The candle still flickered inside the black bottle, and the golden feather was still there. Chase worried a spoon this size would not fit into a satchel this small, but this was a magic satchel and the spoon slipped right in. Chase watched the parade of stars around him and found the brightest in the sky. He made a wish. He wished that he could return to the garden now and get the sweet fruit filled with memory and the nectar of peace. He was certain that since he had successfully collected the candle, feather, and wooden spoon— everything The Professor told him to get—he would be able to complete this perilous journey.

Chase thought about his grandfather. Chase had been running all night and had never felt more scared, tired, or determined. And it was just one spring night! His grandfather had survived many long winters. How many monsters had his grandfather had to escape? How did he break his arm and lose his toe? What happened to his sister? With this thought, Chase didn't feel angry at his grandfather for saying that everything tasted bitter. Chase was brave, but his grandfather must have been braver to survive everything he had gone through. At this moment, the thing Chase wanted most in the world was to sit with his grandfather and learn how to play his bottle cap games.

But when the rope of moonlight lowered Chase down, it was not in the garden. Instead, he was standing on a beach, and there was a family huddled by the shore next to a little wooden boat. Over the sound of the waves, Chase recognized a rumbling. The Plague of Darkness was bearing down on the family, and it was pushing them toward the sea. The family wept:

> "Ve have no vere to run anymore.
> Ve have a boat, but ve have no oar."

Chase ran toward the family, pulling the wooden spoon out of the satchel on his back like an archer pulling an arrow out of a quiver. The family hurried into the boat. Chase climbed in as well. The adults pushed the boat into the sea and leapt in. One person grabbed the spoon and, using it as an oar, rowed them farther into the water. Chase looked at the frightened faces of the family crowded in the little boat. The grandmother, with her hair wrapped in a scarf, was reciting psalms. The parents held their whimpering baby, and two older children—one a toddler and one Chase's age—clung to them, watching the disappearing shore with eyes wide with panic. The adults took turns with the giant spoon, straining with all their might to outrun the Plague of Darkness and the threat of hardened hearts.

Chase shouted toward the shore:

> "Go away and let us be!
> Everybody should be free!"

At last the shore disappeared. The sea was calm. On the horizon was a golden glimmer. The sky was becoming lighter. The sun had not yet risen, but Chase knew it was getting close to dawn. He wondered what would happen when there was no more moonbeam to take him home. The baby and the toddler were sleeping now. The child Chase's age touched his hand and said, "Thank you."

Before Chase could respond, there was a great frothing of water in front of them. The children screamed as out of the sea rose the head of the Leviathan, a giant sea dragon. Chase screamed too. It had the jaw of a prehistoric crocodile and was covered in spiny scales. "No," Chase thought. "This can't be happening!" But the beast sucked air into its huge nostrils, opened its giant jaw, and breathed out fire at the little boat. The heat singed the grandmother's scarf. Then the Leviathan sucked the air into his nostrils and again blasted its fire. Sparks landed on the baby's blanket, and the mother quickly unwrapped the baby and threw the burning blanket into the sea.

Chase held up the golden feather. The Leviathan sucked in air to make more fire, and Chase let the feather go. The monster sucked it into one of its huge nostrils. It looked startled, and then it started to sneeze! The Leviathan sneezed and thrashed, its tail flailing wildly in the air and slapping down, making a wave that lifted the boat high into the air.

Chase and the family held on to the sides of the boat as the wave carried them to a new shore, throwing the little vessel down so it spun across the beach. They were all drenched and cold, but happy and relieved. When they stepped out of the little boat, the family kissed the ground.

Chase walked with them along a wilderness path. The moon was still visible in the early morning sky, but it wasn't as bright. The sky was melting into shades of cobalt and periwinkle, with orange gathering at the point the sun was preparing to emerge. The family started preparing a camp to sleep. Everyone was tired from so much adventure, especially Chase. Chase put down his magic satchel. He sat down and leaned against a rock. Perhaps he would go to the garden the next night, as day was just a few moments away. But before he could close his eyes, he heard the familiar thundering roll surrounding them all. Colors were swallowed up, one by one. It was a darkness so thick, Chase could not see the family. The Plague of Darkness was upon them and there was nowhere to go.

> "Run, run, through the night.
> We'll blow out your little light.
> Run, run, through the dark.
> We'll blow out your little spark."

But Chase wasn't listening to the Plague. Standing and grasping the black bottle, Chase was remembering his grandfather's words. He had said, "In life, there has to be just enough bitter to make you appreciate the sveet. And there has to be enough sveet to make you think that the bitter vas vorthvile. Vell, in my life, there hasn't been a balance. And now, it's all horseradish." Chase knew it was true for this family too. Too much bitter. Every time they thought they were safe, there was another danger to overcome. No wonder some people can no longer taste the sweet.

Chase held the black bottle high in the air. He yelled at the Plague:

> "No more running! No more fear!
> It's time for darkness to disappear!"

All at once, light burst out of the black bottle in a great shining pillar. It was bright and warm and seemed to reach to the very heavens. The Plague faded into mist and then into nothingness. The air was clear, and the crown of the sun lifted over the horizon. The moon was still in the sky, low on the horizon. It was pale and delicate, like a soap bubble sailing toward the floor. A soft gray and pastel pink moonbeam unrolled before Chase like a carpet, and he stepped on, waving goodbye to the grateful family as the moonbeam swished him away.

The powdery moonbeam lay Chase down before the glistening gates of the garden. In the light of early dawn, Chase could see all the rich and beautiful colors of the garden. The angel bowed to Chase and said:

> "Come in, come in. Come walk forward,
> I lay down my fiery sword."

The gates opened and Chase walked in. He was overcome with a tingling sensation, as if all his body was waking up in a new way. His senses were magnified. The colors were dazzling, the perfume glorious, the birdsong magnificent.

There was the woman, on her knees planting and singing:

> "Bitter herbs, luscious vines.
> Pretty maples, fragrant pines.
> Start as seeds and grow up right.
> Morning always follows night."

The woman looked up to see Chase watching her. She stood, took Chase gently by the hand, and led him to a tree in the middle of the garden. Together they filled his satchel with its beautiful, sweet fruit.

Part 4: A Sandwich Once Saved My Life

Chase was again in his bedroom, and the room was filled with morning sunlight. At first, he again thought all his adventures were just a long dream, but then he looked in his satchel at the bright fruit.

"It looks like you made it," The Professor said. Chase looked over at the large dog, with its emerald eyes.

"What do I do now?" he asked.

The Professor said, "A sandwich once saved my life. A sandwich will save your grandfather."

"The Hillel sandwich," Chase said, and The Professor nodded.

Just then Chase heard his father say through the door, "Time to get up for school!"

Chase looked at The Professor and they both laughed. The Professor licked Chase's face and then pushed the door open with his nose. When the dog looked back, his eyes were brown, and his tongue was hanging out. Chase hid the satchel under his bed and exhaustedly prepared to go to school.

Chase's whole family was together for seder—his parents, his aunts and uncles, and his cousins. The Professor waited under the table for scraps to fall. Chase sat next to his grandfather the whole time. When it was time for the Hillel sandwich, Chase said to his grandfather, "I want to make it for you."

"Bitter, bitter, bitter," grumbled Grandpa.

"I know," said Chase. "But taste this."

Grandpa shakily held up the sandwich Chase handed him. He studied it: two misshapen pieces of matzah, a smear of bright purple horseradish, and *charoset*. But this *charoset* looked different from the *charoset* on the table. It looked like it was made from the colors of a sunrise, and it smelled like a field of lavender and roses. Earlier in the day, Chase had made it with the sweet fruit from the magical garden. He had seen his parents cook and bake so many times and had helped them make *charoset* for the family seder. But this was a recipe Chase created all on his own, and he made it just for his grandfather. Grandpa looked at Chase, and his eyes twinkled. He looked as if he had finally found something he thought he'd lost forever.

Grandpa took a big crunchy bite, and a smile spread across his face. He ate the whole thing and licked his fingers. He looked at Chase again, and Chase could see his grandfather's eyes well up with tears. His grandfather took a deep breath and reached his arm out to Chase, drawing him into a hug.

"I am sorry I didn't appreciate the Yiddish flags you made," Chase said into his grandfather's shoulder.

His grandfather waved his hand and said, "Feh, never mind that." He let go of Chase and studied him as if for the first time. "I vant to tell you my story."

"And I *vant* to hear it," Chase said. They both laughed at Chase's attempt to sound like his grandfather.

That night Chase heard not just the story of Passover and how the Jews were freed from slavery. Chase heard the story of his grandfather's life. He listened as Grandpa told him about the Old Country, about shadows and cobblestone streets, angels and monsters, fiery swords and fiery breath, fear and courage, and the delicious, bittersweet taste of finally being free.

QUESTIONS

1. What do younger and older generations have to gain by talking with one another more? What stands in their way?
2. What might the Plague of Darkness in the story represent?
3. Chase's grandfather cannot experience the joy and sweetness around him because of the trauma he carries inside. What is it about this particular Hillel sandwich that opens his eyes? What can we do to help survivors of trauma?
4. The candle, feather, and wooden spoon are used in traditional households the night before Passover. Children use the candle to search out ten pieces of *chameitz* (leaven) that the family has hidden. When they find it, they brush it onto the spoon with the feather. Then, the *chameitz*, candle, feather, and spoon are all burned to symbolize that the home is now

chameitz-free and ready for Passover. In this story, the candle, feather, and wooden spoon are used to find something else that has been hidden— answers to why Chase's grandfather is so bitter. Is there someone in your family or community whom you wish to understand better? What tools can you use to help that understanding develop?

5. Imagine you are using a candle, feather, and wooden spoon, but instead of searching a home for *chameitz*, you are searching your mind for clutter you'd like to clear. What are you finding there?

Catching the Wind
A Tallit Origin Tale

CORA AND HER *IMA* stood on the starboard side of their family's sailboat watching the sunset. The sea was awash in gold and ruby sparkles. Cora loved spending this time with Ima. She loved hearing about Ima's adventures at sea, like the time a wave washed a squid over a fishing boat's bow, and the time she swam with a pod of whales.

Cora's *ima* shifted the sail as they headed back to the marina.

"We can't control which way the wind goes," her *ima* said, "but if we learn to catch it just right, we can always get home."

Cora looked at the seagulls with their streamlined wings riding the invisible air. In the marina, all the boats bobbed on the gentle waves, with their tall masts reaching toward the darkening sky.

Cora's *ima* navigated into the marina. Most of the boats had names painted onto their sterns. Cora liked to read them, although she had already memorized them, since each boat was always docked in the same place. *Floatus*, *Causing a Com-Ocean*, and *Bye-Bye Wi-Fi* were among the boats lined up along the south side of the dock. *Second Wind*, *License to Chill*, and *The Cod Father* graced the north side. And along the west were *Seize the Bay*, *Sea Señora*, *Dream Weaver*, and Cora's family's boat, *Why Knot*.

However, when they pulled into their slip, Cora saw that *Dream Weaver* was not there, and a different boat was in its place. It was a small houseboat named *The Saltbox*. Cora's *ima* tied the boat to the dock while Cora helped tie down the sails. Cora kept glancing over at their new neighbor. *Dream*

Weaver had been a twenty-five-foot racer-cruiser that had been in many competitions. Cora's family's boat, *Why Knot*, was a twenty-foot sloop, with a two-mast rig. A little four-rung ladder led to a small cabin below, with built-in upholstered benches that could be easily folded into a bed for Cora, and a separate little room just big enough for her moms. There was a tiny kitchen with a cooler, a two-burner electric stove, and a sink. There was also a little bathroom. Cora's family had slept on the boat only a few times. It felt adventurous, but it wasn't that comfortable.

But the new boat, *The Saltbox*, didn't just have a cabin hidden in the hull. The whole boat looked like an actual cottage, but in miniature, on a floating platform. Instead of fiberglass like most of the boats, *The Saltbox* was made of wood. Instead of having sleek curving lines, *The Saltbox* was boxy, with straight lines and corners. It had a shingled roof and painted shutters, with checkered curtains in the windows, and instead of a metal railing, there was a real wooden fence, making it look like the boat had a porch instead of a deck. The boat looked a little beaten up. The wood had salt streaks, and the paint was peeling. But it gave Cora a warm feeling, like finding an old bench on a trail when you are tired from hiking.

Cora saw Barnacle leap from the dock onto *The Saltbox* and then onto the roof, laying himself out. Barnacle—at least that is what Cora and her *ima* called him—was an old orange tabby cat who lived in the marina, wandered the docks, and looked for nibbles of fish. He made every boat his own home. But when he jumped onto *The Saltbox*, a little black pug came bounding out of the houseboat's door, jumping up and down and yapping up at the roof.

"Pugboat!" called a man as he followed the dog onto the deck. The man looked over at Cora and her *ima*. "Hey, neighbor! Hope Pugboat didn't startle you."

Cora's *ima* lifted her straw hat and said, "Welcome to the marina!"

Cora saw a little face appear in the window of *The Saltbox*—a little girl with her hair in pigtails. She looked a year or two younger than Cora.

Cora's *ima* said, "I'm Steph, and this is Cora. She'll be nine in November."

"I'm Gary," the man said, and then he called, "Sabina! Sabina, come on out and say hi."

The little face in the window disappeared, but no one came out to say hi.

Gary said, "She's a little shy. And she's having a hard time adjusting to living on the boat. We just moved up here from Florida. Can't afford to move inland right now. Plus, I really like the salt life."

"I'm sure she'll adjust," Steph said.

"I can show her around," Cora offered.

"That'd be great," Gary said. Just then, Barnacle leapt off the roof of *The Saltbox* onto Gary's shoulder. Pugboat jumped up and down barking while the cat clawed into Gary's shirt, afraid to jump down. Gary pulled Barnacle off and gently tossed him to the dock. Barnacle walked slowly away with his tail in the air, utterly dismissing Pugboat's barking.

"Ouch," Steph said, seeing the scratch on Gary's neck.

"Aw," Gary said, "s'nothing. Well, I better start getting dinner ready. See you around."

Cora saw a light go on in *The Saltbox* as Gary ducked through the small door. Cora could hear Sabina say, "I want pizza."

"How about I fry up fish fillets?" Gary said just as the door closed behind him.

Cora and her *ima* finished tying down the boat. It was dark when they got into the car. All through the drive, Cora thought about *The Saltbox* and what it was like to live there.

✡ ✡ ✡

The next morning, Cora wanted to go to the marina after school. Her *ima* said she couldn't today, so Cora begged her mom, Jill. After much pleading, her mom finally said, "Fine, I will swing by from work, pick you up from school, and take you. I have to return Sherrie's wrench anyway."

Sherrie was the captain of *Floatus*, an orange catamaran with flowers on its sails. Cora knew everybody in the marina, and she was interested in finding out more about her new neighbor there. But the school day moved slowly.

Finally, the last school bell rang, and Cora rushed out the door to her mom's car. Soon they were at the marina, and Cora ran down the dock. Sabina was sitting on the deck of *The Saltbox* reading a book. Her father must have been cooking, because there was a thin line of smoke rising out of the roof. Pugboat lay beside Sabina, lazily licking her arm.

"Hi," Cora said.

Sabina looked up, but she didn't smile.

"I'm Cora. You're Sabina, right?"

She nodded. Cora got the feeling that she didn't smile very much.

"Oh," Jill said as she caught up to Cora. "A new neighbor! Hello there."

Sabina looked back down at her book. Pugboat growled softly.

Gary poked his head out of the door and then fully emerged with a big smile. "Hey, I'm Gary."

"Nice to meet you. I'm Jill. My wife Steph and I own the *Why Knot*. What a charming houseboat," Jill said.

"I met Steph yesterday! And Cora of course. Sabina, you want Cora to show you around?" Gary asked. He explained to Jill, "We only moved here a couple of days ago from the Keys."

"What brings you to Bluffton?"

"I'm opening an office in town, but it takes time," Gary said.

"Of course," Jill said. "Where's Sabina in school?"

"She's starting Bluffton Elementary on Monday. Third grade."

"That's where Cora goes," Jill said. "She's in fifth."

"Oh, great!" Gary said. "Hear that, Sabina?"

Sabina answered, "I don't want to go to a new school. I want to go home."

Gary looked pained. Cora felt bad for them both.

Gary invited Cora and her mom to come over. Jill was oohing and aahing at everything about the houseboat. Cora sat next to Sabina on the deck. Sabina crossed her hands over her chest.

"My mom really loves *The Saltbox*," Cora said.

Sabina's shoulders drooped. "My mom loved it too," she said softly.

Cora wanted to ask where Sabina's mom was, but she stayed quiet. Pugboat nuzzled against Cora's leg, and she pet the little dog.

"Do you want me to show you around? The captain of *The Cod Father* sometimes has candies."

Sabina just shook her head.

"And there's a box of games on *Bye-Bye Wi-Fi* that they let me play with. They're never there. And the people on *License to Chill* have a projector and lots of movies. You can project movies against a sail."

Sabina did not look impressed.

Cora's mom stepped off *The Salt Box* to visit Sherrie and return the wrench.

"I'm making burgers," Gary called from inside. "Sabina, invite Cora to stay!"

Sabina looked at Cora and then looked away. She went into *The Saltbox* without saying anything, leaving Cora sitting on the deck with the dog.

Gary came out. "Sorry, bud," he said. "Let's try again another day."

Cora returned to *Why Knot* and put on a Beatles playlist. She did her homework on the deck while she waited for her mom to return.

Cora had to wait until Saturday to return to the marina, but it didn't bother her. She wasn't anxious to get to know her neighbor anymore. Sabina didn't seem very friendly.

Saturday morning, Cora's family took *Why Knot* out sailing. It was a beautiful day, with a crisp, playful breeze. Cora leaned her weight on the jib to catch the breeze and change course.

"Whale!" Jill called, pointing in the distance. All Cora saw on the horizon was a poof of mist, but it signaled that a whale had just surfaced to take a nice gulp of air. The ocean was so mysterious. Cora marveled at the idea of all the life swirling beneath them. She turned the winch to trim the sails and felt the whole vessel pick up speed. When all the elements aligned on the sailboat, Cora could feel the boundaries between herself, the sea, and the sky dissolving.

When they returned to the marina for lunch, Sabina and her father were sitting on the dock, dangling their feet over the edge. Sabina was eating a sandwich, and Gary held a fishing rod, its line disappearing into the water. Barnacle was sunning himself on top of a piling, while Pugboat watched from below, tail wagging.

"Hey, Gary," Steph called. "Come aboard and have a drink with us."

Gary climbed aboard, with Sabina sullenly following, and Jill poured three glasses of white wine on the deck of *Why Knot*. Sabina immediately sat in the corner, staring out over the rail. Cora listened to the adults' conversation, since it was clear Sabina wanted to be alone.

"When Eloise died, everything came undone," Gary was saying to Cora's parents. "Our whole lives unraveled."

Eloise must have been Cora's mother, Cora realized.

"Time will help tie it all back together," Jill said, while Steph squeezed his hand.

"To time," Steph said, and the three adults clinked glasses.

Sabina was sitting now with her back to Cora. Her hair was in a messy braid held together with a barrette. Cora thought about what it would mean to have one's life come undone. To have everything unravel.

Barnacle leapt down and let Pugboat lick his face before sauntering off.

Cora had an idea. She said to Sabina, "What do you think about knots?"

"Knots?" Sabina asked, turning around a little bit.

"I think they are so cool. There are hundreds of kinds of knots," Cora said. "I can make a lot of them."

Sabina turned a little more.

"Want me to teach you?"

Sabina looked at Cora and said, "I don't need you to teach me. I know a ton of knots!" For the first time, Sabina was animated instead of withdrawn.

"Oh yeah?" Cora said. "What are your favorites?"

Cora ran into *Why Knot*'s cabin and grabbed a couple of lengths of rope. The girls showed each other knots that looked like a number eight and others that were square. Sabina tied a clove hitch, and Cora tied a rolling hitch. While the adults talked, the girls tied knots.

Eventually Cora said, "We know all these small knots. Wanna explore and see some really big ones?"

Cora and Sabina walked around the marina, looking at the riggings of *Floatus*, the moorings of *Causing a Com-Ocean*, and the crusted knotted fishing nets on *Sea Señora*. They got candies from the captain of *The Cod Father* and climbed onto *Bye-Bye Wi-Fi* to play a game of mancala. As the sun got low, they watched *Pinocchio* projected on the sails of *License to Chill*. By the end of the day, Cora and Sabina were chatting and laughing.

"*The Saltbox* was my grandpa's boat," Sabina said as they strolled along the dock. "My dad lived on it as a boy. My mom loved it too. She sewed the curtains. She sewed a lot of things—my clothes and gifts for friends. She was starting to teach me how to sew too. We lived on *The Saltbox* during the summers. I was really little, but I remember it was fun. But then my mom got sick, and we stopped going. And after she died," Sabina's voice became quieter, "we had to sell the house and move onto the boat and come here."

"Bluffton Elementary is not so bad," Cora said. When they reached *The Saltbox*, they noticed there was no little dog rushing to greet them.

"Where's Pugboat?" Sabina asked.

Cora and Sabina's parents looked all around, but they didn't see the little dog. It was dark now, and lights were swaying on the masts. Steph grabbed flashlights, and she and Jill walked along the south side of the marina, calling after Pugboat. Gary walked up and down the west side, and Cora and

Sabina walked along the north. They shone their flashlights over the boats, the pilings, and the heaps of ropes and into the water. Looking into the dark water was the scariest. They did not want to find the dog there. Every now and then they heard the barking of seals nearby, which made it harder to listen for Pugboat.

As they approached the end of the north dock, Sabina suddenly gripped Cora's arm and whispered, "Sh!" They held themselves very still and listened. They heard whimpering.

"That's Pugboat," Sabina whispered.

Cora scanned the flashlight all around them. She shone it into the last slip by the mouth of the marina. *Second Wind* was docked there, a seven-foot rubber dinghy with a simple small sail. There was Pugboat, huddled at the bottom.

"I'll bet she was chasing Barnacle," Cora said.

"Come here, girl," Sabina said, patting her knees. "Come on. Come out of there."

Pugboat tried to scramble up the side of the dinghy, but she couldn't.

"I'll get her," Cora said.

"I'm coming with you," said Sabina.

Cora climbed into *Second Wind*, and she helped Sabina climb down as well. Pugboat leapt into Sabina's arms, and Sabina petted her, telling her everything would be all right. Soon, Cora noticed that she was crying.

"It will be all right," Cora tried to comfort her. "Eventually."

Sabina cried and clutched her dog, and Cora put her arms around Sabina and held her.

Suddenly, Cora heard Sabina's father cry out from the dock, "Sabina!"

That's when the girls realized that *Second Wind* had not been properly tied to the dock and was drifting toward the ocean. Cora looked for a rope to throw to the dock, but there was none. Sabina yelled, "Daddy!" just as the boat bobbed out of the marina.

Cora knew her *ima* and mom would untie *Why Knot* and come after them. Still, she was frightened. She knew how quickly everything moved and changed on water. She found two life vests and put one on Sabina and the other on herself. Sabina wiped her eyes. Her face was pale. Her sudden silence was more upsetting to Cora than her tears. She put her flashlight in Sabina's hand and said, "Just keep waving this toward home so they see us."

She prayed the batteries wouldn't go out. She said to Cora, "My *ima* always tells me, we can't control which way the wind goes, but if we learn to catch it just right, we can always get home."

Cora's hands moved quickly. She tightened the sail with a bowline knot. She adjusted it to catch a gust, tacking into the wind to change course. She could see the waves whitecapping in the beam of the flashlight. The little boat skipped over swells as it made its way back to the marina.

"I want to go home," Sabina said.

"We are almost there," Cora promised.

Sure enough, *Second Wind* was pulling into the marina just as *Why Knot* was pulling out, almost capsizing *Second Wind* in its wake.

"You all right?" Cora's *ima* called from the bow.

"Aye aye!" Cora called back, drenched in sea spray.

Cora navigated the boat back to its slip. Sabina's dad lifted Sabina, Cora, and Pugboat out of the dinghy. Sabina and Gary hugged each other while Pugboat jumped happily around them.

"I want to go home," Sabina said.

"I know," Gary said helplessly. "I know you do."

"No," Sabina said, looking up at her father's face. "I want to go home to *The Saltbox*."

The next morning, Cora and her family returned to the marina. Sabina came out brushing her teeth. She smiled a big toothpasty smile and waved to Cora. Cora waved back. She ran inside and then came back out patting her face with a cloth and carrying a small box under her arm.

"I sewed something for you last night," she said cheerily.

Sabina handed the small box to Cora while Gary and Cora's mothers looked on. Cora opened it. Inside was a stitched rectangle of white sailcloth, fringed at the corners with knotted string.

"What is it?" Cora's mom asked.

But Cora knew what it was. "It is my own sail," she said.

"Yes!" Sabina said. "I made one for me too. I'm going to wear it the first day of school, hidden under my shirt, so I won't be scared. I think if we could get through last night, I can get through going to a new school. This will help remind me."

Cora swung her gift over her head and around, so that it landed on her shoulders. She held it around her body. It felt good. Cora helped Sabina put on her own sail. She thought about putting the life vest on her the night before. That was different, but it felt the same. She thought about knots and how they help tie things together. Cora knew she and Sabina would always protect each other. She knew their friendship was something that could never unravel.

QUESTIONS

1. Cora's *ima* said, "We can't control which way the wind goes, but if we learn to catch it just right, we can always get home." When things don't go the way we want them to, how do we adjust our sails/attitude?

2. This story uses a sail as a metaphor for a tallit. What item would you choose to represent the tallit, and why?

3. The knotted fringes on the corners of the tallit are supposed to remind us of the mitzvot. What Jewish reminders do you have in your life?

4. Sometimes people refer to getting married as "tying the knot." We also talk about "family ties," the "parent-child bond," and the "bonds of friendship." Why do you think the knot is used for talking about relationships? To whom do you feel you have "ties"?

A Pock-Faced Beauty

Based on a True Story

LEXI WAS BECOMING BAT MITZVAH in two days, but they were taking the formal photos today. Everyone had to get into the same clothes they would be wearing for her bat mitzvah. They even hired a makeup artist to apply makeup to the women in her family. Lexi knew she was lucky to have four generations of her family present. Her great-grandmother was 102 years old and still sharp as a tack! Lexi took her blouse out of its dry-cleaning bag and slipped it over her head. It was silky and lavender and matched the *kippot* they had ordered. It also matched her lavender-striped tallit. She tucked her blouse into her black slacks and slipped into the little heels that Aunt Remy said were "smart," though Lexi didn't understand what was smart about pinchy shoes. She would have much preferred to wear her Doc Martens boots on her bat mitzvah day. But she was afraid to say anything.

Crazy as it sounded, sometimes Lexi missed the pandemic days when everyone in her school had to wear masks. It relieved so much of the pressure and anxiety she felt about how she looked. At night, when she scrolled through social media, she couldn't help but compare herself to everyone else. She knew so many selfies were staged and set up with ring lights and perfect angles, overlaid with filters and photoshopped to give people fuller lips and higher cheekbones, edited to make people look smoother, thinner, taller, or whatever. She knew the people she saw on Instagram and TikTok didn't always reflect reality, but it still got under her skin and made her feel insecure.

Lexi's Torah portion mentioned mirrors. It talked about how the washbasin just outside the holy Tabernacle was to be made from women's mirrors. Lexi had mixed feelings about mirrors. On the one hand, she loved the mirror in *Alice Through the Looking Glass*, because it was a gateway to a world of adventure and fun. On the other hand, she hated the mirror in *Snow White*, which generated envy and wickedness. She did not know how she felt looking at her own reflection in the mirror.

Lexi opened a plum-tinted lipstick and drew a big circle on the mirror in front of her. Then she drew a circle inside the circle. She positioned herself so her face was reflected in the inner circle. She looked like an astronaut.

"Houston to Bat Mitzvah One," she said in a crackly walkie-talkie voice. "Do you read?"

Lexi came out of her room. Her mother's and aunt's faces were finished. Mother looked beautiful, with her smoky eyes and shimmery cheeks. Aunt Remy's lips, with the lipliner, looked fuller than usual.

Lexi sat and watched the makeup artist fill in her grandmother's eyebrows. The makeup artist had a big black box with movable palates of colors.

"Can you make me an astronaut?" Lexi asked him.

The makeup artist laughed. He then asked Lexi's great-grandmother, "Would you like a little foundation? A charcoal gray around your green eyes and they would steal the show."

Lexi's great-grandmother shook her head. She said, "You know, I was a beautician too. And I was very much in demand. I made up the faces of many famous movie stars back in the day. Have you heard of Ingrid Bergman? Katharine Hepburn? Judy Garland? Lana Turner?"

"Of course!" the makeup artist exclaimed. Lexi did not recognize any of the names.

Lexi's great-grandmother's face was pocked. Craters stippled her face. Some were deep and the size of a lentil, and others were shallow and the size of the head of a pin. Lexi always assumed that she had had terrible acne as a child and thought it was ironic that she had been such a famous makeup artist when she never hid the blotches of pocks on her own skin. Her hair was white and thin, held back with a black velvet clip.

Lexi looked away from her great-grandmother and picked up a makeup brush, twirling it around her fingers.

"There," the makeup artist said to Lexi's grandmother, "beautiful."

Lexi's grandmother got up from the chair and air-kissed Lexi.

"Now for the main attraction," the makeup artist said, gesturing for Lexi to sit in the chair. Lexi hesitated. She felt anxious about having a stranger decide how she would look. Then her great-grandmother said, "May I?"

The makeup artist said, "It would be an honor," and stepped aside from his black box.

Lexi's great-grandmother studied Lexi's face for a moment. She picked up a little jar and dabbed a brush in, sweeping the clear gloss on the back of her hand. Her knotted fingers trembled a little. "You really don't need any makeup," she said. She held her hand up to Lexi. The skin on her hands was pocked as well, but not as badly as her face. "Perhaps just a little powder and a touch of clear gloss, do you think?"

Lexi's great-grandmother touched Lexi's face with a wide brush. "Just a little," she said. "You don't need it. You have nothing to conceal." Lexi closed her eyes. The brush felt soothing.

Lexi opened her eyes and looked into her great-grandmother's soft green eyes, with their wispy lashes.

"A little mascara?" her great-grandmother asked.

"No, thanks," Lexi said. She had tried mascara once. She didn't like putting that inky wand so close to her eye.

"No need, really," her great-grandmother said. "Then you are ready. You have a natural glow." She held up a hand mirror for Lexi to see herself. Lexi looked instead at the pocked hand holding the mirror.

"It's okay," her great-grandmother said, noticing where Lexi was gazing. "You can look."

"What happened to your skin?" she asked quietly, worried she might offend her.

"I was hoping you would ask," her great-grandmother said, laying the mirror down. She smoothed a loose strand of her white hair away from her face. "When I was a baby, in Ukraine, I had the chickenpox. A bad case. The doctor bandaged me up like a mummy."

"Oh, I'm sorry," Lexi said.

Her great-grandmother laughed. "For what? I don't remember it myself. I was a baby!" She smiled at Lexi. "It is what happened next that matters. We lived in a shtetl. A little Jewish village. And one terrible day, a mob of peasants gathered just outside, holding pitchforks and axes and knives, ready to attack our village."

"A pogrom!" Lexi gasped.

"Yes," her great-grandmother said. "That's what they wanted to start. But my mother was a very clever person. She took me and tore off my bandages, showing all my scabs. She came out to the mob, and she held me out to them. And she said, 'Smallpox.'"

"You mean chickenpox," Lexi corrected.

"Yes. I had chickenpox. But they didn't know that. My mother said 'small-pox,' and they all ran away. Lexi, these scars saved a village—hundreds of people." Lexi's great-grandmother took Lexi's hands in her own and brought Lexi's hands to her face, pressing them against her scarred cheeks. "*True beauty*."

"Picture time, Lexi!" Lexi's mother called. "Come outside while the light is good!"

Lexi threw her arms around her great-grandmother and said, "Thank you."

"The perfect light comes from inside," her great-grandmother said. "Now go. Shine."

Lexi ran to her room and changed her shoes. She hurried outside where the photographer was positioning family members in front of the flowering bougainvillea. Lexi stood in the middle between her parents.

"Doc Martens?" Aunt Remy shook her head. "Really, Lexi?"

Lexi nodded. She thought about how silly it seemed, worrying about how someone might judge you for wearing the shoes you like—to style yourself after what you think others would approve, instead of letting yourself shine. She wondered at the pride her great-grandmother had, moving through the world of movies and movie stars with a face full of pocks. Surely, she must have been teased. But there she was, painting the faces of some of the most glamorous people in Hollywood, all the while showing her naked scars to the world. No mask, and no filter.

Lexi remembered studying her Torah portion with the rabbi and learning a legend that said Moses was angry about the mirrors being used to make the washbasin outside the Tabernacle. Moses thought they were instruments of vanity. But God said to Moses that the mirrors were more precious to God than anything in the world. Lexi didn't understand that at the time. But now, she thought about her own quirks and imperfections, the things that made her real and unique, and not some two-dimensional photoshopped card-board cutout. Nearly 102 years ago, Lexi's great-grandmother's scars saved hundreds of people, and today, Lexi realized, those same scars saved her as well.

"Say 'Lexi,'" the photographer said, and everyone smiled.

At the very end of her bat mitzvah, Lexi stood across from the rabbi before the open doors of the ark. When the rabbi held his hands over her head and pronounced the blessing, "May God's face shine upon you," Lexi imagined God's face to be her great-grandmother's face, dotted and dappled with scars, creased and lined with age, and shining with wisdom, courage, and love.

> *Lexi's great-grandmother's character is based on Carolyn Gomberg, of blessed memory, born in Kiev. Her mother did in fact unwrap her bandages when she was a baby with chickenpox and held her up to a gathering mob, telling them it was smallpox. Carolyn became a Hollywood makeup artist and was very proud of her scars.*

QUESTIONS

1. How has your relationship with mirrors and looking at yourself changed over time?
2. Who defines what is beautiful? How do *you* define what is beautiful?
3. Former prime minister of Israel Golda Meir once said, "Not being beautiful was the true blessing. Not being beautiful forced me to develop my inner resources." Greek philosopher Epictetus said, "If your choices are beautiful, so too will you be." What are your thoughts about these statements?
4. Do you have scars—internal or external—that make you proud?

The Magic Word

"**M**ORE MACARONI!" Chantal said, stretching her arms toward the serving bowl that was just out of reach.

"What's the magic word?" her mother asked.

Chantal thought for a moment and then said, "Abracadabra."

The whole family laughed. Chantal loved the way each of her family members laughed. Her mother laughed deeply from the belly. Her father made one loud, fantastic "Haw!" and slapped the table. Her oldest brother laughed with a "Hee hee hee" while shaking his head in disbelief. And her other brother had developed a habit of laughing through his nose with his lips held tight because he was embarrassed about showing his braces; but this time, he laughed open-mouthed and out loud, and Chantal loved his wonderful smile.

"'Please,'" her father said when he finished laughing. "'Please' is the magic word."

It became an ongoing joke in their family. Every time one of her parents asked her, "What's the magic word?" Chantal would say something other than "please."

First, she started with other magic words, like "alakazam," "hocus-pocus," "presto chango," and "open sesame." Then she looked for magic words in television and movies: "Ala peanut butter sandwiches," "bibbidi bobbidi boo," "miraculous ladybug," "wingardium leviosa." Her father taught her magic words and fun-sounding phrases from his favorite songs: "oo ee oo ah ah ting tang walla walla bing bang," "boom boom acka-lacka," "shimmy shimmy ko ko bop," and "shama lama ding dong," which made

Chantal laugh. Chantal also sometimes used words that weren't really magic words but sounded like they could be, like "roasted pistachio," "Zamboni," "valedictorian," "escalator," and "gobbledygook."

Throughout middle school, she kept a list on her tablet and wondered what it was that made a word sound magical. She learned how to say "please" in a dozen different languages, and they all sounded vastly different: *s'il vous plaît, por favor, qǐng, min fádlak, bevakashah, bitte, pazhalsta, onegaishimasu, tack.* She loved the feeling of these words in her mouth. And the American Sign Language word for "please" was especially meaningful, rubbing the palm of the hand in a circle on the chest. It created a warm magic you could feel.

In Hebrew school, when the teacher read from the Torah, "And God said, 'Let there be light,' and there was light," Chantal asked what the Hebrew word was for "Let there be," and the teacher said, "*Va-y'hi.*"

Chantal added that to her list, thinking it must be an especially magic word, because any time God said it, creation happened.

When studying for her bat mitzvah, she learned from her tutor that there was magic in the very shape of the letters. She learned that the four letters that spelled one of God's names were considered so powerful that if you wrote them on a piece of paper, that paper should never be thrown out. Rather, it had to be buried in a special place called a *genizah.* People didn't even pronounce the letters of God's name. Those four letters even had a word to describe them. They were called the "Tetragrammaton," which itself sounded like a magic word!

Some people were even afraid of writing the word "God" in English and sometimes wrote G-d or GD or simply G. Chantal added all the names for God that she knew to her list.

Her mother's question to her when she was a child, "What's the magic word?" led her down a path of wonder and discovery that continued even after her bat mitzvah. When she went to college she majored in linguistics, and Chantal researched magic words from around the world. The Iranian equivalent of "abracadabra" was *ajji majji tarajji,* and in India it was *jantar mantar jadu mantar.* When researching the etymology of "abracadabra," she was especially delighted to learn that it had ancient Hebrew origins, translating to "I create as I speak"—just like God created the world through speech. Chantal believed in the power of words and the way we use words to create—and destroy—worlds. The pen is mightier than the sword, as they say.

One day, Chantal's favorite linguistics professor said to her, "I wish you could meet Rabbi Chaya Yisraela Kagan. If anyone knows magic words, it's her."

"Who's Rabbi Chaya Yisraela Kagan?" Chantal asked.

"She is the direct descendant of nineteenth-century rabbi Yisrael Meir HaKohen Kagan, also known as the Chofetz Chayim, who wrote a book about *lashon hara*—evil speech and gossip. She is a wise teacher and a mystic," her professor shared. "But she is very hard to reach."

A mystic, Chantal thought, maybe a mystic of magic words. She asked her professor, "Have you met her?"

"I have," she said. "When I was about your age."

"What did she tell you?" Chantal asked.

"I can't tell you," the professor said. "The wisdom she shared with me was meant only for me."

Chantal was intrigued. What powerful insight Rabbi Chaya Yisraela Kagan must have if her beloved professor treasured her words so much! Chantal had always wanted to travel to Israel. Perhaps this was the sign she should go.

That summer Chantal boarded a plane to Ben Gurion Airport. Upon arrival, she lingered under the words "Welcome to Israel" spelled out in tall silver letters. She stared at the Star of David in the center of the flag beside the sign. The star wasn't a word, but it was a symbol, and it felt magical, made up of one triangle pointing up and another triangle pointing down. A covenantal symbol, Chantal thought. God and us, together. She hoisted her backpack over her shoulders and headed out to find a cab, stopping to get a pita stuffed with falafel, fries, tahini, and pickles.

"You have never been to Israel," Chantal's cabdriver said, "and the first place you are going is Mount Meron?"

Chantal looked out the window, fascinated by the signs on the Yitzchak Rabin Highway that were in Hebrew, Arabic, and English. It was amazing to see the same letters she read on the pages of prayer books here on highway signs. She thought again about the Star of David, pointing up and down at the same time. She felt she was somewhere in the middle. The undulating Arabic letters beautifully matched the landscape, with its hills and valleys, mountains and trees.

"Why not Jerusalem," the driver continued, "or Lake Kinneret, or Eilat?"

"I will visit those places," Chantal said. She was planning to stay for two weeks, exploring. "But first I have a rabbi I need to see on Mount Meron."

"A rabbi on Mount Meron?" the driver said, pondering. "Well, if you are going to see the great Rabbi Shimon bar Yochai, he died about eighteen hundred years ago."

"I am actually going to see Rabbi Chaya Yisraela Kagan," Chantal said. "She is a mystic."

"*Nu?*" the driver said. "Isn't everyone in Israel?"

Just then the cab swerved to avoid another car that was switching lanes. The driver rolled down his window and gestured at the other car, yelling, "*Idiyot!*"

When they arrived at the foot of Mount Meron, the driver said, "If you need somewhere for Shabbat, go to the Haifa Shuk on R'chov Yechiel and ask anyone there for directions to my mother's house. Her name is Yael Mizrachi—everyone knows her. I will tell her you are coming. She makes the most incredible lamb tagine."

Chantal thanked the driver and checked into the guesthouse she had reserved. Her host Shireen greeted her warmly.

"Three weeks ago you would not have been able to find an available room," Shireen told Chantal. "There were thousands of people here to visit the grave of Rabbi Shimon bar Yochai for Lag BaOmer. But you will be able to visit when it is nice and quiet."

"Actually, I am here to visit Rabbi Chaya Yisraela Kagan," Chantal said. "She is a mystic."

"Ah," said Shireen. "Did you know that throughout all of Rabbi Shimon bar Yochai's life, there was never a single rainbow in the sky? Because Rabbi Shimon was so righteous, there was no need for a rainbow to remind God of the promise not to destroy the world with flood."

"Wow," Chantal said. "That is truly a magical story."

"Indeed," Shireen continued. "And on the day he died, the daylight lasted into the night so that he could reveal all the deep mystical truths he knew. That's why thousands of people come to Mount Meron on the anniversary of his death and build bonfires, to celebrate the light he shared with the world."

Chantal imagined what mystical truths Rabbi Kagan would reveal to her tomorrow. The fatigue from travel crept over her, and she prepared to go to sleep.

Chantal began her hike bright and early. As she walked, she remembered the first time she heard about magic words at her parents' table. Now here she was walking through the Mount Meron Nature Reserve in the Upper Galilee in Israel, every step bringing her closer to a master of magic words.

She walked through a grove of evergreen trees. Through the trees, Chantal admired the rolling hills blanketed with green, fading into the distance as if they were painted with watercolor. Looking further, she could see horizonal stripes on some of the hills, hints of vineyards and orchards. Looking up, she saw flocks of birds crisscrossing the sky. Chantal wondered where they were all going on their migratory paths between Africa, India, and Europe.

Chantal followed the Amud Stream as it twisted through the reserve, admiring the waterfalls and clear pools. She thought about more words that had the power to open worlds. "Thank you" was considered magic. "I love you" of course had magic powers. Those words, when her parents said them at the end of a phone call, made Chantal feel safe. "I'm sorry" had magical properties. It could transform relationships, alleviating years of anxiety and pain.

Chantal took in the beauty all around her. She thought about the words "bless you" that we say when someone sneezes. People used to believe that the soul entered and could exit through the nose, and that is why we say "bless you" when someone sneezes, but not when they cough. "Bless you" was a magical phrase to keep the soul from falling out. Chantal breathed in the aromatic air and said a prayer of gratitude for being part of this wonderful, complex, breathing world.

Chantal continued walking as the path became steeper. She climbed over thick tree roots and boulders. She thought about how the word "yes" was a magical, courageous word. And then she realized that "no" was also a magical word that was courageous and powerful.

Chantal walked and repeated the magical words she had collected, savoring each one. *Aloha. Namaste. Om. Shalom.*

Finally, Chantal reached the dwelling her professor had described, where

the mystic lived. It was a small house built inside a cave. There was an attendant standing outside the front door.

"I am here to see Rabbi Chaya Yisraela Kagan," Chantal said to the attendant.

The attendant responded, "Everyone who visits the rabbi can ask one
question and one question only, and after she answers, you must leave."

"I am ready," Chantal said, brushing her hair away from her face and
straightening her back. *Hineini*, she thought—the Hebrew word for "I am
ready." That too is a magic word.

The attendant ushered Chantal into the dwelling. Chantal followed him
down a hall and through a door that opened into the cave. The cave was lit
with lanterns, and the walls were draped with beautiful tapestries. Sitting in
the center on a rug was a diminutive woman with long dark hair that looked
like it was threaded with tinsel. Her hair was so long, it pooled around her.
Her hands were resting on her knees with the palms facing up, and she was
softly chanting with her eyes closed. Chantal thought about what the driver
had said about Rabbi Shimon bar Yochai and what her guesthouse host
Shireen had said—that he had shared so many magic words on the day he
died that the sun didn't set until late into the night. She anticipated the font
of wisdom Rabbi Kagan might share with her about the magic of words and
language.

Suddenly, the rabbi's eyes opened. She nodded her head toward Chantal.

"Ask your question now," the attendant whispered.

Chantal cleared her throat. Then she took a breath and asked this wise
rabbi the very same question her mother had asked her when she wanted
more macaroni. "What's the magic word?"

The mystic took in the question. And then she lifted both of her hands,
palms to the ceiling, lifted her shoulders, shrugged, and said, "I don't know."

"What?" Chantal asked.

The attendant quickly ushered Chantal out of the dwelling in the cave.
"You cannot ask a second question," he said sharply.

"But," Chantal protested, blinking in the sunlight, "she didn't answer my
first!"

"Rules are rules," the attendant said. "Come again next time you are in
the area."

Chantal was dumbfounded. "I don't know"? *That's* what the great Rabbi

Chaya Yisraela Kagan, descendant of the Chofetz Chayim, had to say to her? What a joke! She thought about turning around and marching right back in. She wasn't afraid of the attendant or the mystic. But she didn't. What was the point? She had hundreds and hundreds of words on her list. The rabbi probably was just going to say one of the words that Chantal already had. But why would her esteemed professor encourage her to take this journey?

And technically, the rabbi didn't even really say, "I don't know," Chantal realized as she stomped away, growing more and more angry. Nor was it a half-hearted "I dunno." It was more like that nasally version of "I don't know" that children say when they are being obnoxious. It was a whiny, slurred "n" sound in place of the syllables. It was more like a "nn-nnn-nn-nnn." She thought about her phonetics studies. Yes, it was what they called a "voiced velar nasal," intoned in D then G then F#, and it was annoying.

Chantal fumed as she walked. She had traveled halfway around the world to ask a mystic a question, only to have her shrug and dismiss her. It was horrible! She paused at a campsite and stood over the charred remains of a bonfire. Probably one celebrating the great Rabbi Shimon bar Yochai and all his magical, mystical words. She kicked a hunk of coal.

"I don't know," Chantal said, mimicking the rabbi. "She doesn't know," she said to a white crocus. "She just doesn't know," she told a rock badger. "She doesn't know," she explained to a woodpecker. "Don't ask her, because she doesn't know," she warned a Levant green lizard.

She walked on, sharing her frustration with all the flora and fauna she passed. "Rabbi Kagan doesn't know, you see? If you ask Rabbi Kagan what she knows, she will tell you that she doesn't know. But she won't even *bother* to articulate the consonants. She will just say nn-nnn-nnnnn, like a *child*. I should be the one sitting in that cave. People should be trekking to ask me questions. Imagine, someone coming to see me, asking me, 'What's the magic word?' I would say . . ."

Chantal paused, standing under a cypress tree. The long list of magic words that she had kept since way back in middle school faded from her mind. She looked up through the waving leaves at the sky. "I don't know," she whispered to herself. Her thoughts quieted. Suddenly she became aware of the thrumming of life all around her, the life of this great tree bridging earth and sky. She saw a mint-green chameleon holding onto a twig. She looked past the branches and saw the tail of an ibex dart into a cluster of

Jerusalem pines. And the hills themselves seemed as alive as the animals and trees. Everything around her was shifting and growing. Chantal slipped down and sat on a mossy cushion at the bottom of the tree. She shrugged her backpack off and rested the back of her head against the trunk.

"I don't know," she said gently. She looked at a beetle crawling on her pant leg, its tiny antennae twitching, picking up scents and signals. "What is having faith," she asked the beetle, "but to trek into the unknown?" She pondered this thought, and then added, "What is God but Unknowable?"

The chameleon watched Chantal as she watched it. She wondered if the chameleon ever said to itself, "I don't know," or if that was purely a human trait. "The more I know," she thought, "the more I am aware of how much I don't know. And the more I am aware of how much I don't know, the more curious I am. In fact, didn't Socrates say, 'The only true wisdom is knowing you know nothing'? And didn't Martin Buber say, 'All journeys have secret destinations of which the traveler is unaware'?"

"None of us know," Chantal told the beetle on her knee. She wondered what the world would look like if people were more comfortable saying "I don't know" instead of working so hard pretending to know everything. Maybe there would be less arrogance, less insistence on being right all the time, and more humility. Chantal realized that saying "I don't know" makes you more appreciative of the vast world, and that is how we accept God's invitation to explore, learn, and grow.

The beetle flew away, buzzing into the sunlight. Chantal picked up her backpack and stood. She thought about how far she had traveled and how many more places she wanted to go. The world is so big, she thought, and I am a part of it.

Perhaps, she mused, all words have the potential to be magic words, depending on the intention with which they are spoken. God created the world with words, and we create worlds with words as well. Maybe that was what Rabbi Kagan was trying to tell her—that to be wise, one must be humble enough to be open to learning from everybody, open to receiving language and stories and words. Even the animals, the trees, the mountains, and the earth itself were speaking magic words, if we could be still enough to listen and interpret them. "I don't know" was the key that opened the door to it all.

Chantal walked through the shuk in Haifa, surrounded by bins tumbling with colorful vegetables, fruits, spices, and grains. There were dozens of vendors. She thought to herself, "This can't possibly work." Then she walked up to a vendor selling figs and dates and said, "I am looking for Yael Mizrachi? I was invited for Shabbat. Her son is a cabdriver?"

"Yes, of course!" said the vendor. "Yael Mizrachi. She makes an incredible lamb tagine. I will tell you how to get there."

Chantal marveled at the way life was like a stream, twisting and turning, carrying you to places unplanned, and how beautiful it was to let go of certainty and discover the magical unknown.

Just then her mother texted her: *So what's the magic word?*

Chantal replied: ¯_(ツ)_/¯

QUESTIONS

1. Erich Fromm wrote, "Creativity requires the courage to let go of certainties." Why does it require courage to let go of certainty? How might uncertainty lead to creation?

2. The Talmud says, "Teach your tongue to say I don't know" (*B'rachot* 4a). How has saying "I don't know" been an opportunity for your own growth and learning?

3. Confucius taught, "Humility is the solid foundation of all virtues." Rabbi Bachya ibn Pakuda taught, "All virtues and duties are dependent on humility." How does humility lead to virtue?

4. What words have felt magical in your life, in that saying or hearing them caused something to transform?

WOODEN SPOON

Stories That Stir Food for Thought

Lace Theory

DURING THE TIME that nearly everyone in the world was mesmerized by the first deep space images from the James Webb Space Telescope, Dr. Gibbous A. B. Zickel discovered something equally, if not *more*, astonishing.

It was a beautiful summer night. Dr. Zickel was in his lab in Honolulu reviewing incoming data from the Keck Observatory when he detected a wobble in a particular star he had been monitoring. He leapt up so quickly that he catapulted his rolling desk chair backward, knocking over a stack of overstuffed notebooks and disturbing his iguana, Zenith, who was halfway up a bookshelf. Zenith turned his spiky green head to the sound.

Dr. Zickel adjusted his glasses and exclaimed to Zenith, "I have just discovered a new planet, or my middle name isn't Asteroid Belt!"

Zenith just licked his eyeball and resumed climbing.

Discovering the new planet was not what was astonishing. To be fair, it was definitely a cool thing. But Dr. Zickel had discovered planets before.

Astronomers know that planets have a gravitational influence on the stars they orbit, so when you measure a star's wobble, you can be sure there is a planet there, even if you can't see it. Dr. Zickel had spent twenty years co-leading an international team developing AI software to survey distant stars to measure their wobble and detect heavenly bodies. The program was simply called X70, since there were seventy people on the original development team. Similar technology existed, but not with nearly the sensitivity and accuracy of what they had been working on. When they were finally ready to release it, it would be a great breakthrough.

Even though today's planetary discovery wasn't the discovery of a lifetime (it certainly wasn't going to share the limelight with the James Webb images), Dr. Zickel was happy. Mapping the cosmos was exciting! He could still remember when his fascination first began, when his parents used to take him outside to stargaze.

Gibbous was eight years old, lying between his parents on a blanket in the backyard of his childhood home, looking at the night sky. His mother was saying that when we look at the stars, we are actually looking at the past, because of how long it takes light to travel.

"In fact," she said, "the star that made the light might be long gone by the time we see it."

Gibbous was contemplating this when he wondered aloud to his parents, "Why is nighttime dark when there is so much light coming at us all the time?"

His father said, "Why don't you become an astronomer and find out?"

He decided then, as they lay there making wishes on shooting stars, that that was exactly what he wanted to do.

On his tenth birthday, one of his wishes came true. His parents bought him his own telescope.

He still had that telescope, folded in its case in the corner of the lab. He decided to celebrate the new planet by taking out the telescope and giving the old brass spyglass a whirl. He carried it out onto the deck and opened the wooden tripod. As he positioned the telescope to face the moon, he could remember his mother's hand on his back when he looked through it for the first time the night of his tenth birthday. He remembered his father saying, "Do you see the man in the moon?" and his mother adding, "Or a woman?"

Dr. Zickel remembered calling his parents after attending a lecture about lunar geology. "There are three craters on the moon named after rabbis!" he exclaimed, breathlessly reading his notes. "The Rabbi Levi Crater, named after Levi ben Gershon, the Zagut Crater, named after Rabbi Abraham Zacuto, and the Abenezra Crater, named after Rabbi Avraham ibn Ezra!"

"Any named after Jewish women?" his mother asked.

He was ready for that question, and said, "Not as many, but there is one! The Nöther Crater, named after Emmy Nöther, a brilliant mathematician."

"Did you find out yet why the night is dark?" his father asked.

"Well," he answered, "space is so unfathomably big, and it is expanding and getting even bigger." The infinitude of space made it even more wondrous to discover anything at all, Dr. Zickel thought. Imagine trying to find a small glass bead in the ocean, he would tell his interns. Now imagine trying to find that same single bead, but instead of searching an ocean seven miles deep, searching the cosmos, which is thirteen billion light-years across.

"*Mah gadlu maasecha, Adonai*," Dr. Zickel said as he peered through the telescope from his childhood. "How great are Your works, God. And how humbled I am to witness them!"

Dr. Zickel could smell the fragrance of flowers and the ocean on a warm Hawaiian breeze as he focused the telescope on the moon's craters, naming them in his head. The image was very low resolution, but the memories it stirred were crystal clear.

His parents had both died in the past year, a few months apart. But Dr. Zickel could still feel them, even though he couldn't see them. That made him feel they were still orbiting around him, influencing him and giving his heart a little wobble.

That's when Dr. Zickel had an idea. He went back into the lab and rolled his chair back to his desk, ignoring the notebooks and papers tumbling all over the floor. He powered up his program with the same childlike giddiness he had felt as a ten-year-old looking into that telescope for the first time. Zenith was now lying across the top of the computer monitor, with his long green fingers gripping the screen. On the bulletin board above his computer, Dr. Zickel had printed out his favorite verse of Torah, from Genesis chapter 15, verse 5: "Turn your gaze toward the heavens and count the stars, if you can count them!"

Now, as it has been mentioned, nearly everyone in the world was mesmerized by the images from the James Webb Space Telescope, but there were many other space telescopes out there besides Webb and Hubble. One of them was on its last legs—solar panels to be exact—and had been orbiting space for  nearly sixty years. However, Dr. Zickel felt the same nostalgia about these nearly defunct satellites as he did about his childhood telescope. Low resolution, but they still had something valuable to offer before they became cold aluminum, eternally adrift. Dr. Zickel synced X70 to the old space telescope and calibrated its curved mirrors toward earth.

"What would happen if this software, designed to seek out wobbles in deep space stars, was instead directed toward earth?" he asked Zenith, chuckling. "We are made of stardust, after all."

Zenith raised his natural mohawk of spikes and then lowered it again.

Dr. Zickel busily adjusted indicators and controls on his touchscreen, watching the cutting-edge technology in front of him integrate with the decades-old mechanism in orbit. He worked through the night, hardly noticing the passage of time. At 6:00 a.m., an image began to come into focus. Filled with anticipation, Dr. Zickel was a child again, his mother's hand on his back and his father helping him with the telescope dials.

Anyone else might have expected X70's resulting image to be a blurry version of Google Maps, but Dr. Zickel knew it would be different. X70 was designed to record wobble, not cartography. Still, what he saw was not at all what he expected.

"Zenith," he whispered, "are you seeing this?"

Even though the ether hypothesis—the belief that light, which was thought to travel in waves, could not travel through a vacuum, and therefore space must be filled with an invisible material called ether—had been disproved over a hundred years ago, the first words that came to Dr. Zickel's head were "luminiferous ether." He knew that what he was seeing couldn't be the luminiferous ether from the debunked ether hypothesis. There was no ether. But then, what was it that he was seeing? What was this dazzling, vibrating framework enwreathing the planet upon which we lived?

Dr. Zickel startled at the sound of a voice. "What are we looking at, Gibbous?"

"Zenith?" he looked at his iguana who lay sleeping on top of the monitor.

"No, dummy," the voice said, "it's Linda."

"Linda?" Dr. Zickel said. He saw her image on his computer. "Linda! Are you seeing what I'm seeing?"

Dr. Linda S. Leib was looking at the same dazzling spectacle on her screen in Sydney. "Yes. I never logged out of our session yesterday. What is this?"

"Isn't it 2:00 a.m. there?" Dr. Zickel said. "Why aren't you sleeping? We have work tomorrow."

"Yes, but it's already tomorrow over here," Dr. Leib said. "And winter. You are talking to the future while I look into the past. Anyway, I'm up the same reason you're up all night."

"Why are we up all night?"

"We're star-crossed dreamers, that's why. Now, what is this? Why are you directing that floating tin can at earth?"

"I wanted to see what kind of wobbles there were here on earth," Dr. Zickel said.

"Wait," Dr. Leib said, "this is an X70 reading? What are we reading, ozone? Electricity?"

"I don't think so. My first thought, crazy as it sounds, was ether."

"What? No. Ether's been disproved," Dr. Leib said, as she stared at the moving image. It looked like a network of luminous neural pathways. Then she posited, "Strings?"

"String theory?" Dr. Zickel responded. "I mean, it does strangely look like strings. A tangled, living mess of strings. But strings are not visible."

"String theory says that everything is made up of itty-bitty one-dimensional vibrating strings," Dr. Leib said. "Gibbous, does that not look like itty-bitty vibrating strings?"

"But, they aren't one-dimensional. And string theory hasn't been proven." Dr. Zickel squinted into his monitor and added, "Yet."

Dr. Leib said, "String theory suggests that there is one unknown unifying force that ties everything together, and visually, it looks like something is tying everything together."

"One unknown unifying force," Dr. Zickel repeated. "It sounds like a description of God."

"*Adonai Echad*," Dr. Leib said in agreement.

The two astronomers were silent for a few moments. Zenith stretched out his front leg and held it motionless in the air, fingers pointing.

"String theory suggests there are hidden dimensions beyond the four we know," Dr. Leib said.

"Linda," Dr. Zickel said softly, "I think our X70 has discovered a hidden dimension."

"Let me take control for a moment," Dr. Leib said. Dr. Zickel watched his screen as she began making small adjustments to the satellite's mirrors. "The X70 is designed to enable telescopes to detect the slightest wobble of deep space stars," she said. "The earth, well, is not deep space. Somehow, the program is enabling us to see deeply into the world we know. Now, when testing it out on distant stars and galaxies, we've never seen anything like this before. So, why earth? Is the program glitching? I don't think so. Earth is different. Why?"

"Earth is full of life," Dr. Zickel said.

"Not just any kind of life, Gibbous," Dr. Leib said. "Complex life. Intelligent life. Emotional life."

Dr. Zickel clapped his hands. "You are right! *Everything* is wobbling and vibrating. It's all about the wobble. Electrons orbit around neutrons in atoms the same way planets orbit around stars the way galaxies orbit around black holes, and we . . ."

"We orbit around each other," Dr. Leib said.

"Yes, yes," Dr. Zickel affirmed. "That must be what the X70 is picking up. The way we are connected to one another, the way we influence each other, the way our actions tug and affect the network to which we all belong. The tug we have on each other as complex emotional lifeforms, that causes our hearts, our minds, our *souls* to wobble."

"Is that what we are going to publish in the journal?" Dr. Leib asked. "That X70 is mapping the wobble of *our souls?*"

"Maybe," Dr. Zickel responded. "Maybe this is a spiritual dimension."

"Let's see if we can test that empirically." Dr. Leib zoomed closer and closer to the exact point in space where Dr. Zickel sat. There were countless strings connected to him, some fainter than others. Some strings passed right through him, and others seemed to start or end with him. Dr. Leib shifted one mirror ever so delicately and spotlighted a single string that was brighter than the others. "It looks almost umbilical," she noted. "Look, there are thousands, maybe millions, of strings all around you. But this one is peculiarly charged. It is . . . jumpier than the others. It seems more alive. And *flowing* with light." She zoomed in even closer. "Light, or . . . information."

"Let's follow it and see where it leads," Dr. Zickel said.

Dr. Leib directed the satellite to follow the string. X70 was performing exquisitely in its precision and detail.

"Well, well, well," she said, "if my middle name isn't Syzygy."

The other end of the jumpy, flowing filament led to ten-year-old Gibbous looking into his brand-new telescope on his birthday in the backyard of his childhood home.

"I knew it!" he said. "I knew there was a connection between this night and that moment. I even took out that telescope tonight! Now that I think about it, it was as I was looking through that telescope that I originally got the idea to use X70 on earth. I could feel my parents' influence on me."

"Spiritual dimension indeed." Dr. Leib shifted the mirrors and singled out a twinkling string that ended where she sat. She traced it to discover that it led to the moment, seven years ago, when she closed her laptop after typing the last words of her dissertation and her roommate surprised her with cupcakes.

"What is that?"

"What?"

"There," Dr. Zickel said. "Next to the twinkling string, there is a broken one, dangling. Let me see something."

"That's painful memory," Dr. Leib said. She didn't know how she knew, but as soon as Dr. Zickel pointed out the broken string, she was certain that it led to the time her mentor published her work under his name and didn't give her any credit. It was like looking at her own timeline, punctured with an old trauma that still felt fresh.

Dr. Zickel found fissures and tears amid his strings as well. "This is where I broke a promise I made. It brings me a lot of regret." Even as he said it all these years later, he felt the sting of shame in his heart. He shifted the satellite. "But I'm surprised this string here is broken," Dr. Zickel said. "I didn't *intentionally* steal that bagel. You can clearly see that I thought I was buying a baker's dozen. I didn't realize I had taken fourteen until seeing it this moment. Why should a mistake cause the same breakage as something I chose to do? Is a transgression committed without intention equal to an intentional transgression?"

"Look," Dr. Leib said, "this string was once broken. You can see where it was torn. I remember this moment too! This was when I was very jealous of my sister, and I said some mean and unfair things. I was so insecure then! But if you zero in a little more, you can see it was repaired. I apologized to her, and our relationship became strong. That must be what repaired the string."

The two astronomers marveled and explored this strange new dimension, recording their findings and making notations. As scientists who understood general relativity, the curvature of space-time, and the oddities that Hawaii is twenty hours in Australia's past, that many of the stars we see at night died billions of years ago, and that if an alien in galaxy NGC 4845 could look at earth today it would see dinosaurs . . . they weren't incredulous at the idea that the past, present, and future are all intertwined. What they were seeing and exploring was always theoretically probable.

Dr. Zickel said, "What if this is not a dimension, but a *force*. Not gravitational or electromagnetic or nuclear, but . . ." Dr. Zickel hesitated.

"Go on," Dr. Leib said.

"What if it is *moral*."

"Moral," Dr. Leib repeated. "Huh. I can see that in some cases. However, what about the string connecting you to your first telescope? Or the string connecting me to finishing my dissertation? Are those moments about morality?

"Or, is it all about relationship? What if the theory of relativity leads to the theory of *relationality* when applied to complex life?" Dr. Zickel said excitedly. "What if everything is operating under the same force?"

"If what we are saying is true," Dr. Leib said, zooming out so they could see the whole shimmering, vibrating filigree, "then maybe they aren't strings, per se, but connections created by our relationships."

"The way neural pathways are created by our behavior," Dr. Zickel said.

"Is this our collective consciousness?" Dr. Leib wondered.

"A tattered mesh of responsibility toward one another, holding us all together," Dr. Zickel mused.

"And accountability," Dr. Leib added.

"Einstein said that human beings are delusional to think we are separate from the rest of the universe," Dr. Zickel said. "He said, 'Our task must be to free ourselves from this prison by widening our circle of compassion to embrace all living creatures.'"

"Look at all these interlacing circles of compassion," Dr. Leib said as she scanned the living fabric. "It's beautiful." Then she added, "It's not string theory. It's more like . . . lace theory. It looks like lace. A gorgeous antique lace."

"So," Dr. Zickel said, "God is a lace maker?"

Dr. Leib laughed and said, "I think She is."

Zenith began to climb down from the computer monitor, his prehistoric-looking body silhouetted against the screen. Dr. Zickel scratched his scaly cheeks. Then he noticed something new.

"It is torn," he said. "The lace." The Yom Kippur liturgy came to his mind. "For the sin we have committed before You by hard-heartedness. For the sin we have committed before You with an utterance of the lips. For the sin we have committed before You openly or secretly. Forgive us. Pardon us. Grant us atonement."

"Perhaps God is the lace maker," Dr. Leib said. "But we can be the lace menders."

"Let's see if we can test that empirically," Dr. Zickel said, echoing Dr. Leib's words earlier.

Over the next few weeks, Dr. Zickel and Dr. Leib tested their theories. Dr. Zickel revisited the bagel shop from which he had bought bagels many years ago to pay, with interest, for the extra bagel he accidentally stole. When the bagel shop owner told him not to worry, it's on the house, Dr. Zickel donated the money to MAZON: A Jewish Response to Hunger instead. Returning to the X70 data, he found that the connection that had been broken was now repaired.

"Interesting," Dr. Zickel thought. "So even unintentional sins require repair."

Emboldened, Dr. Zickel revisited a broken engagement from his mid-twenties. His head was in the clouds then—so much so, he could not appreciate the relationship that was right in front of him. He had been engaged to a wonderful woman named Amelie, but he had broken his promise to wed, canceling the wedding the month before it was scheduled. In the presence of Amelie's sorrow and anger, he had believed he was misunderstood. But he was much older now. His head still in the clouds, but he had matured and was now more earthbound and grounded. He wondered what his life would be like had he married. Would he have children? Would he still be working in a lab on this archipelago in the Pacific Ocean? Looking at the lace, he realized that he wasn't the one who was misunderstood; rather, he was the one who didn't understand. He did not understand the impact of his actions, the power of the promise that he broke, the lack of trust he had in his fiancée. There was so very much he didn't understand. He mustered the courage to reach out Amelie, to see if, after all this time, it was still possible to apologize for the hurt he had caused.

When he called her, a child answered the phone.

"Hello," Dr. Zickel said tentatively. "Is Amelie available?"

"You mean my *grandma*?" the child said.

"Yes," Dr. Zickel said, a little shocked at this evidence of the passage of time. He waited while the child went to get their grandmother. Then he heard Amelie's voice.

"Hello?" she said.

"Amelie, it's Gibbous. I'm sorry to call out of the blue like this," he said quickly, afraid his courage would fail. There was a brief pause.

"Gibbous," Amelie said. "I used to wonder if you'd reach out. But I stopped wondering maybe thirty years ago." She sounded a little bitter, but also amused.

"I wonder if we could talk? That is, if you are open to it. I am sorry for so many things."

"I'm sure," Amelie said. "Listen, Gibbous, I am getting ready to take my beautiful grandchildren out, so I can't talk now. But frankly, I don't feel the need to talk. I am happy with the direction my life took me—truly happy. I hope you can be happy with yours. I don't feel like any more needs to be said. Thank you for calling."

"Thank you," Dr. Zickel said, holding his phone to his ear long after the call ended.

Dr. Zickel realized that some reparations were not simple or complete. They were messy. But there was still meaning in the effort. Dr. Zickel returned to his X70 program. He paused before adjusting the mirrors. He thought about Amelie taking her grandchildren out. Dr. Zickel decided not to examine the string between him and Amelie to see if any repair had been made by the phone call. She had been gracious to talk with him even for a moment. He was grateful for that, and it felt intrusive to look any further. That data would have to remain inconclusive.

Dr. Leib sought to confront the mentor who had plagiarized her work but found he had died. Even with the work of repair, some connections would remain broken or frayed. But she discovered ways to integrate the hurt and gain wisdom from it. Pain and the wisdom acquired from it were the weft and warp that formed the beauty and integrity of the lace.

Dr. Zickel and Dr. Leib shared their findings with the rest of their X70 team, keeping the discovery out of the public eye until they could verify their conclusions. On Tishah B'Av, the team embarked on a bold project, delving into the torn lace and countless broken connections tangled around that date in ancient history when the Temple in Jerusalem was destroyed. They found connections between that destruction and other historic persecutions, the living lace raw with exposed nerve fibers.

During *Kol Nidrei* on Yom Kippur, Dr. Zickel stood amid the congregation, wrapped in his tallit. He held the knotted strings in his hand, thinking about the theory of lace. He listened to the cellist draw notes out of her instrument like genies from a lamp. He imagined the lacework that connected him to everyone there and to those who were not there. He could still feel his parents' celestial spirits, and it comforted him. He was bonded to them by a force that could not be broken. He glanced around at the worshipers in the sanctuary.

"This is the lace workshop," Dr. Zickel thought. "This is the where the Lace Maker invites us to learn Her craft. This is where we acquire the pins and bobbins and learn to mend the pattern."

A few days later, Dr. Gibbous Asteroid Belt Zickel and Dr. Linda Syzygy Leib met in Santiago, Chile, to prepare their presentation for the Astronomy and Astrophysics Conference. It was the first night of Sukkot, and they were invited by a mutual friend for a festive meal. After shaking the *lulav* and *etrog* in all directions and dining on corn casserole and vegetable empanadas, they sat in the booth talking, singing, and looking up at the moon and stars shining through the leafy branches that made the sukkah's roof. There was nowhere in the world like the Chilean countryside to look at the night sky.

"When I was a child," Dr. Zickel said, "I asked my parents why the night is dark when there is so much light coming toward us all the time."

"What did they say?" Dr. Leib asked.

"Become an astronomer and find out," he said.

"And what did you find out?" Dr. Leib asked.

Dr. Zickel thought for a moment. "That prayer, repentance, and *tzedakah* can repair torn lace."

"You know what I think?" Dr. Leib asked.

"What?"

"The dark is there to help us find the light."

They sat together under the waxing moon, feeling their connections weave delicate patterns across space and time.

QUESTIONS

1. What do you feel when you look at the stars?
2. What are the influences that create your wobble?
3. Lace theory suggests that every transgression, whether intentional or unintentional, necessitates repair. Do you agree?
4. Dr. Zickel is comfortable as a person of science and as a person of faith. Do you consider science and faith to be contradictory?

The Radiant Window

A Zoharic Journey

> *There are many mysteries connected with "I."*
> —*Zohar* 2, 25a, *Va-eira* 5:64, p. 1063[1]

T HE PARTY IS JUST AS YOU EXPECTED. Clinking flutes of fizzy champagne, chiming laughter, and you, uncomfortably nodding at those around you. You don't know many people here, at your cousin's wedding. Your parents passed away years ago. You lost touch with these people long ago. It is a surprise you were even invited and a bigger surprise that something compelled you to say yes.

You may be related by blood to many of these people and have the same bump on the nose, the same dimple on the left side of your face when you smile, and the same sensitivity to dairy, but you still feel untethered. Looking around, you can see nature at work, but inside you feel that others got a lot more nurture than you did. You wonder if you would feel more connected to these people if your parents had been different, more present. You think about your journey. How you fell in love when you were young, got married, raised a family. But now you've been divorced, what, six years? Your own children are in college. You've lived a lot of life already. So why do you still feel so lost?

A magic carpet of hors d'oeuvres sails by, and a vapor of fried phyllo pulls you from your reverie. That's when you notice a woman leaning against a

---

1. Unless otherwise indicated, all *Zohar* quotes are adapted from Isaiah Tishby's *The Wisdom of the Zohar: An Anthology of Texts*, vols. 1–3, trans. David Goldstein (London: Littman Library of Jewish Civilization, 1989).

marble mantle. She looks the way you feel—out of place. You excuse yourself from a polite circle of distant relatives and weave your way toward her.

You don't remember seeing her at the ceremony, which is surprising because she is hard to miss in her black catsuit and velvet cape with deep purple lining. She is tall and sturdy, as if carved from the marble she leans against. She has a large head and a high brow. Her glossy black hair nearly reaches her hips, and a long unpainted nail taps her empty champagne flute. You wonder if she is a magician or a performer of some kind. You used to know some magic tricks. She notices you and shifts her weight.

You introduce yourself and ask, "Who are you?"

"Now there's a question to love and hate," she says. Her eyes flash from violet to black.

"Very true," you say. "I hate that question."

She extends her hand to you and says, "As far as I know, I am Bahira."

You take her hand and nod your head, saying, "And as far as I know is honestly not very far, I'm afraid. Would you like some more champagne?"

✿ ✿ ✿

The blessed Holy One made the earth like a pregnant person who subsequently produces young from within. When the earth was created, it was pregnant with all the elements that had penetrated it, and they subsequently brought forth all its progeny.
      —*Zohar Chadash, B'reishit*, v. 558, p. 573

"I am pregnant," Bahira says, putting her flute on the mantle and resting her hands over her belly. "Aren't you?" she asks.

Your face flushes and you laugh throatily. "At my age? Not possible!"

"Goodness," Bahira smiles, looking you up and down. "I see."

"Is your husband here?" you ask.

"Didn't you see him in the ceremony?"

"I'm sorry," you say. "I don't even know what he looks like."

"That's a shame," she says. "He was the naked one, but for all his clothes."

Despite the odd conversation, you are thoroughly amused by Bahira, and you laugh behind closed lips.

She smiles and says, "You know, the doctors might deny it, but I see that you are pregnant too. If you don't realize it soon, you increase the chance of harming what wants to be born."

Bahira increases her volume a decibel. "We are all pregnant, and the sooner we realize that, the healthier our future will be. Our lives conceal a life that connects us to the great mystery, and we are only due the day we die. Know this secret and see if *your* eyes don't radiate darkly." Bahira says louder still, "Come, everyone, be joyful in your pregnancy! Be full of life!"

Bahira turns her full-mooned face to you.

You say, "Having met you, I am pregnant with expectancy."

"Oh, my heavens! We are full of light!"

How does one come to share in such supreme delights? By giving hospitality.
—*Zohar* 2, 155b, *T'rumah* 47:535, p. 737–38

A tray hovers between you and Bahira, and you both take a tomato tartlet. Bahira asks, "So what brings you to this celebration?"

"It's my cousin's wedding. My cousin who is once, twice, maybe three times removed. Actually," you confess, "it's me who's been removed. A long series of wrong turns. Never mind. And you?"

"I know your cousin's parents. So, I am sure they have you nicely set up at the local Marriott."

"Yup," you answer. "Right next to the ice machine."

"How chilling!" Bahira says. Then she adds casually, "I have a house among the trees. Won't you be my guest? I won't take no for an answer. I have so many empty rooms."

You are taken aback by the offer.

"Ah, I see I've frightened you," she says.

There is something about Bahira—her stature, her rippling cape, her odd conversation—that is a little frightening and also a little foreign. She has a kind of royal otherness. And yet, she is simultaneously strangely familiar. She reminds you of yourself, but how could that be? You are nothing like her. There is a mirror over the mantle behind her, and you see your reflection. When you see yourself through your own eyes, you see a tired face, lined with sadness and longing. But for a moment you see yourself through her eyes, and you see depth you didn't know you had.

"Are we related?" you ask, even though she doesn't have the same family bump on the nose or dimple in the cheek.

"I am going to tell you something that is going to be hard for you to believe." Bahira leans in closer to you. "I worked for your parents in their restaurant. I brought you Shirley Temples with extra cherries from the bar. You were such a soulful child. You were more soul than body, if that makes any sense. I was the one who told your cousins to invite you. I wanted to see you after all these years. I heard about what happened to your parents. I should have looked for you long ago, but I was in my own labyrinth."

You are stunned. You try to process Bahira's words. "But that doesn't make sense," you say, as your mind struggles over the math of it all.

"Yes, you are thinking, if you are fifty, and I looked after you sometimes, that would make me . . ."

You look at her. She seems young, maybe thirty-five at best. Then again, she had lied when she said she was pregnant. Maybe she is exaggerating. Yet, at the dim periphery of your mind, you feel like maybe you *do* remember her, but you remember her faintly—not as a steady presence as she suggests, but as a visitation. A distant dream.

A string trio begins setting up nearby. Bahira then says, "There are people you meet occasionally who appear to you as royalty from that distant part of yourself. They remind you of that palace that is rightfully yours. They remind you of how vast an empire is your spirit and how little of its resources you tap."

"Are you one of those royals?" She only smiles enigmatically.

You think of the ice machine waiting beside your hotel room door, readying itself to rumble you awake in the night. And then you decide.

"I would love to be your guest," you say.

✡ ✡ ✡

Whoever . . . cleaves to the blessed Holy One, God immediately loves that person, and treats that person in the kindest way.
  —*Zohar 2,* 111b, *Mishpatim* 3:323, p. 526

You say your necessary goodbyes and well-wishes to the couple, then join Bahira at the door. She leads you toward her home by way of the forest. In the deepening twilight, the trees arch over you in a latticework of rose gold. Your breath quickens—not from the beauty surrounding you or even the exertion of this walk, but rather from fear.

"Aren't you afraid of wild animals?" you ask. You struggle to keep up. You are not accustomed to navigating the woods, and your dress shoes are not comfortable enough for a hike. Your clothes catch on twigs and leaves.

"Afraid?" she says. "I admire them. Lions and tigers and bears, oh my! How wondrous are God's works. But do you know which creature is the most cunning? The real king of the jungle?" She turns around suddenly.

"Which?" you ask, catching your breath.

"The one we haven't discovered yet."

Eventually you slow down, and you walk for a while listening to the sounds of the forest. Pine needles tickle your arms as you walk. You think about all the places you've never been. The things you've never discovered. When was the last time you walked through the woods? You can't remember. You always had a restlessness, a wanderlust; however, you never answered it. And you don't really regret it. You raised two wonderful children, each of whom is brave and strong in their own way. You are proud of them. Sometimes you wonder if they would have benefited if you had in fact answered the call of your heart, left the desk job and taken more chances. What if you had had exhilarating experiences to share with them—would you have been a better role model? If you had been more fun, would the marriage have lasted? You stop yourself then. You stayed alive, you were always present for them, and that's more than your parents did.

"Is there anywhere left to discover?" you ask Bahira.

Bahira laughs lightly and says, "Plenty. I've been to the edge of the field. But what's most incredible are the regions inside. The inner-life. Self-discovery. Most people are so wispy they'd sizzle up and die if they neared their own burning core." She looks at you slyly. "Better to keep walking and leave self-discovery alone and other-discovery to someone else."

Something in her tone makes you think she is offering you a challenge.

There is not a single blade of grass in the entire world that is not controlled by a star or planet in the firmament.
—*Zohar 2, 171b, T'rumah 86:835, p. 664*

Bahira says, "In the heart of the forest there is an orchard, and in the heart of the orchard is my home."

You sense the air change, and the woods open into a large clearing. The night is tinged with a scent of citrus. Neat rows of trees roll out before you, and as you traipse through a wide aisle, you discern in the brightening moonlight lemon, orange, grapefruit, pomegranate, peach, olive, fig, almond, prickly pear, and palm.

There, in the middle of the orchard, rises a large house with radiant windows.

"Anyone home?" you ask.

"Not yet," she says.

"You left the lights on."

"No. The windows glow."

You are curious. As you near the house, you see that it has two stories. The first story has many doors with no windows. The second story has a window corresponding to each door below. Bahira says, "All the doors are locked so we must climb through a window."

Here there is a door through which secrets may be revealed, but one should reveal them only to the wise in heart, to those who know how to interpret them.
—*Zohar Chadash, Yitro*, v. 333, p. 492

"Don't you have the key?" you ask.

"Yes, but I don't carry it with me. I'm afraid someone will take it."

Before you can offer to help get into the house, Bahira draws a ladder from behind a tree and expertly unfolds it against the house. She says, "Blessed is a person's prayer, for it becomes a ladder.[2] Go ahead—the window is unlocked."

"I thought you were afraid of people getting in."

"I'm not afraid of people getting in. I am afraid of them having my key."

"Maybe there are people inside right now," you say, exposing your anxiety.

"Not likely. The truth is no one ever looks for a ladder."

The ten rungs of the ladder are far apart, so you stretch your arms and extend your legs to make your way to the top. Once there, you peer into the radiant window, and to your amazement you see that the curtain inside is drawn closed. You touch the glass. Indeed, the window itself is glowing and there is no light at all from within. You glance beneath you and see Bahira gracefully climbing her way up the ladder. You slide the window open easily.

---

2. *Zohar Chadash, Sifra Tanina*, v.43, p. 1056.

You wriggle over the ledge, under the curtain, and onto the floor. As you draw open the curtain for Bahira, you see that the window is glowing from the inside too. Through the glass, you can see the whole orchard as if it were day; but when you raise the glass, it is clearly night.

Bahira tumbles in like a gymnast and brushes herself off. Her hair has fallen over her face, and as she draws the silky strands aside, all the curtains in the house do the same. All at once the house is flooded with illusory daylight, and you remain on the floor, too astounded to speak.

"It is an unusual thing about windows, you know. They are the thinnest, most delicate veil between here and the other side. And they look out and in simultaneously. Can you do that? Of course not! You would become altogether mad! And yet the window does this with grace and quiet, as if it were nothing at all."

You sit there in shock, denying that everything you have seen is real. It is not possible that she opened all the curtains by brushing her hair aside. It is not possible that the windows are glowing, turning the night into day. You tell yourself you must be overly tired from the trek here. You tell Bahira that you think you need to lie down.

"Soon enough," Bahira says. "We are only here for a short while. Let's not spend all of it asleep."

✡ ✡ ✡

A house is essential, so that a house can exist below on the model of the house above, to enable the upper abode to descend to the lower abode.
                                        —*Zohar 2, B'shalach 25:336*, p. 1018

Bahira helps you up and shows you around the house. The house is large and circular, with an open courtyard in the center. Around the outside there are forty doors on the first floor, with forty corresponding radiant windows above them on the second floor. Around the inside, there are ten doors below, with ten corresponding radiant windows above. The second story has a ceiling of glass, which slants down toward the surrounding orchard. This glass is not radiant but naturally exposes the star-splayed sky.

Looking up you comment, "It must make a fantastic crystal patter when it rains."

She smiles and says, "I am so glad you are here! Yes, I love when it rains. The whole house rings like a bell!"

The entire second story is unbroken by walls, making it one large circular room. Its floor is a deep purple, and its walls are baby-chick yellow. The windows are all heavily draped with light-blue curtains.

"This is my bedroom," Bahira guides you. The only furniture here are bright-red overstuffed armchairs, spaced every four windows, and a large, bright-red bed piled with pillows.

Bahira shows you where to find the bathrooms and a small kitchen, cobalt blue, toppling with baskets of fresh vegetables and fruit.

"Anything you want from this house is yours," she says.

Bahira leads you past the forty small guest rooms, each with their own separate door to the outer orchard.

"Was this a hotel?" you ask.

"Oh no! My goodness! I designed it this way. I am always pining for guests. Come, let me show you the courtyard."

☆ ☆ ☆

And there is one fountain, hidden and concealed, for them all, which waters and saturates them, and they all produce fruits and plants. There is one garden below them, and this garden is protected on all sides.
—Zohar 3, 201b, Balak 27:310, p. 143

As soon as you step into the inner courtyard with Bahira you are knocked dizzy with perfumes. Stone paths wind through a blossoming garden toward the center where a spring is bubbling.

She explains, "There is an underground river that flows underneath my house and nourishes all of my roots."

You admire the spring when all at once, in the moonlight, you see a person who looks exactly like you standing in the middle of the water, looking back at you. You are visibly startled. Bahira touches your shoulder and says, "Ah, you see my tower."

Rising out of the center of the spring is a tall tower, which—because it is mirrored—appears at first not to be there at all. It almost disappears into the starry night so that you cannot see how tall it really is. There is a little iron bridge that arches over the spring to the door of the tower, which is bolted with a chunky iron lock.

"What is in the tower?"

"A spiral staircase. Nothing more."

"Do you ever climb the staircase?" you ask.

"Just before dawn, but only for a glimpse." Something in her tone tells you that you should not ask any more about the tower. You glance toward it, curiosity flooding your mind, but you remain silent.

You return with Bahira to the upstairs and sink into a red armchair. Bahira hands you a date, which disintegrates into honey in your mouth.

She says, "These dates are from the orchard nourished by the underground river."

"Where does the river lead?"

"Would you believe that it leads to the Garden of Eden?"

You peer out the windows at the lush garden on the one side and the rows of trees on the other and nod, "Yes, I would."

You slumbering beings of the lower world, with the closed pupils, awake! Turn darkness into light and bitterness into sweetness before you come here. Every day expect the light.
—*Zohar* 1, 4a, Introduction 10:53-54, p. 167–68

Morning sunlight beams through the keyhole and tickles you between the eyes. You get up and stretch, slip into your wrinkled-up clothes, and head into the garden. Bahira wishes you a good morning. She is watering her hanging plants.

"Put out your hands," she says.

You do, and she sprinkles them with cold water from her watering can.

"We want these to be fruitful too," she says. Then she waters her own hands.

You feel happy, soaking in the morning sun. Bahira brings a tray of halved grapefruit, peach bread, date honey, and apple almond tea.

You ask Bahira, "Where did you get your name?"

"Which one? The one that I told you or the one that I do not know?"

"Let's start with the one that you told me."

"Ah yes, my outermost name. I am called Bahira, which means 'concealed brilliance revealed.' A deeper calling, however, is what you call yourself. What do you call yourself?"

"I never call myself."

"Your true calling is that name by which you were called long before you were born. It is nearly impossible to recall your true calling. But if you manage to discover it, you will become whole."

"What do you call yourself?"

"You cannot know this name," she cautions, then returns to watering her plants.

You pass the morning in the garden and the afternoon in the orchard helping Bahira prune trees and collect fruit.

As you sit together over lunch, you let her know that you will get ready to return to the Marriott and then home.

"Absolutely not," she says. "Stay. Stay for as long as you want. I've already called the hotel and arranged for your things to be delivered here."

You want to protest. You are not used to being away from home this long or being managed this way. But then you think about your empty apartment, with all the little reminders of your children, who are away at college. They aren't coming home for spring break. Summer is months away. You are due many vacation days from work. There really is no reason to leave, except to rush back to your comfort zone. This is a challenge to you, and it is exciting and energizing. So you stay.

You spend day after day this way with Bahira, chatting over meals and tea, sometimes light conversation, sometimes profound. One time, when you are gathering almonds from the row of almond trees, Bahira exclaims, "There is nothing I love more than a nut tree." She picks up a green almond as if it were a nugget of gold. "Here I hold a tree within a nut within a tree within a nut! This is what we are, you know, an adult within a child within an adult within a child. How many worlds there are in our littlest finger!"

"You once said that we are all pregnant," you remember.

Bahira laughs and twirls, her purple skirt fanning into a giant bell. She tosses her basket of nuts into the air. You duck and cry out that the sky is falling.

She laughs and says with her face blushing, "Not as long as my tower is in place."

You grasp her shoulders and beg, "What is in that mirrored tower?"

She shakes herself loose. She looks annoyed. "I told you. A spiral staircase."

Your curiosity burns. Later, in the inner courtyard, you stare at the tower for an answer, but it only shows you yourself looking back.

Just before the day begins to lighten, it is very dark, pitch black.
—*Zohar* 2, 46a, *B'shalach* 4:48, p. 1139

One night you determine to discover the secret of the tower. You creep into the courtyard and lay flat in the flower bed, hoping to witness Bahira enter the tower. Your heart beats rapidly. Eventually, you see her drift out of the house toward the tower, unlock it, and slip in, closing the door behind her. A few minutes later she comes out, locks the door, and goes back into the house. You return to your bed and ponder this mystery. You cannot get into the tower. You cannot learn much more just watching her enter and leave the tower. She had said she goes in for a glimpse. A glimpse of what?

Then, you suddenly remember what Bahira had said when you first came to her home. "The truth is, no one ever looks for a ladder." At once, you understand. While we are looking for one thing, we really should be looking for another. Instead of staring at the tower, you determine to discover the secrets of the orchard. Whatever it is Bahira is glimpsing, it is out there.

The next night, you wait for Bahira to enter the tower again, and you rush upstairs. You duck behind a curtain and look through a radiant window, seeing the orchard as if it were day.

All is calm, quiet, when *whoosh*, a shadow darts from tree to tree. What is it? *Fring, pow.* Another, and another. You squint hard. You make out two little legs running speedily. *Zip*, there goes another, *shazoof*, and another, *vring*! At once, the orchard is filled with darting shadows. *Vip, woo, pop, swiff*, they are all over the place! You watch as the speedy *somethings* dart from tree to tree. Then you hurry back to your room before Bahira reenters the house.

The next night, you leave your bedroom and sit behind a tree in the orchard. All at once, the orchard is filled with creatures rushing. Are they children? Forest nymphs? Leprechauns? Spirits? They run too fast to be much more than a blur. Then, for a fraction of a second, one stops and glances up. Immediately it darts away, faster than before. Then another stops, glances up, and darts, then another, and another. Shadows dart all around you. You can't turn your head fast enough before they disappear behind trees. A thrill courses up your spine when one hides behind the very tree in which you are hiding! In a flash, it is gone. You can feel the wind from their rushing. You turn your attention to the top of the tower. It is difficult because it is nearly impossible to distinguish the outline of the mirrored tower from the sky. You stare and stare while all around you the orchard is a frenzy of motion.

Then it happens. A window appears at the top, and a curtain is drawn partly aside by a hand. Bahira shows her rainbowed face, her black-jewel eyes, and faint smile. The darting nymphs stop, glance up, and then *vroom* away faster than before. The curtain closes. The window disappears. The darting shadows fade before your eyes.

On the fourth night, you creep into the orchard and do some stretches against a tree, then a quick jog around the orchard to get your blood moving. You are ready. At the same time as the last two nights, the shadows appear. You dash after them, but they are so incredibly quick. The instant it takes your body to respond to a sighting, it is gone. You grow crazed. You feel them flash past. Every now and then you even feel one brush you or step on your foot, but you cannot catch one. You lunge and leap, sprint and careen into trees, swipe and dive—ugh! You are not lithe. They are too darn quick. You collapse.

Night after night, you play the same game. You run. A clumsy gladiator chasing bolts of lightning. After many weeks, however, you notice your body getting stronger. The running gets easier.

✡ ✡ ✡

When the most secret of secrets sought to be revealed, God made, first of all, a single point, and this became thought.
—*Zohar* I, 2a, Introduction 4:13, p. 331

At the end of the sixth week, an amazing thing happens. You are standing, tensed, ready to bolt, when one of the shadows collides into you! You swing around and grab its ankle. It squirms and struggles like a lizard, and you are afraid you might pull its little leg off. You wrestle with it until you finally manage to pin it under you. It is a wispy child with enormous eyes! "Where do you come from?" you demand.

The child is terrified and shaking. It cries, "From a cave in the forest."

"Where are you going?"

"I am on my way to be born. You must let me go before I'm too late!" The child's eyes stream giant tears.

"Are you a soul?" you ask.

"No," the child weeps. "I am a First Thought."

"Tell me your name."

"You must not know my original name!"

"Why do you come here every night?"

"We are different First Thoughts that come every night on our way to being born!"

"Why do you look up?"

"To see Concealed Brilliance Revealed. We glimpse her face and long for beauty, and it is for this longing that we bear the trials of the physical world. Let me go! I am going to die before I am born!"

You release your grip on the child, but just as it wriggles out from under you, you grasp its ankle and demand, "What about my name? What is my original name?"

"It cannot be voiced!" The child breaks free.

You call out after the shadowy child, "How can I find it?" but the child is gone across the orchard, faster than a blink.

Later in the afternoon, you ask Bahira how one might go about finding one's original name.

She says, "It is so far gone already. How many shells you would have to crack to find it!"

"How would one start?"

"Oh, my heavens, what a difficult question. It is the mystery of Creation, the question of who or what triggered it into being. How does one take a first thought and make it into something tangible and real?"

"Yes," you say, leaning forward. "How then, does a First Thought come into being?"

"Awakening below stimulates awakening above, and awakening above stimulates a yet higher world, until stimulus reaches the place where the lamp is to be lit, and it is lit."[3]

"I don't understand," you say.

"Knowing that you don't understand is the beginning of awakening," Bahira smiles. "Come, let's pick nuts and figs to make butters and jams."

You follow Bahira into the orchard, thinking about the running First Thoughts. You remember Bahira saying at your cousin's wedding that her husband was "the naked one, but for all of his clothes." You consider this and then say quietly, "Your husband, he is a First Thought."

---

3. *Zohar* 2, 244a, *Va-y'chi* 69:715, p. 1042.

Bahira turns. She smiles her pregnant smile and her eyes flash. She says, "There are First Thoughts, and then there is the Original Thought. The Original Thought is beyond sequence and cannot be included in first, second, or third. This thought is concealed with the thickest garment of all."

That night you sneak out into the orchard and wait for the First Thoughts to appear. This time, instead of trying to catch them, you just run with them. You do this for many nights, and your running becomes lighter. You hurdle over low branches, leap and fling your body into a midair twirl, diving into somersaults while First Thoughts zing past you.

Eventually, your running becomes dancing. You whip your body about ecstatically, like a blade of grass in a windstorm. You are filled with joy. Your upper body and your lower body are equally strong. You realize that you are ready—ready to leave Bahira's home, leave the garden and mirrored tower, leave the orchard bustling with life—ready to continue your journey.

In the morning you tell Bahira that it is time for you to go. She embraces you tightly and then pulls back, looking at you kindly. "You want to ask me something," Bahira says.

You take a deep breath. "You have been exceedingly generous, Bahira," you say. "I hesitate to ask for anything more."

"Surely, you have found your courage and strength to do so," Bahira coaxes. "My good friend, ask."

"I have come to learn that when you speak, you choose your words carefully, and your words contain many truths. You always mean what you say."

"Indeed."

"On the first night of my stay here, you said, 'Anything you want from this house is yours.'"

"I did. And that is true."

Your heart beats faster and you start to shake. How will she respond to your request? "A radiant windowpane," you say.

You are afraid to look at Bahira's face. You look down, ashamed of wanting too much. And then you hear her: "What an absolutely perfect request. I shall give it to you, and you too will know light in the dark."

Rabbi Abba said: This cave is crowned with words of Torah. . . . Rabbi Shimon said: I saw from the walls of the cave that the Shechinah was here.
—*Zohar* 1, 244b, *Vay-y'chi* 71:730 and 245b, *Vay-y'chi* 71:737, p. 366-367

You head off into the forest to find the Cave of the First Thoughts. There, you imagine, you will find your true name and calling. You walk well into the night, holding the radiant windowpane before you, so that you can see the forest as by day.

After many days of wandering and foraging, one evening between dusk and dark, through the radiant windowpane you see a glimmer in a rock. You rush to the glimmer and discover that it is a cave, and inside is a river of light. This must be the same underground river that nourishes Bahira's garden! You wade against the stream deeper into the cave, eager to reach its source. You tuck the radiant windowpane into your backpack and swim with long strokes. You feel as if your body is constricting while your spirit is expanding.

After a few hours, you see a glow in the distance. You sprint and splash to the finish. The low-ceilinged cave suddenly opens into a vast green and golden space. From the top of a high rock cascades a waterfall in a rainbow-flecked shower. The air glistens with spray. Trees hang with heavy flowers like deep bells, and their branches droop with the weight of fruit.

You are floored by the beauty. You stand, stunned in your place. Then you are snapped back into consciousness by a crescendo of giggling. A group of happy First Thoughts are sitting nearby in a circle, playing a game. They notice you and look confused. You take out the radiant windowpane and extend it to them. Slowly, the First Thoughts approach, taking the gift.

"Is this the Garden of Eden?" you wonder aloud.

The First Thoughts don't answer you. Instead, they slowly draw closer to you, hesitantly at first, then with more courage. When they see you intend no harm, they climb onto your shoulders, one by one, to cannonball into the water. You decide to join them in playing in the river of light. After frolicking in the river, you emerge sparkling clean, and you lay on the grass. The children emerge, too, and join you on the plush riverbank.

You ask the First Thought beside you, "Can you tell me, please, what is my true name?"

All the happy First Thoughts jump up and rush to the flowering fruit tree. They all stand on tippy-toes, reaching for the farthest flower but do not pick it. Then they laugh and tumble beside you.

One of them tugs at your hand and says, "Now you understand!"

"But I don't understand at all," you say.

Then a First Thought says, "It cannot be voiced."

You again ask them to tell you your true name.

They start teasing you. "Silly earthling!"

"Why am I silly?"

"Your true name should be Silly One!"

"Is it?"

"No!" they tumble back with laughter.

"What is it then?"

"Every morning you ignore your First Thought!"

"What is my First Thought?" I ask.

"You know! You know!"

"My First Thought every morning is to find my true name."

"Oh, no! Before that thought, before you are fully awake, your *very* First Thought. Your First Thought is to go home!"

"Go home! Go home!" They all cheer together.

It is true. You hadn't fully realized it. You desperately want to go home. They are right. Just before you are fully awake, you have a sense of wanting to go home, but you've suppressed it.

You begin to sob. You crumple over. Tears splash onto your hands. The First Thoughts are a little frightened by this display. They rush over to you and stroke your back.

"We will show you the way."

The good deeds that a person performs in this world are made into a glorious and precious garment to wear in the world-to-come.
—*Zohar* 3, 101a, *Emor* 40:232, p. 1476

You sit in your favorite chair with a quilted blanket tucked around you, a morning cup of apple cinnamon tea beside you. Your partner is walking out the door but stops for a moment to ask, "Do you want anything special from the store for your birthday tonight?"

"No thank you," you say. "I love you."

"Love you too."

Tonight, you and your partner will be having dinner together in front of the computer; children and grandchildren and Bahira will all Zoom in to toast your eightieth birthday. You gaze out the window at a squirrel padding around in the garden. It is looking for nuts it buried in the spring. The squirrel darts back and forth and reminds you of yourself so many years ago, in Bahira's orchard.

You remember that you did want something for tonight. Champagne. You think of calling your partner but then decide instead to go yourself. It will be nice to take a long walk and think about what it means to reach this milestone age.

You stroll through the neighborhood to the main street, appreciating the details all around: ivy climbing a brick chimney, a row of tulips along a stone wall, the shadows of a willow dancing against a weathered barn with a rooster weathervane on top. In town you stroll past the shops. There is a child sitting on a wall, blowing bubbles. A beautiful bubble whirling with rainbows floats just above the child. You stand on your toes, reaching for the bubble. Extending your finger, the bubble pops, and you and the child laugh.

The child then looks at you with a glimmering eye and says, "Aren't you...never mind. I thought at first I recognized you."

You startle at these words and repeat them to yourself: "I thought at first I recognized you." I thought at first. I thought . . . at first. A First Thought!

You ask, "Your first thought, when you saw me, was that you knew me. Who did you think I was?"

The child considers you for a moment and then says, "You reminded me of someone when you were reaching for the bubble. I was in an orchard once, and I remember."

Suddenly you understand what the First Thought meant when it told you your original name could not be voiced. It could not be voiced because it is not a word or a sound. Your name is a motion.

You remember when you had begged the First Thoughts, "Can you tell me, please, what is my true name?" They had all rushed to a flowering fruit tree. They all stood on tippy-toes, reaching for a flower, and then they told you, "Now you understand!" They were telling you your name. They were telling you that you were Reaching For.

"Like this?" you ask the child, reaching your hand up, "When I am reaching for . . ."

The child interrupts you and says, "Yes, yes! That's exactly who you are."

On the day when one's allotted span is completed, and one is about to leave the world, the day when the body is broken and the soul seeks to part from it, one is permitted to see what one was not allowed to see when one's body was healthy and in control.
                    —*Zohar* I, 79a, *Lech L'cha* 8:5, p. 844

You are overcome with a profound sense of understanding. You know who you are, and you feel a great sense of peace spread from your very core out over the landscape of your past, healing every memory it touches. That same sense of peace illuminates the future. You know who you are and what you have always been. You have found your calling. You are Reaching For. For what is not what matters. You reach for reaching higher. You reach for reaching closer. You reach for reaching deeper. You are Reaching For, and you are content in not always grasping the thing for which you reach. There are others whose true names are Grasp and Conquer, Learn and Teach. But you are Reaching For, and there is beauty, meaning, and courage in extending yourself in pursuit of the sunray that is always a little out of reach. You are filled with longing, and longing is the birthplace of poetry. You are pregnant with poetry, you realize, and you feel radiant.

And after a long journey, you have reached your place at last, your own home. You step over the threshold, sit down in your favorite chair, close your eyes, and marvel as your spirit expands past your body's mortal boundaries, reaching for its rebirth.

God made this world to match the world above, and whatever exists above has its counterpart below . . . and all is one.
                    —*Zohar* 2, 20a, *Sh'mot* 50:359, p. 569

QUESTIONS

1. Why do you think the author chose to write this story in the second person? How did it feel as a reader to step into the protagonist's shoes?

2. A First Thought says, "We glimpse her face and long for beauty, and it is for this longing that we bear the trials of the physical world." What is something that you hold onto that sustains you when you need it most?

3. Two of the central works of Jewish mysticism are *Sefer HaBahir* (*The Book of Brilliance*) and *Sefer HaZohar* (*The Book of Radiance*). Both propose to reveal the mysteries of the Torah. They are dense and esoteric, but studying them, especially the newer translations, one finds sparks of enlightenment. Both emphasize that the lower world (our world) matches the upper world (God's world). In other words, they are reflections of each other and essentially the same. Where do you encounter godliness in our world? Where do you have trouble recognizing godliness in our world?

4. The upper world can also represent the mind and soul, while the lower world can represent the body. What can we do in our lives to better align our mind, body, and soul?

The Goat Keeper

Part 1: Azarel

Now Mount Sinai was all in smoke, for the Eternal had come down upon it in fire; the smoke rose like the smoke of a kiln, and the whole mountain trembled violently.

—Exodus 19:18

AZAREL WORE LONG BLACK ROBES that billowed with pockets of air. They swallowed her sandaled feet in waves of thin gauze. Her head rose from her robes as a bird rises from dark waters, stretching to take flight. She carried a jar on her shoulder as she walked to the well, her robes rippling around her. She saw a man—a stranger—at the well.

"Peace be upon you," the man greeted Azarel as he drew water for his camel. "I am looking for a village where I can sell my spices. I have heard there is one nearby, but I don't know its name."

"Edge," Azarel answered, glancing over the camel laden with leather sacks. "It is beyond the dunes, toward the setting sun."

"You came from that direction," observed the stranger. "Would you like a ride there on your return?"

"No, thank you." Azarel approached and scratched the camel's neck. The camel knelt first on its forelegs and then lowered itself so it was resting on the ground. She patted its head and admired its long lashes. "I prefer to carry myself."

The stranger laughed. "I am Omar," he said, "and this is Jamali. Jamali doesn't usually lie down before new people we meet."

"I am Azarel," Azarel said. "Welcome to Edge, Omar and Jamali."

After filling her jar, Azarel walked toward Edge as the sun cast rosy shades over the desert. Smooth sheaths of chalk jutted high above her. The rolling landscape gradually drank up the light, except for a drop that clung moments longer atop a twisted peak. It appeared to Azarel as a glowing crown.

"Fire on the Mountain!" Azarel exclaimed. "You are my God!" She nestled her jug safely in the sand and bowed to the ground. "I betroth myself to You," she declared and then collected her jar. As she continued walking, she saw Omar and his camel riding past toward Edge.

✡ ✡ ✡

Through the dusty weaving that hung over the entrance to their dwelling, Azarel could see her father Korav talking with Omar. She stepped in.

"This is Omar," Korav said. "He is a dealer of spices. Omar, please meet my daughter, Azarel."

"Azarel," Omar said, extending his hand, "as fate would have it, we meet again."

"Dealer of spices indeed," Azarel said to her father, ignoring Omar's hand. She turned to Omar. "I can already tell that you sugar the brew too much."

"You are probably right," Omar laughed, dropping his arm. "Azarel," he said, "you could sting a bee with a sidelong glance." He continued pitching his wares to Korav.

✡ ✡ ✡

Korav invited Omar to stay the night to eat and rest before returning to his travels. Omar helped Azarel and her mother Zilpha to light oil lamps that were nestled all around in wall crevices. The lamps created soft circles of flickering light that clung to the walls, while a small fire in the middle lapped around a pan of sizzling lamb meat. The family moved about in the band of dim light between the fire and the wall, their edges frayed and their actions obscured by the reflected dance of the flames. Zilpha lay down handwoven rugs, and the family and their guest took their places around the fire. While dusk gradually became darkness and stars announced the arrival of night, a lazy peace rolled into the home.

"The seventh day is precious to us," Azarel said, smiling. She tossed two handfuls of incense onto the fire, and they disintegrated into a cloud of sparks. A delicate fragrance mingled with the aroma of lamb. Azarel reclined on a pillow and said, "For six days we sweat for survival, and at times we cannot help but look up from our toils and ask, 'To what end?'" She leaned forward, her face animated by the flames, "I am all things during the week; we all are. I am tipping the kettle, I am digging the sand, I am tending the sheep, I am drawing water from the well. On the seventh day I just am. I am that I am that I am. The seventh day teaches us that being, not doing, is the end."

"I am grateful for your hospitality," Omar said to the family. "Thank Pharaoh for these abundant blessings."

"Thank Pharaoh?" Zilpha said, looking around her. "What dish did Pharaoh bring?"

Korav could see Omar's confusion and said kindly, "Around here we thank the Fire on the Mountain."

"Are you Hebrews?" Omar asked and then added playfully, "Have you lost your way to Canaan?" Looking at Azarel's expression, he was sure he had offended her.

"It is possible we have," Korav said as he began to ladle the lamb into clay bowls filled with cooked lentils and grains. "What do you know of the Hebrews?"

"The legends were abundant. I remember my mother, tale-teller supreme, holding me on her lap and telling me of a strange people. Locust breeders, she called them."

"Oh really," Azarel said, her arms crossed.

Omar knew she was offended, but he didn't understand why. Korav encouraged him to say more, and so he added what he remembered, "They followed a great column of smoke. And they went to a mountain."

Azarel said, "Mount Sinai."

"And where are the Hebrews now?" asked Korav.

"They are building cities in Canaan, as far as I've been told."

The family was silent while they ripped pieces of warm bread to sop up the fatty juices that ran off the meat. Zilpha shook her head in disbelief. "Locust breeders, of all things."

Omar was confused.

Korav said, "My son, I was once like you. But I have come to know the Fire on the Mountain and the prophetess Geula."

"You are Hebrews, then," Omar confirmed. He had never met Hebrews before.

"I really do not know," Korav contemplated. "What makes one a Hebrew? Is it enough to have slaved under Pharaoh? Had one of the enslaved still been chained to a rock at the time of the Exodus, are his children Hebrews? Well, we were freed from Egypt, so I guess then we would be Hebrews. But then there is Mount Sinai. They say just having been witness to Sinai is enough, and then we would be Hebrews. But I wonder, because they also say they're the ones who received the word at Sinai. We were at Sinai. But when Geula stood at the foot of the mountain, before the rock trembling with fire and smoke, she exclaimed, 'We are about to receive and be received!' Her husband was afraid and could not bear to look. You must understand, his heart was as solid as your own, perhaps more so! He was a great and mighty soldier, but to stand before the mountain trembling violently with the presence of God, crown blazing on the top, to bear witness to such a spectacle, you cannot merely be human. You must yourself be mountain!"

"I do not know this legend," Omar said.

Zilpha smiled and said gently, "Oh Omar, you are so honest and open. But our story is no legend. It is not even ancient history!"

"We come from the line of Geula and Zelophehad," Azarel said. "On the day of Revelation, all the people gathered around the mountain, careful not to come too close. When the mountain began to shudder, the people were gripped by fear. A dark cloud enveloped Mount Sinai, and the people threw themselves on their faces. A blast of trumpets exploded from the mountain. There was lightning and thunder, and the whole mountain burst into flames and beamed with searing light. The mountain shook violently as their leader, Moses, began to climb.

"There was one man who was more afraid than anyone else: Zelophehad. He could not bear to witness such a terrifying sight. He was sure he would die. Zelophehad leapt off the ground, lifted his wife Geula in his arms, and shot forth like an arrow. He ran away from the blasting trumpets, away from the heat of the Fire on the Mountain, away from their daughters, their people, and their God. He ran with Geula's black hair streaming behind him like a banner. Geula wept the whole way, sobbing, 'Alas, the word we will never receive, and who will receive the deserter?' Zelophehad ran for days, until he finally collapsed. Geula tumbled from his arms and said, 'We have run so long, this surely must be the edge of the world.' Thus, they called the place Edge."

Azarel added, "Geula left Zelophehad there in Edge and set out alone to return to the mountain and find the Hebrew tribe of Manasseh, where they were from. She went to find her daughters, whom they had left behind. Blinded by hunger and thirst, she collapsed, alone and defeated. And then she heard a voice. The voice said, 'What troubles you, Geula? Your daughters are strong and wise, and they will be leaders. All will know their names. As for you, you have conceived and will give birth to a son, and you shall name him Mehar, for you have come from the mountain. Return to Edge and know that one day, a child of your descendants will help the people and save them.'"

"And you are of the line of Mehar?" Omar asked.

"We are of the line of Geula," Zilpha corrected. "And Azarel is the child of her descendants."

"My mother is convinced I am the one who will help the people. Me, among all my cousins," Azarel said. "That is why she named me Azarel, which means 'God helped.'"

"She has the light in her," Zilpha said. "I see it. Animals know it. Would you believe when she was an infant, a falcon came to the basket she lay in and brought her a sprig of sage?"

Omar thought about his camel Jamali lying down before her, and he nodded. "I can believe it."

Korav was the first to put down his plate. He said, "From the moment they turned their backs on the Fire on the Mountain, I would argue, they were cut off, and their line is their own. So no, we are not Hebrews. The Hebrews, like you said, are building cities in Canaan. No, we are Edge. That is what I would say, but of course, I am just a straggler to this young tradition. I married Zilpha and converted. Still, I have never received visions of Geula. But if I did, I would thank her for putting lightning and thunder into the hearts of my loved ones."

Omar felt himself grow heavy with the warmth of the food and the heat of the day's travels. Korav prepared a bed for him, and Omar stepped outside to get his sleep clothes from his belongings. He stood next to his camel and looked out over the valley. It was too dark to see shapes in the distance, but the half-moon allowed for shimmering hints of the depth and height in the landscape. "A comfort to see you," he said to his camel Jamali. When he went back inside, he lay down on the soft green mat and barely uttered his heartfelt thanks before drifting to sleep.

Part 2: Ezrael

Aaron shall take the two he-goats and let them stand before the Eternal at the entrance of the Tent of Meeting; and he shall place lots upon the two goats, one marked for the Eternal and the other marked for Azazel. Aaron shall bring forward the goat designated by lot for the Eternal which he is to offer as a purgation offering; while the goat designated by lot for Azazel shall be left standing alive before the Eternal, and to make expiation with it and to send it off to the wilderness for Azazel.
—Leviticus 16:7–10

Azarel was working on her loom late one afternoon, her mother weaving by her side. Her father was with Omar, tending the sheep. Omar had decided to stay in Edge a while longer and had set up his tent in the shade of the cliff on which Azarel's family lived.

Suddenly, Azarel heard a child calling her name. It was the voice of a child, but it was coming from far away. Still, Azarel heard it clearly, as if the voice were right in her ear.

"Do you hear that?" she asked her mother.

"Hear what?" Zilpha said. "The sheep bleating?"

Azarel didn't exactly hear it either. She *felt* it. And it wasn't sheep. Whatever it was, it rattled her so much that she stood up and stepped out of the dwelling to see where it was coming from. Outside, she heard her name more loudly, felt its resonance more deeply. So she began to walk toward the source, walking faster and faster with each step, until she was running. She stumbled and fell on one knee, but she was up and running again in an instant. Soon, she had left Edge. She followed the voice, turning around a dune, across a flat stretch of cracked land, between jutting cliffs, climbing up a rocky mound. A sharp stone cut her toe, but it did not slow her. By now, her throat felt raw as she struggled to pull in air as she ran. Her eyes were nearly blind with sweat from her brow. Still the voice called to her, filled with agony. Azarel's legs ached and her arms were beginning to feel limp, but she gritted her teeth and drove herself harder. "Almost there, almost there," she thought without knowing where "there" was. She was dizzy with thirst. Her armband pinched her as her arms swelled with heat. Her hair was plastered around her neck. Finally, she collapsed, gasping for air. A fit of coughing racked her body, and her heart felt as if it would explode. When she lifted her eyes, she saw that she was on the edge of a cliff. Had she not collapsed at that moment, she would have tumbled down and broken her neck. Azarel scrambled back from the edge. The voice that was calling remained just as strong, and Azarel knew she had to continue following it.

It was a dangerously steep slope, but Azarel collected herself and began to descend, clutching onto ridges and feeling for footholds. Halfway down, Azarel's robes got in her way, and her foot slipped. She almost panicked. She pressed her cheek to the rock and whispered, "Fire on the Mountain, help me!" She swung her legs and found a cleft, where she rested for a moment before continuing down.

Finally, Azarel's feet felt the ground below, and she let go of the cliff. She had not anticipated that the ground would have such a sharp slope where it met the cliff, and she rolled over backward before finding herself facedown with a mouthful of sand. She raised her head and spit it out. Her body ached, but Azarel hardly noticed. She was overcome with a different sensation. She felt someone there, watching her.

Azarel stood. Despite the feeling of being watched, she felt calm. She wiped her nose and walked with her shoulders back and her chin high. She wove through pillars of rock. Until she saw it.

There before her, waiting for her, was a beautiful creature with golden eyes and a halo over its head radiating in the twilight.

She approached slowly, entranced. As Azarel came closer, she could see the creature had a long white beard that touched the ground. A step further and she could discern the creature's hooves. When she was but a couple of handbreadths from its face, she could see the horizontal pupils in its golden eyes.

It was a goat; however, it was unlike any goat she'd ever seen. Perhaps, she wondered, it was part angel.

And then, in a voice as clear and hollow as breath through a flute, the goat spoke, "I have run many days to find you."

As far back as she could remember, Azarel's mother had told her that she was the descendant in Geula's prophecy. And while animals had never spoken to her before in a language she understood, she had always felt a relationship with them. Doves would land and sit beside her, singing their special songs. A family of gazelles circled her when she was a child. Recently, an ostrich followed her for an entire moon cycle wherever she went. Perhaps this was why she was not stunned to hear the goat talk. She realized that in a way she had been expecting something like this.

Azarel sat before the goat, and the goat sat as well. The halo, she realized, was its horns, clear as glass and touching at the top to form a nearly perfect circle. The goat began to tell its story.

"My mother was a beautiful goat who grazed by the shores of the river Jordan. Birds made their nests between her shoulder blades and whispered songs under her ears. Almond trees showered her with pink and white blossoms whenever she passed. God sent a cloud to protect her in the night. She was the most beautiful goat in all the land.

"My mother had twins in her womb, and the pain became too great to bear. She cried out, 'Blessed One, generous and merciful, why do I live if it is so?' God answered her, 'You have two goats in your womb, and they will be My messengers of peace. One will bear the sins of humankind on its back. The other will fall under the knife and be gathered unto Me.'

"My mother birthed us when the sun was high, in emerald grasses dotted with orange poppies. My mother's milk was smooth and sweet as cream. We frolicked about, my brother and I, and the sun always lingered on our heads a bit longer than the day lasted.

"One day we saw three men approaching. They came to prod and investigate the herd. They pulled at the lips of the goats. They examined under eyelids. They lifted their tails and inspected their bellies. When the men came upon my brother and me, they rejoiced and danced about. My mother did not cry. She told us, 'The day has come. Do not be afraid.'

"They brought us to the house on the hill, which gleamed in the distance. Thousands were gathered with prayers on their lips. When they saw us, the musicians put down their instruments. A majestic priest in flowing garb came to greet us with the words 'Holy unto God,' and we felt God was there. The priest led my brother up the white stairs. My brother's hooves clip-clopped behind the priest. His head was held high.

"At that moment I was led away. I was led to the farthest gate of the

House. Hands were laid upon my head. The gate was lifted before me. The men in white robes urged me to run. I cried, 'I will not leave the House of the Eternal to go into that wilderness,' and then my eyes became my brother's eyes, and I saw the flash of the blade, and a searing pain shot through my neck. In fear, I leapt from the House and I ran. As I ran, I felt a fire on my back, but nothing was there. I felt people straddled upon my back, kicking my sides. I felt children jumping on my head. I felt the blood drain from my neck where there was no cut. I lost sense of who I was or where I was. I ran for days until I began to sense that I was no longer running away, but running toward. I was running toward you."

Azarel wrapped her arms around the goat and stroked its silky hair. "I have been running toward you too," she whispered into its ear. She pulled back and looked into its golden eyes. "I see the pain in your eyes. I feel the suffering in your heart." She combed her fingers through its beard. She thought about the prophetess Geula and the monumental task she had accepted, to establish a new line far from her people. She, like the goat, had been thrust into the wilderness, at the moment of Revelation. And the Fire on the Mountain had told her to stay in Edge.

"There is a reason you came to Edge," Azarel told the goat. "There is a reason you came to me. We've been told that there would be a day that the people would need help. I think this is that day. I will keep you safe. The pain they placed on your head, we will contain it. We will hold the suffering together. We will bind it in bonds of love. You will be my goat, and I will be your keeper."

"Your name shall no longer be Azarel," the goat said, "but Ezrael, for you are the Goat Keeper—the *Ez* Keeper."

Ezrael's goat was three times as large as the heartiest goat gathered at the well. Ezrael walked through the flocks, slow and regal, with the goat and its majestic crown sailing through the sea of fleece. Its horns were like the circle of light that often circumfuses a full moon. The shepherds stared, astounded. They had never seen a goat so large or one with horns that shone. Omar, however, was not surprised. Somehow it all made sense. He remembered Zilpha saying that their story was no legend. He understood that now. This was the wellspring of legends, right here, right now. It wasn't ancient history.

He could feel his faith in the Pharaohs fading before the mysterious Fire on the Mountain. As Ezrael watered the otherworldly creature, Omar knew that she was this goat's keeper. He made a twofold vow to himself: to stay in Edge to watch over her, and to stay out of her way.

Omar surveyed the green wadi snaking its way through the rolling hills. From here he could see six large prismatic rings casting rainbows all around. Omar never ceased to be amazed by the incredible appearance of Ezrael's goats. A new one joined her herd each year at the same time. Ezrael told him that one was sent into the wilderness each year by priests in a great temple as part of a ritual of atonement.

Over the years, rumors spread about Ezrael's goats, and there developed many folktales. Some said the goats were secretly princes under a spell. Others said they were visiting angels. Some believed they were messengers of Hathor, the Egyptian goddess of love. After hearing the stories so many times, one tribe was inspired to plot a heist. If indeed the horns were made of diamonds, their eyes of gold, and their size extraordinary, they could bring fortune. What use were they in the hands of some woman from Edge? And they figured, if the horns are not diamond and the eyes are not gold, they would roast the stolen goats over a bonfire and enjoy their meat.

Meanwhile, Ezrael settled under a date palm. It was early morning and the shadows were still long and cool. Each year a new goat arrived with a similar story, having been exiled from the House of God. She closed her eyes, listening to her herd of scapegoats as they spoke with each other. They shared stories about their brothers. They wondered why their brothers were chosen to climb the altar while they were sent here. They spoke about Ezrael and how she soothed their anguish with her gentle listening and filled their hearts with hope. No one else heard their stories and conversation. It was a gift handed only to her, and she attributed it to the prophetess Geula. Suddenly, Ezrael heard a rustle and her eyes snapped open. People—strangers—were descending into the wadi. Thieves! She bolted upright, and one of the goats rushed toward her, flipping her onto its back. She grasped its horns and they started running, the other scapegoats running alongside. The thieves chased them, but the goats were faster. Then Ezrael heard galloping. Hunters on horses came around a bend to cut off Ezrael and the goats' escape. They would be trapped.

In the chaos of dust clouds and shouting, one of the hunters leapt down onto the back of one of Ezrael's goats, wrangling it to the ground, while another swiftly threw ropes around its head. Ezrael clung to the goat that carried her as it maneuvered around the bandits. All at once one of the horses reared up and its rider fell backward, shouting. Ezrael saw Jamali, Omar's camel, stomping and snorting, kicking at the horses. One by one the horses reared up, bucking the hunters to the ground. Then there was a great whoosh from the sky. A falcon, then two, and then three, swooped down and pecked at the raiders as they scrambled away. Emboldened, Ezrael told her goat to charge toward the remaining thieves. One bandit slashed at the sky with his sword, chasing the falcons away, and then turned his gaze toward Ezrael. Ezrael stared back at him through the shining circle of horns of the goat upon which she rode.

"Shall I charge?" the goat asked her.

"No," Ezrael said.

The man pointed his sword toward Ezrael and began running at her. She and her goat stood their ground, and just when he was a few cubits away, one of the horses came charging at him from the side, catapulting him off his feet and through the air. The horse then turned to Ezrael, its nostrils flaring. It came so close to her that its hot breath blew her hair back. Then it galloped away.

Omar came rushing through the wadi, followed by other Edge shepherds and villagers. Ezrael slipped off the goat and looked around her.

"You are all right," Omar said, rushing to her side.

"They took one," Ezrael said, counting her goats. There were only five goats remaining.

"Tell me what to do," Omar said.

"There is a storm coming," she said. "The herd has to be whole."

Ezrael climbed back onto the goat to follow the thieves. Omar climbed onto his camel and followed, along with the four other goats. Shepherds and villagers followed after.

"They will be buried," Ezrael's goat said to her.

Ezrael turned to Omar and told him, "Tell the people not to follow. Tell them to get to safety."

Omar delivered the message to all who were following. Before their eyes, the wind picked up, increasing velocity with supernatural speed, carrying sheets of sand. The people hurried to safety behind rocks and in caves.

Ezrael and the goats marched onward, heads down, cutting through the storm. Soon the sandstorm blotted out the sun, and the day became dark as night. Ezrael heard the same cry as the time she ran into the wilderness to meet the first goat. She felt that cry in her bones. She knew which way to go.

Omar rode up to Ezrael, following the light emitted by her goat's horns.

"Edge will be destroyed," he called to her.

"Not only Edge," Ezrael said, filled with dread. "All the world is dark. All the wells are dry." But Omar didn't hear her response. A gust of wind knocked Omar off his camel. He smacked the side of his face against a rock. He struggled to get up. It had become so dark, he couldn't see his hand in front of his face. He felt his back growing heavier and heavier. The wind was blanketing him with sand. With all his might, he could not lift himself. He tried to cry out, but the pressure was pushing his mouth into the earth. He could not find which way was up. He was drowning, his thoughts fading.

Omar felt a sharp pain on his shoulder. One of Ezrael's goats was gripping him with its teeth, pulling him from the sand. The others were digging around him. With their help, Omar managed to shake free and climb out of what was almost his unmarked grave. When he was above ground and could suck in the air again through his teeth, his eyes filled with tears.

"Thanks be to the Fire on the Mountain," Omar said, the howling wind drowning his words.

Ezrael and Omar each rode one of the goats, with Ezrael at the front and the others following in a V formation. Omar knew his camel Jamali would survive. It was built for storms like this and would be hunkered down, waiting it out. The wind parted before them as they continued, as if there were something cutting it for them. Omar imagined perhaps it was the pillar of smoke he had heard rumors about.

Ezrael gripped the goat's glowing halo as she instructed it where to go. They crossed through the mountains, the sandstorm whipping the world around them. The wind picked up rocks like they were dry leaves, but the glow of the goats shielded Ezrael and Omar.

Ezrael saw fires in the distance. As they got closer, they saw an encampment at the foot of a mountain, partially shielded by a cliff. They rushed inside the encampment and found tents torn apart and wagons on fire. They heard people shouting to be saved. Omar and the four other goats began moving from tent to tent, rescuing people who had been trapped. Omar recognized a man he rescued as one of the thieves who had raided Ezrael's herd. Omar became angry, but the man fell to his knees before him and begged, "I am sorry! Let me live, and everyone will know that the goats are not to be touched."

Ezrael rode toward the cliff, where she spotted a cave. She knew the stolen goat was inside. She could hear it crying out to her. Ezrael dismounted and stepped into the cave, winding her way toward the soft glow shining from the cave's depths. As she got closer, she saw the glow formed a crescent, not a circle. When she reached the stolen goat, she noticed that one of its horns had been shorn off. The goat was tied up and helpless. The shorn horn lay on the ground, ashen and dead. Ezrael grabbed it and held it close. A man stepped out of the shadows and said, "You have five of them already. We are keeping this one."

Ezrael held the horn out before her, with the tip pointing at the man. As she stepped toward him, he stepped back. She said, "Listen to me carefully. I am the keeper of a herd of scapegoats. Each carries a portion of the world's pain." As Ezrael spoke, the sawed-off horn in her hand began to glow, becoming brighter and brighter. She continued, "If one of them is harmed, all the suffering they keep inside is released." The man kept stepping back until his back was against the wall. "The only way to stop the storm is to unite the herd and bind them to me in bonds of love. Now, you will leave this place and tell everyone you see that I am the goat keeper. I protect the goats, and the goats protect humankind." She held the glowing horn right up to the man's trembling face. "Now, go," she ordered him.

The man ran out of the cave, and Ezrael quickly untied the goat. She and the goat reunited with Omar and the rest of the herd.

The wind had begun to die down, and the sun was visible through a veil of dust. Ezrael surveyed the destruction around them. People were huddled and weeping together in the aftermath of the sandstorm. As they marched out of the encampment, rain began to fall from the sky, extinguishing the fires across the camp.

Omar watched Ezrael move up the mountain, with her black robes billowing and her long white hair flowing like a banner. Behind her marched her herd of magnificent goats, with glittering silken beards and radiant halos. How many were there now—forty? Fifty? More? Omar had lost count. He watched until he could no longer see her. He smiled and praised the Fire on the Mountain and the prophetess Geula.

At the summit, Ezrael stepped up onto a flat rock. She blew the crystalline sawed-off horn, and its long resonating sound caused wayfarers to stop and look up.

Ezrael's herd gathered close, and she spoke to them saying, "The Fire on the Mountain has not forgotten you. Geula counts your tears and tallies them. One day the blast of this horn will issue all the nations into paradise. Families will be reunited, and running will be only for play. So lift your hearts, exalt and sing, for the Fire on the Mountain delights in you!"

Passersby in the flatlands below saw the mountain top and thought it was crowned with fresh snow, for the gleaming backs and radiant halos of the assembled goats glistened so brightly in the sun.

QUESTIONS

1. The people of Edge's ancestors witnessed God at Mount Sinai but did not stick around to receive the Torah. The characters discuss whether or not they are Hebrews. What does it mean to be a Hebrew/Israelite/Jew?
2. A scapegoat is a person who is blamed for the wrongdoings or faults of others. It originates from the Torah where the High Priest would send a goat out of the Temple after symbolically laying the people's sins upon its head. Similarly, we cast out bread for *tashlich* to symbolize the casting away of sins. How do we create scapegoats in society today?
3. In the story, the scapegoats find a haven in Ezrael's herd. Where can people who are scapegoated, persecuted, and maligned find refuge? How can we help create a safe haven in our society?
4. Zelophehad ran away from his experience at the mountain, but Azarel runs toward her feeling of mission. What is something you have run toward or away from?

Two Rocks
A Very Long Legendary Love Story

Everything is energy and that's all there is to it. This is not philosophy. This is physics.
—Albert Einstein

MEI WAS A SCULPTOR, and her medium was stone. She traveled the world to find the right types of stone to carve. Her studio was filled with raw hunks of rock she had collected, some from spelunking deep caves, others from scaling high mountains. She had rocks chipped out of glaciers and rocks she dug up from wild fields. Mei would run her hand over the great slabs of granite, marveling at the natural ribbons of color throughout. She caressed the soft soapstone. She was awed by all the colors and textures around her: bright-red desert rocks, smooth blue river stones, pocked black lava rocks, wood that had petrified into green stone, translucent alabaster and moonstone. Many of the rocks were formed over billions of years, and when she touched them, Mei felt that she was touching the very mystery of the universe.

Mei would sit in her studio and listen to the rocks, living with them and getting to know them before transforming them into a work of art. She found that rocks from Thailand had a different vibration than rocks from the Ivory Coast. There was a different character to the geology of one place over another. It wasn't exactly that the rocks spoke to her in any familiar language. Mei began to sense that they emitted silences and that the particular silence of this cut of quarried quartz was different from the particular silence of that block of marble or that chunk of pink tourmaline.

Very few people realize that a silence is not uniform and empty. Silences are powerful communications filled with information. An astute and sensitive listener could discern a sort of rhythmed silence coming from the stones, like Morse code drummed with feathers on marshmallows. For instance, to Mei, the silence of limestone was fuzzed and heavy, with pockets of warmth throughout, while the silence of sandstone was long and hollow, punctuated by short staccato holes, as if the air was being gauged by an invisible awl. The silence of obsidian stone was open and giving, while the silence of serpentinite stone was glittery and ticklish. Mei would listen to these patterns emitted by her global collection and imagine what they wanted her to understand.

Mei knew she had listened long enough when the vision came to her of what a rock wanted to become. Sculpting, she believed, was a conversation between the material and the artist. When she developed her vision, Mei would wet down the stone, put on her safety goggles and dust mask, and start redeeming the vision from inside the rock with her hammers, chisels, electric grinders, and sanders. It was alchemy, this transformation from rough ancient unhewn mineral to beautiful modern languid form.

There were two rocks that had lived in Mei's studio for many years. Every time Mei thought she was ready to carve them, she drew back. There was something very sad about the rocks, and it was not clear yet what they wanted to become. The first one was a rock she had found on a windy hillside in central England, jutting from the ground near the ruins of an ancient church. The second one she found embedded in a cliff east of the mountain Jabal al-Lawz in northwest Saudi Arabia. Mei believed these rocks longed to become something, but she could not discern exactly what.

It happened that late one afternoon, after a long day of artistic and geologic alchemy, Mei took off her safety goggles, cleaned the dust from her workspace, then turned off the lights of her studio and locked the door behind her.

When Mei was in her studio, there was constant motion and sound. Her hands fluttered over the stones. She caused sparks to fly and filled the space with the deafening screeching peal of the diamond-tipped circular disc and electric sawing blade. Then there were her own dynamic vibrations, her heartbeat, her breath, her heat, her synapses firing with ideas, all rippling into the chalky air as she worked. But when she left, the stones, minerals, and crystals filled the void with their own vibrations and frequencies. The studio became a thirty-two-foot by twenty-six-foot universe energized by the signals of geometric patterns of molecules and space dust that had blasted out of exploding stars billions of years ago.

The English rock and the Arabian rock were on opposite sides of the studio. Despite being from different parts of the world, they shared a unique wavelength. While the other stones in the studio exuded steady, stable vibrations, the English and Arabian rocks shared a wobblier frequency, filled with longing and lament.

The English rock emoted, "Men came from many lands to lay the sole of their boots against me for leverage."

"I understand," emoted the Arabian rock.

"I was touched by prophecy," the English rock continued.

"As was I," the Arabian rock commiserated.

"The prophecy said, 'Whoso pulleth this sword from this stone is right wise the king born.' Princes, noblemen, and commoners came to me to try to pull out the sword. But I held Excalibur fiercely."

"I know you did," the Arabian rock affirmed.

"Right in my heart."

The two rocks contemplated each other. The Arabian rock had been brought here first, to this studio in Sedona, Arizona. It was a strange world, surrounded by red mountains of iron oxide sediment completely foreign to the Arabian rock, and the rock felt alone, an asteroid adrift. But the moment Mei touched the English rock, even across continents and oceans, the Arabian rock felt it. They were not of the same star, but they shared something deeper than space dust. And now here they were, in each other's orbit, dancing.

"I was filled with purpose," the English rock continued. "When the men came and yanked on that sword, I believed they admired me, my power and strength. I believed we shared a glimmer. But they did not care for me at all. They did not think of me. They would blast me to bits if they thought it would release Excalibur. I was a burden. A boulder. A dead thing. They only thought of the penetrating sword, that killing thing."

"I understand," said the Arabian stone, its frequency quivering. "I know better than anyone. I know."

"I know you do," the English stone pulsed.

The night grew dark as the planet rotated on its poles, and beneath them, they could sense the slow creeping of the earth's silicate mantle, its pressure, depth, and heat.

The Arabian rock emoted, "I had been content in the desert heat. Lizards warmed their tummies upon me. Dew evaporated into manna on my planes every morning. I remember receiving the rumblings that a man was crossing the desert with a mass of people in his wake. This was a man who knew rocks. He had nestled himself in the cleft of a rock to receive visions. His name was Moses, and he called God 'The Rock!' He knew that the rock the others discarded would one day become the cornerstone of the House of God. He knew how to bring forth honey from a rock and oil from a flinty stone. Moses could even harden a human heart to stone."

"Yet he did not know the heart of you," the English stone empathized.

"I waited for him to pass my way. I waited for the prophet whose name meant 'Drawn from the Water.' I prayed he would choose me. That he would draw forth water from me. I prepared myself to quench this weary people. I realigned my chemistry for him. I changed my nature."

"What rock in history could do this?" the English rock marveled.

"You," the Arabian rock responded, and they both were still, contemplating billions of years.

The English rock emoted, "By the time Arthur came to me, I had already learned that they only cared for the sword and not for me. I succumbed to him and was promptly abandoned. For a time I thought he'd return to me. Pour water into my wound. Plant it with fresh earth and a snip of budding vine, that butterflies might visit. I had thought he would make something of me. Turn me into an altar."

"Ah," the Arabian rock echoed, "altars."

"Yes," the English rock emitted, "but they are all returned now to the earth, and we are still here."

"Yes," the Arabian rock agreed.

They both paused to bathe in the rotating frequencies of the moon, Mercury, Venus, and Mars.

The Arabian rock shared, "I had heard how Moses had stirred up all the sediment of the Nile so that it became blood red. I had heard about the splitting of the sea. I heard about the smashing of stone tablets. Such power and might! I was ready."

"And when he finally arrived?"

"And when he finally arrived, he did choose me. He took his rod and he struck me. Twice."

"I know," the English rock soothed. "I know."

"I was stunned and ringing. The copious waters were my tears. The people drank what I had to give, and then I was abandoned. I thought he might return and make something of me. Turn me into an altar. A place upon which people would lay their offerings of gratitude and love. A place that connected the heart of humanity to the Creator of the world."

"Where earth offers up and God touches down," the English rock dreamed.

The two rocks oscillated and hummed together until the morning, when Mei turned her nickel key in the brass lock and returned to the studio.

Mei was neither prophet nor king, but an artist with a sculptor's calloused hands and a creator's listening heart. She stood in the center of the studio, the vibrations of the English rock and Arabian rock passing through her body, resonating in her bones. She held herself very still, letting their cascading silences fall over her. She could feel their vibrations, and she understood that they held stories and that their meaning was far weightier than their mass. The rocks were soothed by her presence.

Mei meditated on the silences radiating from the great stones and finally understood what they wanted to become. Mei brought the two rocks together into the center of her studio so that they were touching each other. Immediately, the air around them changed from an aching throb to a gentle purr. The English rock was a pebbly dove gray, and the Arabian rock was a fawn beige. Mei wet them down and put on her goggles and mask. She started to chisel them, moving from one to the other and back again. She was like a surgeon, carving out the tumors to restore the bodies to health. As she worked, Mei had the sense that these two rocks were in love with each other. The form that emerged from each rock was the perfect puzzle piece for the other. Mei sanded them together with the finest grain, smoothing their surfaces to satin. The dove gray and the fawn beige blended into a fluid and seamless landscape. The rocks fused, holding onto each other as if they had been born together, soulmates erupting out of earth's crust onto different continents, worlds apart.

Mei's work united them, and united they would remain. After bearing witness to prophets and kings, earthquakes and eclipses, fire and brimstone, and ages of aloneness, they were pressed into permanent embrace by the skillful touch and precise torch of a sculptor. Their curves and contours melted into each other, their arcs and bends melded. Together, they became the altar they dreamed of becoming for so many centuries, a place where earth offered up and God touched down. They pulsed with gratitude and adoration, generating a new electromagnetic wave different from x-rays, gamma rays, and ultraviolet waves. Their vibrational frequency was a steady, reliable, unfluctuating love.

Mei left the piece untitled. It needed no title because the work spoke for itself in its own language. Every person who saw it resonated with the love and devotion of those two stones carved into one. The piece was purchased by the Israel Museum in Jerusalem, where it lives still, pulsing long, slow waves over the world, two stones unhardened into one heart.

QUESTIONS

1. Why do you think the author brought together a legend from Jewish history and a legend from British history?
2. Geologists think of time in a unique way. While we may think in decades, they think in millions and billions of years, in which our human lives are so brief. How do we reconcile our allotment of years with the long chronology of earth?
3. In Yehuda Amichai's poem "Mayor," he writes, "At night, the stones of the hills round about will crawl down toward the stone houses, like wolves coming to howl at the dogs who have become men's slaves." Do you think stones and earth have feelings?
4. Mei's medium as an artist is stone. What medium do you or would you like to create with, and why? What type of sculpture do you most like?

Abraham's Return

A True Story of T'shuvah

We each have countless stories about our families,
some passed down through the generations,
some unfolding this very day. This is one of mine.

MY FATHER JAMES GRASHOW once told me that if you go into a kindergarten class and ask everyone, "Who here is an artist?" everyone
will raise their hand. However, if you go back a few years later and ask the
same question, everyone points at one or two children and says, "They are."
My father told me that in the beginning, we are all artists. He said, "As we
grow older, we unlearn how to dream."

My brother once said, "You know all the stuff you did in kindergarten?
That's what my father does for a living."

My father didn't unlearn how to dream. He became an artist.

I like to imagine my father as a child, making rockets out of refrigerator
boxes. And he continues to make amazing large-scale sculptures out of card-
board, even today! One of the many things he loves to create is woodcuts.
He was a freshman at Pratt Institute in 1960 when he was first introduced to
the art of woodcutting. Other students struggled with the tools, but for my
father, the tools glided beautifully over the wood. As children, my brother
and I loved watching our father engrave the polished, silky blocks of Swiss
pear wood and then, when the engraving was finished, roll the ink onto the
block and press a delicate sheet of rice paper onto it. Finally, he would peel
the rice paper off the block, and there would be the finished artwork: a print
with beautiful fluid lines. Even though we saw the process from beginning to

end, it always felt magical when it was complete. He became a well-known woodcut artist and made many iconic posters and album covers. His prints have appeared in nearly every major periodical and publication in the United States.

But it is the story of one particular print, early in his career—the year before I was born—that I want to share.

My father was hired by Barton's Continental Chocolate Shop in 1970 to illustrate their new advertisement. He made a powerful and beautiful woodcut and called it *Abraham: The First Jew.* My father smoothed ink over the block and hand-printed a limited edition of one hundred on rice paper, each one signed and numbered.

The ad for Barton's Candy appeared in *The New York Times* and included *Abraham: The First Jew* alongside legends of the biblical Abraham's fight against idolatry. The text concluded, "Monday, September 23rd is Rosh Hashanah and we are reminded of Abraham once again. The shofar (or ram's horn) blown during the synagogue services is a symbol of the ram which Abraham offered as a sacrifice in place of his son, Isaac. His willingness to sacrifice even his own son is further proof of Abraham's undying devotion to the Lord. One Lord, the Creator of Heaven and Earth." I hope the ad led to a lot of people buying Barton's Candy for a sweet new year!

Well, a Swedish art dealer saw the ad and fell in love with the illustration. He found his way to my parents' apartment and offered them a deal. He said that he would sell the prints in Europe, for a commission, and send my parents the money from the sales. My parents were excited about the idea of my father's art being shared. They happily agreed and put aside one print for themselves.

As the dealer was walking out, my father told him how much he admired his keychain, which had a little foldout scissors on it. The dealer gave him the keychain . . . and my parents never heard from him again.

When I became a rabbi, my parents gave me the one remaining *Abraham: The First Jew* print to display in my study. It felt symbolic because my journey to the rabbinate began with my father's woodworking. When people used to ask me, "Why did you become a rabbi?" I used to answer, "Because my father is an artist!" To me, that answer made complete sense. I go back to my childhood, sitting in a bin of cloth and string in the studio watching my father woodcutting. As he worked, he would talk about creation and destruction, life and death, the beauty of blank space and the human impulse to fill it. To me, it made complete sense that this setting led to me being a rabbi.

But I soon realized that people needed a little more explanation. I see the work of an artist and the work of a rabbi as very similar. We are both taking delicate fibers and trying to weave them into something meaningful and lasting. I love having *Abraham: The First Jew* looking at me, reminding me of that connection. Whenever my parents would visit, they would look at the piece and wonder what happened to the rest of the edition all those years ago.

Forty-seven years after the print first appeared in *The New York Times* promoting Barton's Candy for the new year, my father received the following email:

> *Dear Mr. James Grashow:*
> *My father passed away a couple of years ago. Now my mother also passed and we found a series of "Abraham" when cleaning out their estate. It's a series of 100, and we've got lots of them. We are three siblings that live in Sweden, Norway, and California. We would love to have your input and look forward to hearing from you.*

Stunned, my parents responded immediately:

> *Hello and thank you for reaching out. This answers a mystery that started 47 years ago. Your father visited us in Manhattan and looked at prints. He ultimately wanted the edition of Abraham, promising distribution and payment. We remember distinctly he left with the prints and handed me a keychain with a foldout scissors. We never heard from him again.*
>
> *We were very naive at the time and often laughed at how foolish we were then to let so much go for what turned out to be only a keychain . . . We would personally love to have some of the Abraham prints because your father had all of them.*

The art dealer's children, now fifty-seven, sixty, and sixty-two, were mortified. They loved the print, which hung over the mantle of their childhood home. When they discovered the prints among their deceased father's belongings, they researched my father on the internet, saw the extent of his work, and wanted to find out what they might be worth. After learning the truth, the siblings wanted to atone for their father's wrongdoing.

They decided to return the prints, but they didn't want to merely mail them. They wanted to return them in person. They arranged a date and flew to the United States, then took a train to meet my father.

Stepping off the train, carrying a big, battered suitcase, they greeted my father with smiles and big hugs. My father drove them to his studio, where they met my mother, and together they opened the suitcase. It contained the original cardboard box, wrapped in a quilt. Upon seeing the eighty-seven prints that were left in the box, my parents burst into tears. It was a moment of true redemptive *t'shuvah*—a literal "return."

Afterward, my parents and the siblings shared a toast over champagne and lunch. The siblings said that they didn't understand their father's actions but wanted to make it right. At the end of a wonderful afternoon, my father drove them back to the train.

The next morning, my parents received this email:

> *This day will stay in our memories for all our lives, and we're so happy that we were able to correct one of our father's mistakes. We're so thankful.*

My parents never thought they would see those prints again. But when they were returned, we believed it was for a special reason. After they had been hidden away for so long, we decided to give them the opportunity to live in vibrant Jewish communities. In the summer of 2018, dozens of *Abraham: The First Jew* prints found new homes in synagogues and studies across the land. And there they remain, sentinels of faith, witnesses of *t'shuvah*, pilgrims of hope.

QUESTIONS

1. Over sixty copies of this print were mailed to rabbis all over the country. Imagine you were one of the rabbis who received this print. What would you say in a sermon about the print and its story?
2. What is the relationship between art and religion?
3. Are we responsible to right our parents' wrongs? How far should one go to right a wrong?
4. Is there a *t'shuvah* story in your family? What about a reconciliation in your own life?

Chapter 1:

God Chooses a Genre

When God sat/sits/will sit to write the book of everything, God thought/ thinks/will think, "I am about to become the author of all life. But, what kind of author? Fiction? Nonfiction? Just because I am the God of truth, does that mean that I have to write technical tomes or economic essays? Perhaps journalism. Here's the scoop: I am God. Nothing else exists. The end. What good is that? No plot. No relationship arc. No all-is-lost moment. No resolution. So, ixnay on the nonfiction.

"Fiction is strange. Far stranger than truth. Take any reality and add a jabberwocky in an ill-fitted paisley smoking jacket . . . isn't the situation now stranger? *Way.*

"What is fiction anyway? Artistry and inventiveness. Figments of the imagination are fragments of the subconscious. And everything is a man-ifestation of My subconscious. I once dreamed of shapes that had never been. That dream gives shape to ideas that shape creation."

God mulled/mulls/will mull over this an indeterminable moment longer. "What if I write fictional characters who think that *I* am fictional? Wouldn't *that* be a hoot?"

God laughed/laughs/will laugh and wondered/wonders/will wonder, "But do I want to be a comedy writer? Humor writing is really the hardest type of writing. The creative genius that goes into writing a good joke is infinite. First you need material, and I have none. Literally. The singular point is, to do it right, I'd have to make time. There was evening, there was morning. Done."

God chewed/chews/will chew on the concept of a pencil, reconsidering. "What about writing a romance? The unlikely story of one whose vastitude is limitless and cannot be contained, captivated by one so small and finite. The mortal being, pinched of mud, fragile as earthenware pottery, tethering the heartstrings of the Almighty.

"Oh person, you are flesh and bone, but you are saturated in divinity! Earthbound with inklings of eternity, you eclipse the quasars, the nebulae, the globular clusters, with your tiny tantrums and furious poetry. I write you into being, sentence you to sentience, and in return you invent for Me a heart. It beats and aches and breaks for you. Beloved biped, betroth thyself to Me in covenant. I will arrange the stars into constellations for you to interpret, sequin the grass with dew for you to step on. I will give you breath and you will take Mine away.

"But something is lacking. A plot twist. A change in direction. Temptation, to transform an endlessly amorous ode into a gripping page-turner. The appearance of a tree with luscious yield, dripping with syrup, busting with substance, surrounded by DO NOT CROSS tape . . . now, that is a blockbusting setup for drama." God was/is/will be filled with visions of grandeur. "It could be a screenplay!" God visualized/visualizes/will visualize God's name on the marquee in lights.

FADE IN: EXTERIOR. BARREN WASTELAND—MIDDAY

Sound of iron clinking against rock. Sparks flying. Horizon wavering in desert heat. As camera rises, we see man working the land. ZOOM in on sweaty brow.

WOMAN (*off-screen*): (*Low animalistic howl.*)

MAN (*with urgency*): Now? The baby's coming now?

God woot wooted/woot woots/will woot woot in revelation, "Woot woot! I'll design a Choose Your Own Adventure template. That way, I can interact with My art. Let the characters lead Me as well. They will make decisions but within a controlled environment. Free will, with predetermined plotlines."

CHAPTER 1: If you choose to get up, walk the dog, brew a cup of African rooibos tea with a touch of agave nectar, and get back to writing, go to CHAPTER 2. If you choose to put the kibosh on this author-of-life venture and rewind to the undifferentiated lastingness that predated the very first once-upon-a-time, go to CHAPTER 3.

CHAPTER 2: You are out of agave, so you have the tea unsweetened. You stare at the blank parchment through the fragrant steam. How shall you start? If you look for inspiration in the tea leaves at the bottom of your cup, go to CHAPTER 4. If you start exploring a new genre, go to CHAPTER 5.

CHAPTER 3: It turns out, you cannot go back. You created the clock, you wound the clock, and now the clock won't stop ticking. You encompass all wisdom, but it was a primordial porridge. Now it is solidifying and splintering into synapses. You don't want to return to the solitary nada. Every choice you make as you write this story eliminates other possibilities. With every dash and dot, you are lessened a bit, a quark, a Planck length. If this makes you uncomfortable, go to CHAPTER 6. If you are curious to continue from the point that the story starts to write itself, go to CHAPTER 7.

CHAPTER 4: The tea leaves make a golden spiral. This will be your signature as you compose the cosmos, your fingerprint pressed into the wet clay of your work. You will develop detective work into your characters' backstories, and they who come from dust will dive to the depths in search of evidence of you.

CHAPTER 5: You are intrigued by the psychological thriller genre, which employs an unreliable narrator. This makes for edge-of-your-seat engagement. You will write that all are made equally in your image and then blatantly favor one over the other. You will elect a hero to save all the animals, and then you will write yourself some nostrils and delight in the smell of roasting carcass. But you won't explore this genre for your own base entertainment. No, you are not sick. Rather, you explore it because this is the only way you can learn about yourself. You are the writer, and you are the muse, and you are also the intended audience. That is the ultimate twist—that everyone else, every self-important someone, exists solely as literary devices to move you closer toward your own self-awareness.

*CHAPTER 6: You are uncomfortable with the way choices diminish pos-
sibilities, so you veer into the world of sci-fi and trade the linear scroll
for a Möbius strip upon which you design a multiverse in which every
outcome of every choice you make unfolds in alternate realities and
parallel universes.*

God turned/turns/will turn on the light and considered/considers/will consider the shadows it creates. It was/is/will be exactly this hour that God
heard/hears/will hear a claw scuffing the cold cement floor in the darkest
corner of the study. God squinted/squints/will squint to see a skeletal seraph
with burnt wings, its head pressed against its knees. It lifts its head, thin gray
skin stretched over its skull. Instead of a cherubic cherry mouth, it unhinges
the mandibles of a serpent, with dagger fangs fizzing with venom. God
shuddered/shudders/will shudder the spectral projection away concluding,
"No, ma'am. Horror is unstomachable.

"But provocative and haunting, and hard to forget."

God banged/bangs/will bang out reams of tragedy on God's theoreti-
cal keyboard. God sat/sits/will sit back to read them, reeling from the new
awful stunning breathtaking feelings flooding the megacosm. With each
emotion—dread, sadness, worry, woe—God fathoms Godself more deeply,
developing dimensionality. The world is awash with regret and remorse, but
also resolve, relief, redemption.

God watched/watches/will watch the grass grow and the asteroids orbit.

"Perhaps something in the field of existential literature," God said/says/
will say to Godself while holding up a white dwarf star and turning it round
and round. "Imagine—one teaspoon of neutron star weighs one million
tons. Earth and all it contains—hardly more than tinted vapor. What does
matter matter?"

God skimmed/skims/will skim the draft thus far. "It matters."

"Now fairy tale, fantasy, folklore, and fable," God perked/perks/will perk
up a notch, "How phenomenal to formulate phenomena that inspires belief,
to *make* believe, to fashion faith, and better yet, *fandom*. Do I dare animate
and unleash beings and beasts with wings, wands, secret words, cryptic
spells, fire-breath, and songs of enchantment?" God spritzed/spritzes/will
spritz a little gold leaf on the edges of every folio.

At last God finished/finishes/will finish the book of everything.

"Look at that," God marveled/marvels/will marvel at the complete manuscript. "Turns out it's a Mystery, after all."

CHAPTER 7: *You*

QUESTIONS

1. What if instead of thinking of God as the Author of All Life, we instead thought of God as the Reader of All Life? What if *we* are the authors of life and our deeds are all notes we write to the Reader? How would that change our behavior?
2. Do you agree that we are living in a mystery? If not, what genre do you think we are living in?
3. What would it mean to imagine that we are characters in a work of fiction, living in God's imagination?
4. On the High Holy Days, we talk of the Book of Life. If you could make up a title for the Book of Your Life, what would the title be?

Glossary

Abba: Father.

Adonai Echad: Literally, "God is one," from the Torah (Deuteronomy 6:4); the closing words of the Sh'ma prayer.

Beit Midrash: A "house of study" where people gather for intensive Jewish learning.

B'nei Mitzvah: Literally, "children of the commandments," this is an important life cycle milestone for children who are thirteen.

Chameitz: Leavened food such as bread, which cannot be eaten during the holiday of Passover.

Chanukiyah: A nine-branched candelabra used during the festival of Chanukah.

Charoset: A sweet paste often made of fruit and nuts that is eaten at the Passover table and is part of the Seder Plate. It symbolizes the mortar which the Israelites were forced to make as slaves in Egypt.

Chazan: A cantor or musical prayer leader.

Echad, sh'tayim, shalosh: One, two, three.

Etrog: A citrus fruit that is part of the celebrations of the holiday of Sukkot.

Genizah: A depository (usually attached to a synagogue) for damaged sacred texts that cannot be thrown away.

G'matria: A type of Jewish numerology and kabbalistic textual interpretation, wherein each Hebrew letter is assigned a number (for example, *alef*, the first letter of the Hebrew alef-bet is assigned the number one, *bet* is assigned the number two, and so forth). A common example is the word חי (*chai*, life) whose *g'matria* is the number eighteen.

Ima: Mother.

Kippot: The traditional head coverings worn by Jews.

L'chi lach/lech lecha: Words from the Torah (Genesis 12:1), adapted by musician Debbie Friedman, meaning "go forth."

Lulav: The closed frond of the palm tree, which is combined with myrtle and willow as part of the celebrations of the holiday of Sukkot.

Meshugaas: A Yiddish word meaning "crazy."

Mitzvah: A commandment, often translated as good deed.

Rosh: Head.

Sh'ma Yisrael: Literally, "Hear, O Israel" from the Torah (Deuteronomy 6:4) this is one of the most important prayers in Judaism.

Tallit: A prayer shawl worn by Jews, usually during morning worship.

T'filah: Prayer.

Tikkun Olam: Literally "repair of the world," this is a mystical concept asserting that the world is broken and we are obligated to repair (*tikkun*) it.

T'shuvah: The Jewish concept of "repentance," related to the concept of returning to God.

Tzedakah: Usually translated as "charity," this Jewish concept of monetary giving is related to the concept of justice or righteousness.

About the Author

Rabbi Zoë Klein serves Temple Isaiah in Los Angeles, California, where she brings her unique blend of innovation, tradition, creativity, and wisdom. At Temple Isaiah since 2000, she has served as the associate rabbi, the senior rabbi, and the director of adult education and engagement. A Connecticut native, Rabbi Klein holds a degree in psychology from Brandeis University. She received a master's degree in Hebrew literature and rabbinic ordination from Hebrew Union College–Jewish Institute of Religion in New York and Jerusalem. She pursued the rabbinate out of a passion for ancient texts, mythology, liturgy, and poetry. Rabbi Klein is the author of the novel *Drawing in the Dust* (Gallery Books, 2009) of which *Publishers Weekly* wrote, "Insight into the world of biblical excavation in Israel raises Rabbi Klein's debut novel from a Jewish *Da Vinci Code* to an emotionally rich story of personal and historical discovery." *Drawing in the Dust* has been published in five countries. In addition to this collection of short stories, Rabbi Klein is also the author of a children's story *The Goblins of Knottingham: A History of Challah* (Apples & Honey, 2017), as well as *The Scroll of Anatiya* (Wipf and Stock, 2009). Rabbi Klein's writing is included in *The Torah: A Women's Commentary*, *Teen Texts*, *Holy Ground: A Gathering of Voices on Caring for Creation*, *The Sacred Exchange: Creating a Jewish Money Ethic*, and more. Her poems and prayers are used in houses of prayer around the world.